SWORDS, MAGIC, AND HEART

TALES OF IMAGINARY REALMS

ALSO BY DAVE SMEDS

The Sorcery Within

The Schemes of Dragons

The Wizard's Nemesis

Piper in the Night

Embracing the Starlight

X-Men: Law of the Jungle

Raiding the Hoard of Enchantment

SWORDS, MAGIC, AND HEART

TALES OF IMAGINARY REALMS

DAVE SMEDS

BOOK VIEW CAFE

LAS VEGAS, NV

SWORDS, MAGIC, AND HEART
TALES OF IMAGINARY REALMS

Book View Café
304 S. Jones Blvd., Suite #2906
Las Vegas, NV 89107

ISBN: 978-1-63632-285-8

Publication Date: September 17, 2024

Publication Team:
Cover Art & Design: Dave Smeds, with thanks to Ancello at Dreamstime and Ironika at Depositphotos.
Proofreader: Sherwood Smith.
Book formatter: Dave Smeds.

Copyrights

CONTENTS

The Wind's Kiss

The folk of other lands have a saying: "Ask the wind." They say it as if the wind is mute.

In the Folded Prairie, the wind declares.

Once, many years ago, the king's tax collectors learned that lesson. They crossed the plains to our small corner of the realm, thinking much of themselves atop their stout horses, clad in their hauberks and gleaming helms, bearing swords we haven't the iron to forge even if we could convince ourselves to set aside our bows and spears and slings. They sped from house to shack to granary, a scheme they imagined would deny landholders the chance to conceal their valuables. They demanded the tithe, seized what they deemed right—always more than actually *was* right, of course—and sped on. Better men would have accepted the welcomes they were offered. Those overtures were not uncommon, tendered by those hungry for word from the South and East, or by those whose intrinsic decency made them want to look out for the welfare of strangers unaccustomed to our province. Like any other new arrivals, the kingsmen might have made friends, might have warmed themselves at clan elders' hearths, might have been fortified by the bowls of soup the loomhouse women set down at their common tables.

The windfolk took offense. Wind brothers blasted the intruders' armor until gauntlets froze onto fingers, and the poor horses became blind and fatally stumbled. Wind sisters wormed their way into crevices in armor and up nostrils until the shaking ague took root in lung and in gut. No matter how robust the fellows had been when they had first appeared among us, few survived the sisters' caresses. Some say only one wretch made it back alive to the regions of castles and pageants and grand market faires.

We have not seen the king's tax collectors since. Perhaps we are not even part of the realm now. I suspect only the windfolk have true claim to the Folded Prairie. If we bide here, in our pathetic numbers, it is only by their leave.

And because, they are interested in us.

Can you accept that some of us are interested in *them?*

If Orann the fletcher had been free to do so, he might have followed his young wife into the grave, but he had a son, a mother, and his mother's bachelor uncle dependent upon him, and so he tilled the soil. He harvested his crops. He stocked the quivers of the rangers who patrolled the hinterlands. It was his responsibility to keep living, and so he did.

His grief was not banished. It was merely contained.

One warm evening in high summer his four-year-old, spent from an afternoon of swimming below the mill dam with neighbor children, fell asleep in the straw while Orann was tending to the cow's evening milking. Orann carried him to bed, gave him a kiss, and informed the boy's grandmother he would be out of the house for at least the next two hours.

Braccah frowned but did not insist he stay inside. Later she wished she had.

Orann chose the path north, if only because he had taken the one south two nights before. Whichever way he went, the land rose, because the homestead lay in a hollow, the better to remain in the lee of both the blizzards of winter and the thunderstorms of summer. Not for whimsy do we call this the Folded Prairie.

The last glow of the day was overcome and starlight ruled, abetted by the bent-sickle crescent of the pumice moon in the west. Orann was untroubled by the murk, knowing from memory the height of a raised root and the softness of the places where gophers had worked their mischief. In another little while the agate moon would rise, not far past full, and its luminescence would accompany him the rest of the night, if need be.

Eventually he turned off the beaten trail, climbing up into a formation of rock — once the floor of a great sea, now thrust up at an angle and revealed to the sky, new fossils emerging with each season. A fortnight earlier, in daylight, Orann had found a weather-smoothed shelf near the ridgeline, a natural seat unnoticeable from below. Judging by the scattered twigs, and by the traces of guano and rodent blood upon them, a pair of eagles had once made their aerie here, but had not come back in many seasons.

Orann pulled out his flute, the one made from the wing bone of a great sedge heron. He sat down and began to play.

The tune wafted over the outcroppings and between the tussocks of the heights, down to the fields rich with barley or fallow with bee vetch and mud poppy. A bevy of dance deer lifted their noses and, disturbed at the human character of the noise, bounded back over the fence they had scorned on their approach. Across the dale at the holding of Orann's neighbors, the Quickfollows, the goodwife emerged from her root cellar, caught the rise and fall of the notes, and recognized the song. The tears that came to her cheeks had nothing to do with the onions she carried.

Orann let his awareness of his surroundings fade. On the back sides of his eyelids he saw his Maleene as she had stood by the well at the wainwright's shed to listen to him play for her — that thing he had never had the courage to do until that day.

Some might tell you the wind never ceases in the Folded Prairie, but that is not strictly true. At times down in the hollows the wheat stands as straight as maize, and within the barns the scurry-scritching of resident bats goes unmuffled. But of a certainty, the wind keeps vigil over the ridges, as a mother or father would linger near the cradle of their sleeping infant. When Orann opened his eyes, a dozen heartbeats after the last note had escaped the end of the flute, he found a woman floating in front of him, bedecked in a firefly gleam.

The wind sister regarded him with a confidence that was as intimidating as it was intense. She cocked her head, and it reminded him of a time when he was a boy, and a magpie dropped a walnut onto the canal bridge as he crossed, and waited to see if his foot would crush the shell and expose the treat.

Her form undulated and coalesced, grew opaque and then nearly transparent. Her threshing skirt and loose blouse, so similar to what Maleene had worn that day long ago, alternately billowed and flapped and then clung to her like rain-soaked fabric. She was gaunt and then abundant, short then tall, hair ablaze at first, then dim as fading embers. She smelled of lavender, though the only shrubs nearby were nettle and stranglegoat.

Finally the wind sister held out one hand to him, and with the other, scribed a broad circle in the direction of the sky. She changed again, becoming a helix of whirling air. She left the ground and roamed the heavens above the ridge, making the stars shimmer or even wink out as she passed in front of them.

Back to the ground she came, and back to shoulders and hips and legs and arms and just enough of a face that Orann could read the mix of compassion and…invitation.

"I want to," he said, "but duty binds me here."

Again, she was the magpie, observing something in him that fascinated her, but whose outcome she could not predict.

"Please," he begged. "Do not offer again."

And with that, the stirring of the air that had been pressing him toward her, ceased. She nodded. In the next moment, the only evidence that she had ever been there was the lingering whiff of lavender.

In the morning, Orann sat down to breakfast with every bit of stubble gone from his chin, shaved as adroitly as had once been his habit. He finished his porridge quickly and when his mother set the pot on the trivet, he took a second helping.

Orann himself failed to realize he was not behaving as he had the previous morning, or the morning before that, or for that matter any of the mornings since Maleene had succumbed.

His mother noticed. So did his boy, still known then as Twig because even at four years old, his true name tangled up his mouth and he refused to answer to it. Being four, Twig did not hesitate to exploit the possibilities.

"Can we dig today?" the child asked.

Automatically Orann prepared to tell Twig no. The fields were planted, and no hoeing would be needed for a week or more. Orann had already decided his task for the day was knapping arrowheads in his workshop in the barn. That sort of work was beyond the skill of someone so young, and the obsidian too sharp for him.

But Twig did love to be out in the fields with him, and he did so love to dig.

"Very well," Orann said, tousling his boy's hair. "The furrows need scooping out."

And so they went 'round by the bent path to the reserve garden plot near the creek, Twig scampering ahead of his father and Uncle Wollmew, an elk-bone spade perched on his shoulder.

The reserve garden had not been planted that year. The rains had been and continued to be ample, supplying the cropfields and the pasture and the garden near the house with all the moisture they needed. But as it often happened, the spring had featured a month when ample had become excessive. The creek had overflowed its banks, depositing a layer of mud upon the plot where the reserve garden would have been. As old Uncle Wollmew could testify best of anyone in the family, the year to come might be dry, and then the household would be grateful that a portion of their holding was capable of being irrigated.

Some say that the earthfolk have never forgiven us for cutting the land with metal, back when our ancestors first ventured into the Folded Prairie. Some say that is why, even now, we are visited by the fevers and the plagues, and why women here bear few children. Who can say? The folk of earth and water and fire never deign to speak in the words we use. Only the windfolk will do that. What I do know is that the soil yielded easily and without complaint to the tools of bone and wood and stone that Orann and Wollmew and Twig brought to bear that day, and gave up a fecund aroma of sod and clay, of earthworm castings and beetle husks.

Orann soon worked on ahead of the other two, breaking up the caked mud with grand strokes of his pick, leaving in his wake clumps easily dealt with by the slim little boy and the bent old man.

Wollmew as usual made no conversation. Orann had appreciated that quality over the past year. Healthy and strong and youthful Orann might be, but no farmer could deal entirely on his own with the many tasks of stewarding a holding, even if another's contribution was nothing more elaborate than opening a paddock gate at just the right time, to let in the cow but not the bull. In Wollmew, Orann had his helper, but one whose advice was silent. Unlike his mother's.

But Wollmew was not dull. He observed how his grand-nephew labored, saw the deep full breaths, the muscles bunching and relaxing with each swing, the cleanliness of the sweat that beaded on his brow. Not once did Orann pause, shoulders drooping, and gaze off at the horizon. Not once did he clutch too tightly the handle of his pick.

Wollmew nodded, and began to hum to himself as he worked.

Before they sat down to the noon meal, Braccah made Twig wash his hands a second time, as if that would be enough to rinse the dirt from the seams of his palms, much less from beneath his fingernails. The boy obeyed without a word of complaint.

"Tennie Farrow asked about you at Meditations last week," Braccah said to her son as she ladled soup into cups. "Perhaps you would consent to be her escort at the basket social?"

Wollmew coughed, turned, and headed out again, his mumbles implying he had just remembered he needed to visit the outhouse.

The old fellow need not have fled, because Orann accepted what his mother was asking with neither the pain nor the coldness he had displayed every other time she had indulged in even the slightest degree of matchmaking.

"Very well. I will go," Orann said. "If you will be the one to tell her."

His mother beamed. "Of course."

In point of fact, Braccah could so little contain her enthusiasm that she spent a portion of the afternoon walking over to the Farrows' holding with the excuse that she was out of salve for the milk cow's nagging case of flakeskin. She returned in a fine mood, but wore out early from the exertion and emotion, as did Twig from his hours of digging. Both retired to bed not long after supper.

Wollmew settled by the hearth, as he often did of an evening, and resumed whittling a gamepiece from the mammoth ivory he had so long ago brought back from the moss downs.

Orann was all too free to do as he wished. That, he explained at a later time, was the turning point. Once he finished with his usual chores in the barn and went to the laving stall, he found himself washing his hair and his entire body, though he could not recall having consciously chosen to be so thorough. After he had dressed, he went to his work bench and retrieved his flute from the cubby where he had tucked it amid a set of unfinished arrow shafts, only then becoming aware he had not left the instrument in its usual place in the cabinet in his bedroom.

He headed out along the northward path. He climbed into the rock formation, found the former eagle aerie, and settled down. He began to play.

The wind sister appeared at once. She kept her human form more reliably, as if she had made a recent study of what was necessary to accomplish that. She eased downward until her feet actually touched the ground, and she slid onto the stone shelf next to him. She patted both hands upon the surface and bounced her hindquarters upon it, plainly testing out the experience of pressing against some-thing solid without slipping off or around or over it. She smiled — not at him, but at the world. At the experience.

If he hadn't been occupied playing the flute, he might have laughed.

She ceased to glow, yet paradoxically she was more perceptible than ever, occupying the spot as a woman of meat and bone and blood might, her silhouette blocking the stars and the moonlight, her skirt exuding the grassy scent of weed linen and her hair the now-familiar aroma of lavender.

Orann did not reach out, nor try to speak to her. She did not repeat her offer to carry him off to the clouds. They simply sat there. He played his flute. She listened.

He did not repeat the tune he had played the night before, with its mournful character. He substituted other, livelier songs.

She listened to the first, the second, and the third, but as he was about to begin a fourth, she reached out and touched the flute.

He offered it to her.

She shook her head. "You hold."

Her voice was less a product of throat and tongue and lips than one of the magic of which she was made. She did not say more. Orann sensed how arduous it had been to say even that much.

He understood. He held out the flute in both hands, gripping it securely, fingers away from the holes.

Her solid form evaporated. A current buffeted his hair and ruffled his clothes before she managed to condense herself and pour into the mouth of the flute.

He expected unstructured tone, but what came from the instrument was a line of melody.

Twice more she whirled through the flute, repeating the same sweet sequence.

Orann wasn't sure whether he was being presented with an offer or a request, but he took it as both. He played the fragment as she had rendered it, recreating her version if only to demonstrate that he had absorbed it correctly. Then he did what his musical sense demanded. He played again, but held each note longer.

Done at its original brisk rhythm, the tune was a slice of fruit, sweet and glistening, held up to the nose. Done slower, it was the same morsel nestled between tongue and palate, juices trickling, the flavor released.

He began to extend and shape that beginning, hoping to craft something fine, but happy already just to be involved in the challenge.

The wind sister manifested above him, once again vaporish and glowing, shape molten except for her face. She watched him, smiling.

She stayed as long as she could. It was only a fragment of an hour all told. He expected that. He remained in place until midnight, working out the piece to the best of his talent.

Orann woke to the sensation of Twig bouncing on his mattress, and to the crinkling sound of chaff stuffing being crushed with every impact.

"Pa! Pa! The cow needs milking!"

Orann groaned and pointed toward the door. "I'll see to it. Let me wash my face."

Twig bounded out. No doubt he would be just as exuberant on the way to the barn. Orann wondered how soon his child would cease to think that chores were interesting. Probably as soon as he *had* to do them, rather than being occasionally allowed to participate.

Orann spotted the flute on the nightstand, and recalled why he had not managed to awaken at his usual time.

Ears full of remembered song, he picked up the instrument and almost touched the mouthpiece to his lips. But he heard his mother moving about in the common room, setting down bowls.

Frowning, he tucked the flute away in the cabinet.

Basket socials were great entertainment for the gossips, and as reliable a subject of conversation on market days as crop yields and health. Orann had been spared the embarrassment with Maleene; they had declared their interest early and without overtures meant for others to witness. He was grateful all he had to do was accompany Tennie Farrow up the slope of the picnic hill above the wisdom lodge, find a measure of grass upon which to sit, and eat the food she had prepared for the occasion.

Nervous, he started up the path with more haste than he should have. Even so, Tennie kept up with his strides. It startled him. He had known her when she was barely as tall as her mother's knee, and he had not encountered her enough in the past handful of years to have become accustomed to the grown version.

The difference in their ages was a good thing. Tennie was young enough that she was not one of the women he had passed over when he had chosen Maleene. In those days Tennie had still been chasing piglets with her brothers, as flat of chest as they, and as likely to plunge into the wallow mud to get a grip on her quarry's hind foot.

She now was the opposite of boyish.

"Your brothers are both still away?" he asked. The last he had heard, the Farrow boys were both on patrol, one in the north, the other in the west, Orann's arrows in their quivers.

"Yes. I miss them, but when they're home they won't shut up about all they've seen."

Orann laughed. It was a good beginning, but then he was stumped for a way to continue. The silence went on long enough to be awkward. Fortunately they soon came to a suitable flat spot. He handed the basket back to her, and busied himself spreading out the blanket.

Judging by the weight of the basket, Tennie had outdone herself, but her mother had obviously schooled her well enough that she made no airs about the abundance so as to cultivate the impression she could equal it any old day. Mindful of the flies and the tiny green grasshoppers that had decided to share their blanket, she opened the lid only long enough to take out a small crock of butter and a round of bread that smelled of the oven the moment she broke it open.

"Very nice," he said around his first mouthful. "Is that fennel seed?"

"A little." She smiled. "It spoke to me."

A cook by instinct, not by rote. Given what he'd had to put up with over the past year, Orann found that appealing.

Tennie seized the opening and began to chat about her inclinations in the kitchen, how the texture of foods was as critical to her as the flavors—that cooked carrots must be crunchy, and puddings never runny. The words tumbled out at first with a trace of stutter, but as he nodded and smiled at her, she settled into the sort of easy conversational rhythm he had been so accustomed to hearing from Maleene. Freed from the need to do much more than chew or add a stray comment here or there, he relaxed as well.

Tennie glanced at the henfest of ladies outside the lodge and at the other couple some two hundred paces to the north, and frowned just enough that he knew she wished they weren't there.

Each time she fetched an item from the basket, she ended up sitting just a little closer to him.

So much was so familiar to Orann. Sitting near, almost to the point that warm air forms in the gap. With Maleene, he would find himself leaning in, nostrils widening to absorb her essence, his own heartbeat gradually growing audible in the background.

What he had felt back then, and his reaction, were not of his design. Choice had not been part of it. It had simply *been.*

This day, with Tennie, the closer she moved, the more he leaned back, the less he made eye contact. The less he said.

Orann's mother managed not to race out when he appeared around the bend of the hill. She stayed on the porch mending socks while he unsaddled his horse and rubbed it down. She was still in her chair, needle and thread in her hands, as he trudged up to the house.

"How was Tennie?" she asked.

Orann stopped with one foot on the stoop and looked straight at his mother.

"Mortal," he replied.

The line in the center of Braccah's forehead deepened so severely she seemed, all at once, a decade older than she was.

"As are we all," she shot back. "You can't let that matter. You have to be brave, my boy."

"Courage has nothing to do with it, Mother. The simple fact is, I will never be fond enough of Tennie to give her what she is due. I will not let her attach her hopes to me. It would be cruel and false."

"Do not decide so soon," Braccah insisted. "You're far too hasty. Your feelings *will* change."

Orann sighed. Instead of going into the house, he retreated to his workshop and his arrows.

He did not stay there long. For five days he had done all he could to shut his mind to the memory of his latest encounter on the ridge, determined to abide by the promise he had made his mother. When he had walked up the slope above the wisdom lodge, Tennie's basket in his arms, he had done so honestly, keeping alive the possibility the gash in his heart might have healed.

But now he knew his mind, and he found he could not wait even five more hours. With Twig napping and his mother and Wollmew out back breaking down the retted flax they had recently collected, Orann retrieved the flute from the cabinet and escaped along the northward path.

In full sunlight, the rock formation did not loom as it had in the night. It seemed smaller, not as miraculous a place — instead only a feature of the landscape at the boundary of his family land. Nevertheless, he sat on the platform of stone amid the brooding-eagle debris, and put the flute to his mouth.

He played the song he had worked out, incorporating the final flourishes that had come to him in his dreams over the past several nights.

The song ended, even the echoes, and he saw and felt no indication of windfolk visitation. The distant tendril of smoke from the Quickfollows' chimney barely strayed from the vertical. The wildflowers on the hillside held so steady it was as though they were calling to the bees.

Orann did not reprise the performance. He had made his declaration. Once was right. Twice was pleading.

He waited. He waited until he felt ill from it. Then he heard a noise behind the ridge. He swung about and caught a glimpse of a disturbance. A whirlwind? It vanished so soon he couldn't be sure.

Around the crest of the outcropping walked the wind sister, as corporeal as any other woman he had ever met.

She was naked.

He stood, gaze fixed, taking in the form she had chosen — consistent now, a portrait painted, no longer evolving at every moment. For the first time, he could commit its details to memory, appreciating all the ways it was lovely, and all the ways it was herself, unlike any woman of his own people, and most important, how it was not an imitation of Maleene.

She reached him. Stroked the side of his face. That alone seemed to be an artifact of her unaltered self, a caress not of flesh but of air.

She smelled of lavender, and of woman.

He held up the flute, miming the act of playing it.

She shook her head. She took the instrument and laid it far to the side, almost entirely off the edge of the stone shelf.

With a grin he could only have called impish, she loosened the laces at his collar and pulled his shirt off his body.

She did not stop there. In short order he was as undraped as she was.

She scanned him from toes to face, and smiled. "Oh Rann."

Whispery as her voice was, he adored the emotion and confidence she put into it.

She took his hand and touched it to the center of her chest. So authentic was her fashioning of her tangible body he could detect the pulsing of a heart within her ribcage. He was so distracted he didn't realize at first what she was asking.

But of course she wouldn't have a name. The windfolk must use other means to recognize one another.

"Zhara," he said. When he had been a little boy, his grand-mother had asked who he thought he would marry when he was grown, and not wishing to mention any girl he actually knew or had ever heard of, he had invented a name.

She nodded. She opened her lips. He thought she was going to repeat the name, but instead she placed her mouth upon his.

Her tongue rolled over his, tangible and playful. Her breasts nudged against him. He was already aroused, but now he grew so ready for her, the stiffness actually hurt.

Her manifestation faltered. Her hair began to coil in serpentine arcs around her head, the tips brushing his earlobes, his neck, his shoulders. For an instant, her entire body gleamed as it had that first time he'd seen her, though the effect was not so vivid in the light of day. When she noticed these signs, she solidified, and all was as it had been, save that now she exuded a fresh degree of urgency.

She pressed him down flat on his back on the slab, straddled him, and slipped him inside.

A sound very much like a gasp escaped her. Gone was the assertive manner. Had she not known how it would be? No. She was discovering.

She beamed at him, and began to rock back and forth, experimenting. He took hold of her hips and suggested a rhythm. She followed the cue. Already warm and slick, she grew warmer and slicker still. The fit became more precise as she applied herself in ways only a shapechanger could.

He sensed a pressure in his mind and he yielded. In the next moment his awareness became ductile, no longer confined to one spot. He was simultaneously aware of himself in the usual way, from within his body, and yet also able to look down from above, viewing himself gazing at the clouds with a fool grin on his face, viewing the clenching of Zhara's rump and back and thighs. He wound around and within and through her thoughts as well, almost to the point that it became vague as to which observations and emotions were his and which were hers, aside from those he could not let in because they retained a perspective only an immortal could endure, and the few he reserved, unable as yet to share.

He was the virgin now, learning her way even as she learned

his.

It was a coupling. Yes. But not just that. It was transformation.

The sun was still above the horizon when Orann reached his homestead, but it was the sky to the north, not the west, that demanded attention. Wollmew and Twig stood in the lee of the barn and watched open-mouthed and unblinking as currents of wind stole vapor from the clouds and swirled it, made designs of it, and created rainbow after rainbow. Lightning flashed and streaked and forked. Between the thunderclaps a pure sound flowed across the landscape. When the dog heard it, he began barking as though he had just spotted his litter mates coming toward him across the wheatfield. The old man could not be sure what the sound was, except that it seemed exultant. The boy simply smiled.

Braccah emerged from the house, stopped four steps outside the front door, and began to cry.

Orann approached. Braccah's eyes widened at the sight of his tousled hair, his unlaced collar, and the utter absence of tension in his brow, his neck, his elbows.

She stepped back.

"Not that," she pleaded. "You mustn't."

"It is not for you to choose for me," Orann said gently. "Can you not be happy for me?"

Alas, just as Orann had found it impossible to do as his mother had wished, she found it impossible to do as he asked. For the next eighteen months, she barely spoke to him. She put down plates of food in front of him, she laundered his clothes, she helped with the farm chores when all hands were needed, but she never sent a smile in his direction, nor squeezed his shoulder, nor even looked at him if she could help it.

"Mother," Orann would say, an overture of one word. He did this every other day at first, then every week, then every fortnight. He did not press more than that. He knew it would do no good.

In most other ways, at most other times, his spirit was light. He was no longer a survivor of the past, but a participant in the present. Whenever he could, he slipped away to the ridge, or to the far corners of his fields, or even took his horse and ventured out into the hinterlands. Zhara would find him. She brought warm winds when frost cloaked the landscape. She drove away rain. They wrapped themselves around each other on the grass or in the dirt or on the smooth stone where they had first consummated their interest, and even in the sky, lofted by her magic. Sometimes it was carnal. Often it was playful. Occasionally it was subdued and sweet.

Other times, he went out, he waited, and she did not appear. A touch of his former gloominess dogged him on his way back from those disappointments. He would retreat to his workshop, or tend to heavy work in the field, doing things that would work up a sweat and leave a burn in his arms and legs. He would make sure to go to bed weary, and when he awoke in the morning, he greeted the day fresh of heart and of vigor. At the next opportunity, he would go out again, and like as not, Zhara would be there.

A number of neighbors were unsure how to behave toward Orann, and what their view of him should be. Some resorted to pity. Some to dismay. Most treated him with awe that he had even managed to survive an encounter with one of the windfolk, much less that he shared an on-going bond with one. Yet everyone knew such a union had happened before, and likely would happen again. This was the Folded Prairie, after all.

Tennie Farrow was courted by Abeck Greenleaf and things proceeded harmoniously. A winter betrothal. A few months later, a wedding while flowers abounded across the prairie. Pregnancy announced on Midsummer Day. For the following week, Braccah was listless. She did not send a New Mother gift.

Wollmew alone treated Orann precisely as he had in the past. The old man was there when tasks needed a spare set of hands, even ones as diminished as his, and he let Orann be when his presence was not required. He refilled the water barrel. He trimmed the horse's hooves. He was the first to set out the game board of an evening. Steady he was. Steady he stayed. Orann did not take it for granted. Most of all he was thankful Wollmew was alert to those times when Twig might otherwise have gone unsupervised.

Twig thrived, and by the end of those eighteen months had finally gained enough padding on his ribs that for the first winter of his existence, he was not trapped within doubled undershirts and a cloak so heavy he could barely move. He romped in the snow drifts with the dog and skated on the beaver pond. Most of the shivering he did came from joy, not from the frigidity of the outdoors. He had grown upward as well, and was finally approaching the height of other boys his age.

But the Folded Prairie has a way of bending a stalk that grows too fast, and one afternoon Twig came in early from his adventures and asked to go to bed. By nightfall, the skin of his forehead and neck was mottled, a scattering of pallid oblongs on a field of unnatural rosiness. Sweat matted down his rats-nest hair until he hardly looked like himself. His lips dried and cracked no matter how many spoonfuls of broth and sips of water Braccah managed to get into him.

In those years, the best healer this side of the Endless Butte was Granny Springborn, a matron so old few recalled what her given name had been. Her hair was white as frost, her cheeks fissured almost to the bone, and her fingers would no longer fully straighten, but she could still ride until her horse was spent and she had to borrow another to reach those in need of her skills. She came when others wouldn't. So many of the blights that affect the Folded Prairie are contagious, but Granny paid no mind. She knew death would soon come for her soon no matter what risks she did or did not take. She reached Orann's holding two mornings after Twig had fallen ill.

Twig had met Granny before and liked her, but he gave no sign he was aware of her presence other than to reflexively squirm as she dabbed his nostrils and upper lip with an aromatic salve.

Granny retreated across the room with the adult members of the household before giving them her assessment. "It is the Snow Lung."

"I had it as a child, and I recovered," Orann said.

"As did I, but we were lucky," Granny answered. "This time it has rooted in. The only consolation I can offer is that he is not in pain, nor will he be. He will slip away within the next few hours."

Orann was a strapping man, but he wilted and grew small. He wobbled back across the main room to sit beside the bed.

"I will stay until the end," Granny promised.

Braccah coped by stepping away to make tea for her guest. Wollmew decided to leave the house and find some distraction tending to the animals in the barn. As he opened the front door, he was knocked flat by a gust of wind.

Cups rattled on shelves, dust whirled up from the rugs, and the dog yelped and hid himself behind the woodbox. The blankets fluttered. Twig's mouth and nostrils suddenly widened as Zhara burrowed into his chest.

Out poured a spray of green mucus and diluted blood. It did not stop until all that emerged from the boy was clean, healthy air.

Twig opened his eyes, lifted his head, and blinked.

A soft current fluffed his hair, restoring a bit of the usual tangled chaos. Another stroked Orann on the cheek. On her way out, Zhara lifted Wollmew up and set him on his feet.

"In all my days," said Granny, "*that* is a thing I've never witnessed."

Not until spring, on an afternoon when Twig and Wollmew were off to the creek to check the snares for crayfish, did Braccah sit down at the table with her son and finally speak with him directly of the choice he had made.

"I will forever be grateful to her," she said. "From this day I will say no word against her."

"But…?"

"She comes and she goes. It is the nature of her kind. Surely a man needs more than that from a wife. Deserves more. My heart aches for you, child. I can't help it."

Orann placed his hands atop his mother's.

"It doesn't matter to me that she is steadfast," he answered. "It only matters that I am."

I live and I breathe, and I have told you this story of my father, who went on to a long and rewarding life, and is now at rest in the tiny graveyard on the slope above the butterfly brambles. Sometimes, when the snow is thick against the windward side of the barn and my gregarious orange rooster retreats to his nook behind the stove, I get a thickness in my chest and a cough that lasts for many nights. I always rally, and am doing well all told, despite my sixty-seven years.

I had two mothers. The first, who was made of flesh and made me of it, lies beside my father. The other visits still, and fills me anew with the spirit of her kind. If anything has been troubling me, those worries evaporate and I am left at peace. She assures me I deserve this, because I spring from a father such as mine.

The Nature of Wraiths

NO ONE MAY MURDER a witch. A witch may murder no one.

Four hundred years ago, more or less, Ixus the Eternal found his way to the mortal plane and sired a brace of children. The sons he took home with him. The daughters were left behind. Eleven of them, there were. Protected and restricted by the covenant, they found their places. Many a time, it was the involvement of one of more of them that determined whether a kingdom rose or fell.

It was the second part of the saying that troubled Old Murgen. Witches themselves might not commit murder, but they made poisons for their patrons. They crafted weapons. They trained creatures. The result? Death and more death. None of the Eleven was responsible for a higher stack of corpses than the one who sat beside Murgen on the seat of his farm wagon.

The old man knew this was the last summer he would ever see. If he died on this short journey, what would he be cheated of? A few months of pain in his belly and dark clots in his stool? Nevertheless his hands shook as he gripped the reins.

He flicked his lash. The oxen snorted. Perhaps they sped up.

The sorceress's eyes were closed. She couldn't be asleep, not with all the jostling and bumping as they made their way along the rutted and weedy byway. Was she too weary to hold her eyelids up? The blood of an immortal father might run through her, but the years had touched her profoundly, making leather of her skin and folding deep cracks into it, thinning the hair on her head while thickening the strays on her chin and upper lip. She sat with a twist in her spine, and he doubted she had the option to straighten it. The only thing about her that rewarded a second glance was the circlet of etched gold dangling from her left earlobe.

She was in worse shape than he was.

They made it over another little rise of the terrain and Murgen spotted indications their destination must be near. A decaying siege engine, wheels stolen and timbers charred, crouched in the quail bramble to the left. A series of cairns on the next ridge showed where hundreds of bodies had been laid to rest.

Murgen had helped carry slain comrades to those graves. Helped to stack the rocks. A victory, the duke had proclaimed. Small comfort for the fallen.

He wondered if any of the bones of the losers still lay scattered about, hidden in the tall grass. The crows and the ants had made quick work of the soft parts in the days after the battle, he knew that all too well. Perhaps the marrow dogs had carried off everything that remained. He hoped so.

Finally they came to what was left of the redoubt where the doomed cohort had made its stand. What had once been a fortification was not much more than a circle of raised earth. Erosion had filled in the dire trenches. The flag tower that had stood at the center was crumbled down to a heap of stones save for one flight of its staircase.

"Here you are, m'lady," he told the witch.

Shading her eyes, she squinted. Murgen wondered how much she could see with those rheumy orbs. Apparently it was enough to satisfy her that he had spoken truly. She held out her hand and gestured impatiently. He helped her clamber down.

She wandered around the ruins, swaying on her feet, kept upright only by the grace of her walking stick. She tilted her head back as if trying to catch a scent on the wind. All Murgen detected was skunk mushroom and fleece heather.

A mossy fragment of a cistern remained, its pool sufficient to water his oxen. Murgen left his team in its vicinity, still yoked. He attached hobbles for good measure. Whatever was going to happen, he had a feeling it might inspire them to run off if they had the freedom to do so.

"Build the fire there," said the witch, pointing to some stones that encircled a mound of old ashes and charcoal. Murgen of course had already seen it. He sighed and fetched kindling and cordwood and his tinderbox from the back of the wagon.

He dreaded having to stay into the night. Bad enough that they were even visiting this old killing ground, but to do it deprived of the balm of sunshine and the reassuring company of humming bees and acrobatic grasshoppers? He snuck a drop from his flask.

When the logs were securely aflame, he brought his employer's rations to her. At her gesture, he set the platter on a slab that had long ago tumbled down from the tower. She ate there while he retreated to his wagon bench with his bowl of cold porridge and his jar of five-herb tea, that being as much as his wretched insides could cope with.

The sun set. He slipped on a cloak. Summer or not, he felt a chill.

The witch began murmuring. Murgen could detect a meter and a rhyme, but he did not recognize the language. He wrapped the cloak around himself more tightly.

Twilight became dusk and soon the fireglow was a tiny island of illumination in a shuttered landscape. "We will begin now," the witch announced.

She held out a ring.

Murgen did not want to take it, but he understood he had made the choice the moment he had agreed to bring the witch out here. He held out his palm. The witch dropped the ring into it.

Heavy. Heavy beyond natural law. It was as if the gold contained something within that craved to pull him down an abyss to the center of the earth.

"Do not put it on. Just hold it."

"Yes, m'lady."

"My name is Emeena. Repeat that back to me."

"M'lady?" Everyone knew you didn't utter the true names of the Eleven to their faces, as if they were commoners.

"Say it."

"Emeena."

The ring grew even heavier, and it began to shine as brightly as their campfire. He cringed, expecting to be burned, but the metal was no warmer than blood in the vein.

"You knew me of old, Murgen of Flatmeadow. You saw me, here, in this place, on the day this fortress succumbed."

"I-I-I did," he stammered.

"What was the name of my shieldwoman?"

"Nira," he said at once.

The witch smiled. "Yes. Very good. Tell me what you remember of Nira."

"She was…glorious."

Murgen could tell his companion was pleased by that. He hadn't said it for her approval, though. Nira had been glorious that day.

"She was so fast, she hardly seemed to touch the ground," he continued. "She tumbled and she twirled. I saw a knight swing his sword at her from the saddle, and the next I knew, she was on the horse behind the man, shoving her stiletto in his visor slit."

It was all coming back to him. The magnificence. He had so many vile memories of that battle, he embraced the chance to distill out ones worth exhuming. He had felt such awe watching Nira, felt such relief to know she was fighting on the same side that he was.

"She never seemed to get tired. She would run out of range. She would circle. Her opponents would be breathless from trying to close in, and then she'd strike. Those little blades. She seemed to have an endless supply. She'd find the chink. Open the arteries. Stab the eyes. She'd dodge away and be on to the next foe before the one she'd finished with understood he was dead."

"Yes," the sorceress said.

Murgen pulled up detail after detail. He had not realized what a trove of recollections he had managed to preserve down deep where his awareness had not ventured in many years. What had the witch put in his tea? He was thankful for it now. A measure of his old vigor overcame his debilitation. He threw that energy into his talespinning. The dancer assassin, that's what his friend Bostax had called her. Barely bigger than the boys who ran the messages from the duke's pavilion to the commanders in the field, so small that even Murgen — back then — could have lifted her over his shoulder with one arm and carried her an entire league without stopping. She never wore armor. It would only have slowed her down, forced her to fight like a soldier, and that would have been the end of her.

"Faster than arrows," Murgen said. "That's how she seemed to me. Faster than arrows."

The witch was gazing into the night in the direction they had come. Something was there. A slender, almost childlike shape. Glowing.

"I…"

"Keep talking," she commanded. "Keep remembering. Tell me of the Nira you knew that day. If you run out of words, say them all a second time."

"She didn't use arrows herself. It would have slowed her down to stand and draw a bow, and she didn't have the upper arms for it. She never stayed still…."

Somehow he kept talking. How, he wasn't sure. His attention was fixed on the figure walking toward him. Like a ghost, she was. Filmy and semi-transparent. Yet she was easier to see moment by moment.

It was her. It was Nira. She was as young as she had been on the day of the battle. She wore the same leather tunic and knit hose. Bristled with the same armament. Moved as lightly on her feet.

Wraith.

Finally she was standing an arm's length away. She looked straight at him. He was thankful his bladder wasn't full.

She held out her right hand, lifting the center finger a little higher than the others.

"Put the ring on her." The excitement in the sorceress's voice was palpable.

Murgen's hand trembled. He took a moment, knowing he

would need better control to do as he had been commanded.

That is when he remembered the final part. After the battle, he had brought a pail of clean water to Nira, serving her needs before any other combatant.

She had lifted the pail, poured herself a full mouthful, and swallowed. And then she had smiled at him.

Such a change that had been. For that instant, the fierce bodyguard, the killer, the dancer assassin — gone. She had been a comrade.

The wraith's eyes widened. Her mouth popped open. Murgen knew it was impossible, but he would have sworn she recognized him. A hint of the smile emerged.

He slipped the ring on her finger. It ceased glowing, and so did the wraith.

Now, standing in front of him in the firelight, was Nira the woman.

Murgen's knees buckled. He would have gone down had not Nira reached out and caught him by the elbow. Even so, it was a near thing, because she was too small to serve as much of an anchor.

"Steady now," Nira said. "Sit yourself down." She walked him back a few steps, and helped him sit on the fallen slab. The witch was no longer using it. Emeena was upright, arms flung wide. Her grin somehow embodied joy despite the missing teeth.

"Child." Radiant, the sorceress teetered forward and gripped her restored servant on the outside of her upper arms, a pose that reminded Murgen of the time when his late wife had greeted a beloved niece she had not seen since childhood — not with an embrace, but apart so that the view of her was uninterrupted, as if she might otherwise vanish.

Murgen half-expected Nira *would* vanish. It was easier for him to believe the witch had crafted an illusion than actually brought back a being so long in the grave, enchanted ring or not.

"Mistress, I fear I was taken from you," Nira said. Her brow furrowed. She touched her chest a little to the left of midline.

"It was a crossbow bolt through the heart," Emeena said. "You were older. Slower. Do not dwell on it. You are as you were years before that day ever dawned."

"So I am," Nira replied, voice hushed. She took Emeena's hands from her shoulders and studied the deep, ragged creases in the palms, the gnarled joints of the fingers. "You have endured a great deal while I was gone."

"I have. Some of that can be rectified. Will you help me do so?"

"Of course. Why should it be a question?"

"Death released you from your oath. You are not bound to my service."

"Then we will repeat the ritual as soon as we reach the oath henge. In the meantime, I will see to your well-being as the friend and mentor you have always been to me."

Emeena leaned in and kissed Nira on the cheek. "We have much to talk about."

The witch turned to Murgen. "You have done as I asked. In the morning, you'll take us back to your village. In the meantime, you may claim your reward. It is in the green bottle beneath the seat of your wagon."

The old man, absorbed in what he was witnessing, was reluctant to step away, but the sorceress's expression made it clear he must give the two women their privacy. He made his retreat, unsteady legs managing to serve him.

The bottle was right where the witch said it would be. Clutching it, he clambered onto the bed of the wagon and arranged himself in as comfortable a sprawl as his creaky joints would allow.

He lifted up the bottle to the starlight, but could divine little of the nature of the contents except that the liquid inside was dark. He pulled out the stopper. Sniffed the vapor rising from the opening.

The stuff smelled like every extract an apothecary might have in his collection, blended together. Murgen coughed.

He didn't trust the witch, but he did trust that he had just witnessed the greatest marvel he would ever live to see, and he understood that he had somehow been a vital element in making it possible. If his end came now, what better moment?

He tipped back the bottle and drained it in a single pour, as if he were at his favorite tavern with all the old comrades — blessed be their memories — with the serving wenches cheering him on.

Warmth radiated from his stomach, as would happen with the first gulp of anything with that much alcohol in it. In the next moment, he knew the witch had not played him falsely. He would live to see the morning, and in the meantime, the gnawing agony inside his abdomen was gone. Completely.

He ran his tongue over his gums and the insides of his cheeks. The aftertaste was as strange as strange could be, but he savored it. Then, much as he would have loved to eavesdrop upon the conversation by the fire, he pulled a blanket over himself and let the exhaustion of this remarkable day have its way with him. Soon he drifted into the first good sleep he'd had in over a year.

Noises seemed too loud, aromas too pervasive. Nira had wandered the world as a phantom for so many decades — peering semi-blind through a curtain of murk, passing right through trees and walls and even people without effect — that to be truly *of* the world was disorienting.

But oh, such welcome confusion. She cherished the perceptions, the sensations. She was even grateful for the itchiness of the mosquito bite on her neck, and the tickle in her nose as Emeena blew the dust from yet another article drawn from the storage chest.

"Do you remember this?" Emeena asked, holding up a small mirror. "Shall you have a look?"

Nira recognized the designs on the pewter frame and handle. It was the plainest and earliest of several such mirrors Emeena had made, the rest of which had been sold to noblewomen or the wives of wealthy merchants. The reflections omitted moles and birthmarks and all manner of blemishes. Emeena had been well-paid for the others she had made, wrought of gold or silver or electrum.

"Thank you, no," Nira replied. Vanity had never troubled her.

She had earned her scars and was proud of them. What beauty she possessed had only ever made her a target of interest she didn't want.

Emeena herself indulged, but after one long look, her face clouded over and she put the mirror away.

The sorceress rubbed a crusty patch on her chin.

"Lizard hives?" Nira winced in sympathy.

Emeena nodded. "Sestana's curse. It's the least of what I've had to endure, once my sisters lost their fear of me. I won't burden you with the list."

"You may share whatever you like," Nira said. "If it helps."

"Revenge will be my comfort. Today you will bring me the first small piece of that."

Nira wolfed down another square of bread, again well smeared with jam. Such a hunger she had, as if she were making up for all the years of not eating. Revenge. Yes. Her mistress had already laid out the details of her first mission.

Nira lifted her pike from the corner where she had set it. She reexamined the grain of the shaft, trying to accustom herself to the sight and feel of the new wood, absent the nicks and bloodstains her ownership had bestowed upon its predecessor. The important aspect was, the weapon as a whole was well balanced. It would serve to deliver a slice or a thrust precisely where she meant it to go. She slid the back of her hand along the edge of the blade. The distaff ends of three hairs fell to the floor, severed effortlessly. She nodded, satisfied that the honing she had done earlier was adequate.

She spun the long spear in a circle over her head and began executing her practice form. And then paused six moves in, recognizing that something about her control was off.

Ah. Of course. The ring. Its presence affected her grip.

She lifted her right hand and contemplated the talisman—the shiny gleam, the mysterious glyphs of the inscription, but most of all, the shape and weight. She was primarily left-handed, but she did depend on her right from time to time, and she had never had to accommodate the encumbrance of jewelry.

"Do not remove it," Emeena warned. "Not even when you bathe."

"What would happen? Would I die?"

"Your solid form would be lost. I would have to repeat the summoning. For that, I would need the cooperation of someone like Old Murgen—someone capable of remembering you as you should be. There aren't many alive today who remember you at all, save as a figure in the stories they've been told."

"This magic. It is not something you had in the years I was with you."

"No. I've had to be resourceful. Make bargains."

Emeena's tone made Nira certain she did not want to know all that had been involved. Accordingly Nira did not press.

Nira had no trouble infiltrating the huge dockhouse where her quarry was to be found. She simply walked in past a bee hive of clerks and dispatchers. The lone sentry, a giant of a fellow with a low-slung gut, a metal-capped baton idling on his shoulder, yawned as she passed by, seeing no threat whatsoever in a tiny woman in a service blouse and ink-stained skirts, a harbormaster's message canister in her hand.

Her destination was on the second level, in a vast, cargo-stacked office overlooking the bay, where she found a stout man in apparel that must have cost as much as some of the men in the front room earned in a year. He did not have the mien of a man of leisure, though. A heavy galleon mess table served as his work station. Bills of accounting and lists of inventory littered the area in front of him. At one end stood a lamp. At the other, an iron lockbox was secured to the table by sturdy bolts. He was shuffling through a stack of papers, hot wax and a signet ring within easy reach. This, Nira understood, was a man who knew where every coin in his financial empire came from, and where it was going.

"You are Arras the merchant?" Nira asked.

"Who wants to know?" he huffed.

"I represent Emeena of the Eleven. You have cheated her. That has consequences."

He stood. The latter action put his eye level far above hers, so that to continue the conversation was inevitably the equivalent of looking down his nose at her. She had no doubt that was intentional.

"You're entertaining" he said, "so I'll give you one minute to explain why I should negotiate with you."

"I'm not here for negotiation. You cheated her."

He shrugged. "She wanted certain goods ones of my ships had delivered. I demanded payment. What would you have had me do? I am a merchant."

"She offered her services. That was all that was required. The Eleven are to be respected."

"That spent old hag? She couldn't be counted on to charm the fleas off my dog. It was value I needed. I accepted nothing less. That is all that happened."

"The article you claimed is worth far more than the goods she received."

"Call it collateral against future purchases."

"She will be making no more purchases from you."

He did not call out for assistance. He came around the table and marched toward her with the air of a man of influence expecting only one outcome from his exertion of authority.

Nira withdrew the dagger from the sheath hidden in her skirts and flung it. She moved so quickly and so fluidly, Arras did not even break stride as the knife sped across the gap between her hand and his head.

The pommel struck him hard in the center of the forehead. His eyes crossed and he collapsed to the floor. By the time he regained consciousness, she had gagged him, bound his hands behind his back, and tied him in a sitting position to a post of the table.

Heavy as the table was, it did not shift as he wriggled within his bonds and spewed all manner of muffled curses at her around the gag. She paid no mind as she employed the set of keys she had taken from his belt, unlocked the strongbox, and removed the item Emeena had been coerced into surrendering—a rod of silvery metal, seemingly a tuning fork. Nira knew its true purpose. Strike it upon a coin or an ingot of bullion, and the tone would disclose whether the item was pure, or whether plating had been applied over a core of lead, saving the bother of tedious measurement on the scale of an assayer, and providing a more certain answer.

She knelt down and placed the tip of the dagger at his throat. He ceased squirming and became very, very quiet.

"Insult my mistress again, and I'll make you eat your balls," she said.

The merchant's eyes went wide. She saw that he understood.

Tucking the dagger away, and placing the recovered wand into another hidden pocket of her skirt, she strode out of the dockhouse as innocuously as she had entered and vanished into the throng of longshoremen, sailors, whores, fishermen, and seafood vendors that frequented the harbor quarter.

"You let him *live*?"

Nira was unsure why she had admitted it so readily, so soon after returning to the crumbling barn that served as Emeena's sanctuary. Habit, she supposed. She had never concealed anything from her mistress.

"You remember what men like that did to you when you were weak," Emeena said.

Nira shied back.

"I'm sorry," she blurted. "I did not think killing him was necessary."

"I will be the judge of that." Emeena glared. Her displeasure was so palpable Nira removed herself from the chamber, retreating upstairs to the loft.

Men like that. Nira did remember it. Age ten, thrown down in a livery stall, victim of a man who weighed three times as much as she. A year later, trapped in a gully by a roadside, attacked by a group of four.

The rage. How it had fueled her. She might never have lived long enough to meet Emeena had it not been for that anger, motivating her to survive the shaping she undertook to be an assassin and bodyguard. She had forced herself to remember every specific of the assaults. It made her strong.

Where was that rage now? The memories were still there, but they did not affect her the same way. They seemed like tales told — incidents that had happened to some other person. The Nira she was now? Her most vivid memory was of a knobby-elbowed man approaching across a battlefield carrying a pail. She recalled the blessed sensation of water sliding down her parched throat. And she remembered the smile that welled up to realize she was in the presence of a person whose first concern had been to ease her suffering.

A week after the incident at the dockhouse, at the culmination of a journey that avoided public inns and made much use of obscure routes, Emeena and Nira arrived at a hideaway in a thicket in the midst of a handsome country estate, once a summer retreat the infamous Prince Iglian the Fair had maintained for a favorite mistress.

"Phorenna was given this land forty years ago," Emeena said of her least favorite sister. "Her reward for helping the king with the inconvenient matter of his legitimate brother."

Nira gazed across tilled fields at the manor house, a structure sufficiently modest in scale and workmanship that no member of the nobility would be inclined to seize it for himself, but grand enough that when it was new, Iglian's lady would have considered herself well pampered. A large tower loomed just separate from the main residence, resplendent with flowering vines that rose as high as the crenelated terrace at its crown.

"The upper room of the tower is her den," Emeena continued. "She's there now. I can sense it. It's as I predicted. She is in one of her trances, and will continue to be until supper hour or later. Her guardian will be in the receiving chamber at the base, making sure she is not disturbed."

"He'll be alone?" Nira asked.

"I am certain of it."

A single bodyguard. Phorenna was mighty among the Eleven, with the influence and the means to surround herself with a castle full of men-at-arms if she chose, but that was not her style. Her reputation was heightened by the degree to which she dismissed the possibility she could be threatened. Here, she was in fact well protected by sentry charms and her slaverhounds, and of course by what she herself could bring to bear.

However, at the moment, she was blind to what might be happening around her. Her magical wards and snares, and her dogs? Those could be thwarted with the resources of an opposing sister of the Eleven. Nira faced a clear path to the tower. There she would find Lithus. A veteran of the War of Four Towers, he and his sword had been by Phorenna's side for twenty-two years, serving her as Nira served Emeena.

"You know what to do," Emeena said. "I know you will not disappoint me."

She did not say the words aloud: Kill him. The rules of the covenant were uncompromising on that point. Nira was expected to infer Emeena's desire, and carry out what was necessary to fulfill it. In years past, that process of interpretation had always been enough.

Nira had always been eager to be Emeena's instrument. She had never doubted her purpose. But in times past, Emeena had been different, not as given to grudges, not intent upon enemies but upon her own accomplishments.

Duty was duty. Nira proceeded toward the tower.

She found Lithus at his post in the tower's audience room, stationed at the base of the stairs that led to Phorenna's sanctum. He was nibbling at the fare on a trencher a servant must have recently delivered from the kitchen. He spat out the mouthful the moment Nira appeared in the doorway, recognizing at once what she was — perhaps even who she was.

Nira darted into the center of the space, brandishing her pike.

The spear was a gamble. Such a lengthy weapon was not recommended for enclosed spaces. But Lithus was large and well-muscled. Rumor said he was fast, too, despite his years. She needed something to keep him at a distance, at least at first. So far the plan seemed sound. The chamber was roomy and nearly unencumbered by furniture.

And it was circular. That was key.

He wasted no time with words. He encroached immediately on her half of the space, sword ready, but not committing. She recognized the maneuver. He was trying to corner her. It didn't work. The room had no corners. Her heels never touched down as she sped clear of him, running along a wall for three steps and regaining the major area of the floor, with plenty of margin of safety. His sword was longer than most, but not *that* long.

She reached behind her back, seized a fling knife, and threw it at his head.

He dodged, but she was cobra quick. The point of her spear sank home in his abdomen, just below the ribs.

His sword clanged loudly off the pike as she pulled back. The blow having struck the metal portion, not the staff, her weapon remained intact and in her possession despite the force of the stroke.

They circled. As ever, he made sure to stay between her and the base of the stairs, but his frown suggested he had deduced that it was he who was the target, not the lady he served.

He kept his hand pressed against his side. Blood continued to leak between his fingers. His complexion grew pasty. She suspected she would not have to engage with him again. To ensure his demise, she had only to keep him from retreating to a place where he could be tended with bandages and stitches and doses of his patroness's elixirs.

She was therefore already halfway to fulfilling her instructions. Why was the prospect making her insides churn?

"You needn't die," she found herself saying.

"No?" he asked.

"Not if you leave Phorenna's service. Deprive her. Force her to find a new shieldman."

He laughed. And then winced, because the effort had made use of the muscles around his wound. "Would you do that to your mistress? Who are you to think I might be so false?"

"I am a woman considering mercy to someone she has defeated," she said. "I do not apologize for it."

"I think you are a creature of fumes. You do not belong here."

He charged. This time it was her turn to be surprised. He closed the gap so adroitly she could not bring the spear to bear in time to skewer him.

Her weapon had become a handicap. She dropped it at once and threw herself to the left as his sword cut descended. He missed, in part because he had expected her to dodge right, so as to stay on his wounded side, and forcing him to reach farther.

She drew her long knife. She kept close after that, where the range of his blade didn't matter. He managed to get his shortsword out. After that it became fast and bloody and with no time for thought or speech or second-guessing, just battle. Those were conditions in which she knew herself.

Nira crossed the fields along the hedgerows and between the haystacks and was not seen by the denizens of the estate. The shallow cut in her thigh made her limp, but the makeshift bandage kept her from leaving a blood trail.

She spotted Emeena crouching in the shade of the thicket. The sorceress winced as she noted Nira's gait, but overall her manner exuded triumph. After all, the mere fact that Nira was able to return meant the mission must have succeeded.

"He is dead?" Emeena inquired the moment Nira reached her.

"Yes."

The Emeena that Nira had known would have instantly turned her attention to practical concerns — first to an examination and proper tending of Nira's wound, second to the execution of the escape plan they had made, given the reaction that was bound to ensue once Phorenna awakened from her trance and saw what had happened to her sentinel. Instead the witch actually laughed, and spoke of how this was only the beginning.

She was not, after all, the Emeena Nira had known.

Nira reached up as if to caress her patroness's cheek. Instead, she closed her fingers tightly together and with a sharp jerk, freed the distinctive earring from the flesh to which it had clung.

With shock still evolving over her face and in her posture, Emeena faded and became colorless as fog. Soon she lost her human-like form altogether. Only the slightest vestige lingered, a wisp that could not withstand the force of the breeze and began to be carried away.

"I know there are people out there who remember you at your best," Nira called to the departing figment. "I will look for them."

She tucked the earring in her pocket.

"I will look for them," she repeated, but it did not ease the sorrow.

The Ferryman

AS EROM DRIFTED down the river, the mists appeared. Once again, he had been summoned.

He played his usual game, trying to predict what his landfall would be. He dipped his fingers over the side. Not long after his gondola was enveloped by the murk, the water temperature shifted from bracing to inviting. Seconds later a dragonfly whisked past, wings bright with the color and iridescence of a southron species. In the shallows off to the left, ibis sedge whispered in the breeze, a snakelike susurrus warning him to venture no closer, because even a craft as buoyant and flat-bottomed as his could be stranded.

He sighed. His destination could only be Allistoya. Land of goats and olives, distinctive only for the long tenure of its ruling dynasty. As a young man—before he had ever met an immortal, much less become one—he had blundered through Allistoya.

Even then, he had not liked the place.

The pier loomed, a dark outline in the greyness. Soon he could make out the stone waterfront and its gibbets, a newly executed trio of men suspended from the nooses around their necks.

His frown tightened. Just once he would like to take on a passenger at a normal dock, where commerce took place, where fishermen dangled their lines, where drunk sailors zig-zagged to their berths singing bawdy songs.

The crowd caught sight of him. They called out, not to him but to one another. They began taking their positions, some in order to get the best view, others creating the gantlet down which the condemned person must travel.

The assembly was larger than the last time he had been summoned to Allistoya. When had that been? Not more than half a year.

Did they have nothing better to do?

He poled his way in until his port gunwale bumped gently against stuffed burlap. He tossed up his fore and aft mooring ropes, and teenaged boys fastened them to the cleats.

No one spoke to him. Few were even willing to make eye contact. A pair of stewards brought the usual wooden chests of supplies and tribute, lowering the containers to him by means of pulley and tackle. He stowed the items, taking the opportunity to put away his cloak, his fur-lined boots, and his gloves, reducing his ensemble to a sleeveless shirt and knee-length breeches, as suited the climate.

The convict emerged from the holding house on the waterfront's upper level. For once it was a woman — the first female to be tendered into his custody in a dozen trips, and not what he had expected from Allistoya. A peppering of grey moderated the raven blackness of her hair, but she was not beyond childbearing age, or so he judged from the steadiness of her gait and the smooth lines of her neck.

She began her descent down the ramp. A pair of wardens flanked her on either side. Another followed. All three had their swords drawn, ready to cut her down if she tried to flee. Erom saw no hint she would attempt to do so.

By now, the people had formed into their long lines. The woman proceeded between them down the center of the pier. The wardens remained at the shore end, leaving her both unescorted and un-shielded.

As ever, some onlookers jeered or shouted, cursed or spat. An urchin threw a fistful of mud — or something as brown as mud — and spattered her prison smock. A gap-toothed crone flung a bucketful of fish offal, striking so true the mess drenched the target from neckline to waist.

The promenade of the guilty had been played out before Erom thousands of times. Not once had he derived pleasure from being its witness. He did not turn away, though, because something unusual was going on. Yes, there was cruelty in play, but no one scattered broken glass on the planks in front of the convict's bare feet. No one tore open her garment. Some observers were somber. Others, anguished. A few even went so far as to glower at the wardens. Erom wondered if an attack would break out, no matter that the law's representatives were armed and armored, while the common folk were empty-handed.

No such incident developed, and in due course, the woman reached the end of the pier.

"Zeranna of Fallen Oak, you are condemned to the river," the magistrate intoned, waving a sigil-stamped order. "Step aboard, and be gone."

Another huge pair of wardens stood near the high official, available to enforce the declaration if need be, but Zeranna continued to show no resistance. She went to the wooden ladder to do as commanded.

An elderly woman near the end of one of the rows stepped forward. She held out a covered wicker basket.

Zeranna smiled at the grey-haired matron and took possession of the basket.

To Erom's surprise, she was allowed to keep it. The magistrate and the wardens did not interfere.

Down the ladder Zeranna came. Two steps, then she poised on the third. Erom held out his hand. She took it, and with a light hop, began her exile.

She seated herself near the prow, basket in her lap, facing the river rather than the realm and people that had spurned her. The boys on the pier loosened the ropes and tossed them down. Erom poled out into the current.

"Do not speak of whatever you did that brought you here this day," Erom stated once they were out of the hearing of those behind them. "Especially do not tell me you were falsely accused."

"How weary you are of those words," she responded.

Erom could not recall an occasion when the first conversation out of the mouth of one of his passengers contained any measure of sympathy, yet that was what he sensed from her. Perhaps she was an actress.

"Most who cross the water with me believe I must have the ability to moderate their sentence in some manner, but I am only the ferryman. The river will decide where you are to go. What you might say to me, and whatever I might think of it, will not alter the destination."

When he had been new to his incumbency, hearing his riders' tales had been a diversion. Who else did he have to talk to? What more natural way to pass the time? But long ago, the stories had begun to ring too familiar.

Zeranna did not comment. She kept her eyes forward, her spine straight, as if declaring she was steeled for whatever hell or desolation she was bound for.

They floated on, he making the occasional adjustment with his pole whenever the portents warranted, she waiting on the bench, hands poised on the basket.

Beyond the immediate vicinity of the boat, the vista was unchanging. Just fog. Yet to Erom, a great deal was happening. Pressure nudged from one direction then another. Thresholds were crossed. Voices spoke to him inside his head, most in whispers too soft to decipher, or in languages he had never learned, but the god-touched part of him understood.

Zeranna was detecting none of that. Inevitably she wearied of the featurelessness and turned around. She opened the lid of the basket.

"Would you like some bread?" she asked. She pulled out a braided, glazed loaf.

He shook his head.

"Do you even consume food?" she asked.

"Of course," he replied.

"Obviously not much."

Her gaze tracked up and down his body. He imagined himself as she must be seeing him. "Push a pole in and out of river mud every day for seven hundred years, and this is the result," he told her.

In truth, he had not eaten in a number of hours, and the aroma was seductive, but he had noticed the purple discoloration below Zeranna's eyes and the unsteadiness of her hand as she had lifted the lid of the basket. Each of these things told of how long she had been subsisting on prison fare, and of how little of that she had been given.

"Very well," she replied. She turned her attention back to the bread, and suddenly it was as though she were in her own home, invisible to anyone's scrutiny as she paid court to the first mouthful. Erom felt as though he were intruding on a private moment.

She swallowed. She smiled the most peaceful smile he had seen in a hundred years. And then she began eating more.

"You're sure you won't have any?" she asked.

He found himself raising his hand. He poised his thumb and forefinger slightly apart.

She plucked out a shred and gave it to him.

The morsel clung to his teeth, moist and chewy, rich with the flavors of flour, yeast, cardamom, and especially of butter. He knew he would find nothing of this quality when he opened his supply chests.

"It was so good of Basha to think of me," Zeranna said. "Her baking is the equal of my own grandmother, and I told her so." She took another nibble, and closed her eyes while she savored it. "Though now I think even that compliment was insufficient."

Her placid mood disappeared as a long, disturbing moan pushed its way out of the mists and rolled over them.

"What is *that*?!" Zeranna blurted. She nearly dropped the remainder of the loaf.

He had no comforting answer. "The wretch you hear is the

victim of a contagion. We are approaching the Writhing Shore. Few who dwell there escape its touch. The curse is in the soil itself."

"Is that where I am to go?"

"No. We are only passing by."

A bluff loomed, boulders and shrubs and hanging vines still colorless through the veil of mist but discernible enough to show what they were. Less defined were the large beings that shambled along the top. Links of chain clanked on packed dirt. A stench wafted down that combined the taint of sewage with the fetor of death.

"The wharf is around that bend. The passengers I have delivered there are uniformly vile. Often they are evildoers spared from the gallows only to protract their punishment — make them suffer more for what they've done. I am glad to know you are not that sort of person."

They continued on. The moans and cries began to fade away.

"Has anyone ever jumped overboard to avoid going there?" Zeranna wondered aloud.

"Of course. They drown. The river makes sure of that. If you wish to imitate them, I will not stop you."

"That's not why I asked," she said. "I was just curious."

He caught her glancing at the scars on his abdomen and his throat. She did not ask the corollary question. Obviously there were passengers who attempted to take control of his boat. Just as obviously he had prevailed.

In another quarter hour, Erom lifted his pole from the water. The current was pulling them along more assertively now. The slosh and slap of rapids became increasingly audible.

"Brace yourself," he urged.

The mists hid the cataract until they were nearly upon it. Abruptly the vessel tipped beyond the edge of the shelf of the terrain and lurched down through billows of water, past boulders and over swells. Droplets rose higher than their heads as they splashed into a pool, but they were only moderately soaked. After two lesser plunges they safely reached the end of the turbulence and proceeded into a new stretch of level river, the waters now chummed with flotsam and foam.

The mists peeled away, revealing a sunny sky liberally adorned with clouds. The heaviest of the silt sank out of sight and the water became clear enough to reveal the clam banks and sunken logs. In the far distance the banks were wooded and reedy, a boundary of green just defined enough to confirm that they were still on a river and not on a gulf or bay.

There was however no sign of the cataract down which they had so recently pitched and heaved. It was part of some dimension they no longer occupied.

Zeranna shaded her eyes from the glare and took in the vista, smiling as a trout jumped, mouth wide, at a low-cruising chevron of gnats.

"This is certainly better," she commented. "Not gloomy at all."

"The mists are present when we are shifting between realms. At the moment we are fully in whatever place this is. I don't know that it has a name. I have been here many times but have never noticed any sign of inhabitants. We will go with the current until we are called elsewhere."

"How much time is this trip going to take?"

"Another day at least. Perhaps a week."

"A week?!"

"Possibly. I don't yet know."

Zeranna regarded the fish guts congealing on the front of her smock.

And she wilted. It caught Erom by surprise. Her attitude had been so stoic, but now she dropped her chin and surrendered the air in her chest. Her hands went slack over the basket.

He wondered how long her imprisonment had gone on. Long enough, apparently. She slipped from the bench and gathered into a lame-pup coil on the nearby stack of folded canvas. She did not close her eyes, but if they were focussed upon anything, it was nothing more than the grain of the inner hull in front of her face.

−o−

She was still there, limp and listless, when his vessel ground against sand. Erom tossed a mooring lasso over a tree stump and pulled it tight.

Zeranna sat up. Her brow furrowed.

"I don't understand," she said.

She studied the scene as if expecting to see more than was there. It was, he conceded, not much of a place — an island twenty paces across, fifty paces long, just an outcrop of rock rising no higher than whatever tree the stump had once been part of. Its one structure was a blockhouse of plain masonry brick, the top open to the sky.

"That is the bathhouse." He gestured at the fish guts and mud spatters on her smock. "While you're cleaning up, I'll rinse that in the river."

She blinked.

"You do want to wash, don't you?" he asked.

"Of course."

"Best be about it, then. We've another leg to complete before sunset."

He hopped out, stalked up the incline, and swung wide the door of the bathhouse.

Inside it was just as he remembered, though it had been nearly a decade since the river had happened to guide his vessel to this particular waystation. The interior was a single chamber. Its main feature was a broad hollow of granite, waist deep. A subterranean channel of the river kept it full, the overflow draining away through a gap in the bottom of the downstream wall. A hot spring bubbled at the crest of the rocks in the upper corner of the enclosure, its steaming overflow trickling down, leaving an occupant of the tub able to seek out the place where the temperature was the desired mix. On the wall hung a net with several large cakes of soap that smelled of cedar oil. Two towels hung nearby, and several washcloths lay on a chiselled shelf.

He heard the scuffing of bare feet on stone as Zeranna came up behind him.

"This seems…impossible," she said.

"In the world we came from? Nearly so. But I assure you it is no illusion." He turned to find her holding a folded skirt and blouse.

"Where did you get the clothes?"

"I made them, once upon a time," she replied. "They were in the basket. Under the bread."

"Your friend Basha thinks of everything," Erom said.

He stepped out of the bath house.

"You're not going to watch?" Zeranna asked.

"You want me to?"

"No."

"Then why would I watch?"

"My jailers always watched."

Erom felt his cheeks redden. He faced her squarely, and spoke as plainly as he could. "You are not my prisoner. You are my responsibility." He placed the door against the jamb and pressed until the click of the latch confirmed it was secure.

After a period of time, he heard sounds of sloshing and rinsing. Her cheerless prison garment came sailing over the upper rim of the bath house and landed on the rocks. Erom picked it up with a wand of driftwood and tossed it into the brush at the end of the islet. He then retreated to the mooring.

Finally the door opened and Zeranna emerged.

Her clothes fit loosely on account of the weight she must have lost, but they had been made for her and still flattered her shape. She was transformed. She had gone in as a dungeon wretch and come out as a person.

"Better?" he asked.

"Much," she said.

"Then we are done here." He held out his hand to assist her into the gondola.

The waystation vanished behind them as they drifted down the mid-current of long, lazy bends of river. Eventually Erom's attention was drawn to a pair of crimson herons standing on a barely submerged sandbar. The birds were tossing a small frog back and forth to one another, never eating it. He knew then to get out the steering oar and guide his vessel toward the west bank. The mists thickened around them. A quarter hour later they dissipated, revealing a far narrower version of the river bracketted between sheer cliffs of layered rock. After an hour navigating the twists and whitewater of the channel, he saw and heard a bashhorn ram calling across the water, mocking the cave panther impotently eyeing the flock from a ledge on the opposite face of the canyon. The measure and pitch of the ram's bleats told Erom to drop his anchor and remain in place. The mists wrapped 'round. When they cleared, he and Zeranna found themselves along a placid stretch of river framed by cinnamon dunes and a verge of crocodile shoals.

He contemplated a bevy of day bats that fluttered along, feasting on the insects that cruised in the thermal layer some ten to twenty feet above the water. Finally he was satisfied with the portent, and nudged the gondola in that direction.

Throughout it all, Zeranna had watched him as much as she had watched the scenery. "You really *are* guided," she commented. "You don't choose which way to go."

"Why should that seem odd? I am a ferryman, not a pirate."

When the sun was low in the west they came to a place where he had stopped many times over the centuries — a large island suitable for a night's shelter, in a domain where they needn't fear intrusions by lions or pythons or any other dangerous creatures, especially humans. Erom gathered driftwood and lit a cookfire, leaving it to Zeranna to steward the coals and position the kettle while he brought the supply chests ashore.

When Zeranna saw the ample selection of food, she brightened. Erom, not having been as deprived of late as she, was more critical.

"We'll want something fresh as well," he said.

He climbed a coconut palm and cut down a pair of fat, round nuts. He halved them and set them down on a flat rock near the firepit. Next he foraged in the willow brambles at the upstream end of the island. He returned with a clutch of quail eggs.

It was Zeranna who cooked the meal. He saw the meaning the act held for her and did not interfere, though that went against his habit of self-reliance. To avoid fidgeting he went back to the coconut grove and strung hammocks, making sure both were anchored to thick, sturdy trunks and positioned where nothing would fall on either of them while they slept.

Zeranna did not challenge his wordlessness. Already today he had said more aloud than he typically did in a month. He could tell she had more questions, and was grateful she held them back.

After they had eaten, he spread a large blanket on the sand and settled down to admire the starry sky.

She approached, stood nearby, and likewise gazed upward. The glow of the embers was ample enough to reveal how fascinated she was at the plethora of strange constellations and the tiny red moon hanging near the zenith. He decided he could bear a little conversation, after all.

"In a short while another moon will rise. It's half again as big as the one that hangs over Allistoya, and more argent."

She sat down next to him. There was ample room on the blanket, but he tensed at the proximity. Occasionally in the past, when he was mired in loneliness or desperate for physical release, he had given in to overtures from passengers of his ferryboat. He did not want that now, no matter that Zeranna possessed the sort of unpretentious, villager's-wife appeal he had never been able to resist in his wandering-rascal youth. The overtures seldom had honesty behind them. They were inevitably a form of attempted bribery by convicts who had not fully accepted he could not improve the terms of their sentence.

Zeranna however did not impinge upon the remaining gap between them. She looked at the sky, not at him.

And one thing more. She relaxed. Even in the dimness, he could see it. She was not on guard against him.

He had forgotten how it felt not to be feared, or distrusted, or treated as a means to an end. He wondered if she even realized what a gift she had given. That was the true bribe, in part because she did not mean it as one.

Finally she spoke. "You seem quite at home here. On the river."

"I appreciate its virtues," he answered, "but I long for the day when I cast off my mantle and leave my boat for good, even if that means my bones will finally grow brittle, and my skin become fissured and stained."

"That sounds like regret."

"I do not regret that I am here. Of all the things I have done, that was necessary. It is just that I am weary and look forward to my rest. I regret that I am not stronger."

"That is my regret as well," she said. "That I was not stronger."

All at once, he knew her fate. The river whispered to him, and he knew it as if the magistrate had written it on the parchment.

"What is it?" she asked.

"What is what?"

"You seem different."

"Do I? Pay it no mind."

She let it go. She did not press. Again, a gift.

He leaned back, pillowed his head over his folded hands, and savored the peacefulness. The promised moon crested the horizon and its luster spread across both sky and water.

They were five days on the river all told, and part of a sixth. Gradually Zeranna ceased to brace herself each time the mists pulled back to expose a new realm. When the places were ominous or forlorn, as so many of the lands were that Erom and his boat visited, she studied their natures carefully and seriously, and asked what sort of transgression might have consigned her there. When the places were benign or beautiful, she immersed herself in the moment—fashioning a cowl for herself when they found themselves in bright glare, inventing names for the creatures they saw that were unfamiliar even to Erom, and at his suggestion, learning to fish.

Day by day, her body showed fewer signs of deprivation. The hollows below her eyes filled in and the shadows disappeared.

Day by day, her mood brightened earlier and stayed that way longer. Her questions turned to easy, conversational subjects.

Day by day, she grew stronger.

At last, the river decided she was strong enough.

"In a few hours, if I am able, I will deliver you where you must go," Erom announced on the morning of the sixth day.

"What do you mean *if* you are able?" she asked.

"Today we go the hard way. I cannot be certain either of us will survive it."

"I wasn't certain you *could* die," she said. "Not while you wear your mantle, as you put it."

"I have been spared the touch of old age and disease, but nearly everything else that can kill a man will kill me."

"Do not take this risk on my account." She touched him on the arm. "I would not be the cause of your death."

"Thank you for that," he replied. "But I will do as I must."

Zeranna became very still and quiet. She nodded. The corners of her eyes moistened. But as she had at the beginning, she took her place on the bench near the prow and faced whatever was to come.

They had spent the night in a stilt hut in a mangrove delta. In any normal world that would mean they were at a river terminus, but that was of no consequence. The tide came in and the gondola was pushed into the river mouth and upstream. The mists gathered. When they vanished again, Erom and Zeranna were somewhere in the heart of a great continent where a tributary river, itself vast and wide, poured down as a hundred-foot-high waterfall.

"Now it begins," he said. "I want you to buckle in."

She did as ordered, fastening the safety strap around herself and checking to be sure it was securely attached to its rung.

They proceeded along the waterfall. He waited for the omen. It came in the form of a family of otters. The sleek creatures raced past them and abruptly vanished into the cascade. Erom pushed his pole as hard as he could, pointing the gondola at the same spot.

They were drenched. Zeranna was nearly washed off the bench and he nearly knocked from his feet, but momentum took them through the barrier and into a cavern.

Only a small portion of daylight filtered through the liquid wall, but as their eyes adjusted they made out the tunnel mouth at the back of the grotto. The otters perched on rocks to either side, their chorus of "hah hah hah" barks inviting them forward but far too happily, as if they knew what sort of joke was being played.

The opening resembled a maw. Zeranna leaned away from it, and drew in a sharp breath.

"Yes, that's our path," Erom said. "The gullet of the titan. We will be underground for some time."

No sooner had the tunnel closed around them than the passageway slanted downward. The boat picked up speed, plunging them into acute darkness. The vessel struck one wall or another nearly every moment, the vibrations of impact suggesting the hull might not be strong enough to hold out in the long run. The echoes made plain how closely the walls were crowding in.

Zeranna screamed. Erom would have liked to imitate her, but he needed all his concentration. Though he had no more ability to see their surroundings than did she, he could hear the voices in his mind, guiding him now with outcries instead of whispers. He obeyed without question. He struck out with his pole to shove them away from an obstacle. *There!* went the projection that would have skewered his craft. He dodged. *There!* went the stalactite past his ear that would have knocked his head off if he had not shifted.

Finally he ducked all the way down as far as he could. He pressed Zeranna low as well. The rock ceiling whipped by just over their heads.

And they were in daylight again, thrust out of a mountainside a dozen feet above river level and into the air over a vast pool. They plunged nearly to the gunwales before they popped back up.

Zeranna rubbed her bottom and winced, but otherwise appeared to be unhurt. "Will there be any more of *that*?" she asked.

He sighed. "To be frank, we are in a far more dangerous place now."

She turned to see what he was pointing at. She gasped. Looming into the horizon was a volcano. From a gap in its crater wall a massive flow of bright orange lava was descending inexorably in their direction. It was already more than halfway down, and appeared to have the speed and volume to make it all the way.

The water was too deep for his pole. Erom switched to his rowing oar. He aimed them toward the place where the pool became a narrow river that flowed along the base of the defile that divided the mountain range. "The molten rock is not what worries me. It will take a few more hours to arrive. But ahead of that are heavy gases. They will fill this little valley and push all the lighter, breathable air beyond the reach of our lungs."

"Did we truly have to come this way?" she asked.

"Yes. Don't despair. I think we will make it."

He was afraid he was exaggerating their chances, but it wasn't as though they could scoot back up the gullet of the titan. He put his back into his rowing, and when the channel grew more shallow, got out his pole and propelled them along with as much velocity as his stamina, experience, and sense of self-preservation could provide.

His effort was just good enough. He was finding it hard to draw breath—and not because of any exhaustion on his part—when the mists closed in.

They came out of the fogginess into a scene nearly as grey because of the overcast sky. The river on which they found themselves was wider than the one that had flowed beside the volcano, but still narrow enough that its current was powerful.

That was unfortunate, because their way was against that

current. Worse still, the river was thick with calved-off glacier ice. Many of the chunks were larger than his gondola.

Erom had no doubt of the direction. On a bargelike slab of ice ahead was a troop of seals hooting at them even more enthusiastically than the otters at the waterfall.

Weary as he was, he had no choice but to drive forward, because even a brief lapse would shepherd them in the wrong direction. Within minutes, in spite of the chill air, sweat was beading on his brow. Every bit of progress was hard won. The ice prevented him from choosing the ways of least resistance.

The seals were amused, and followed them much of the way. Finally the mists enclosed them again. The current's viciousness ended and the ice vanished. His ordeal was over.

He combed back his damp hair with his fingers. He drank an entire flagon of water. His shoulders burned from the over-exertion. His palms were blistered.

Soon the water was not just ice-free, but warm. A dragonfly whisked past. The murmur of ibis sedge wafted their way from the unseen shallows to one side.

"This is it," he said.

The mists faded back, slowly revealing a pier whose outlines were familiar not just to Erom, but to his companion.

"How did this happen?" Zeranna asked.

"This is the river's judgment. Your presence is still needed among your own people."

As the waterfront loomed near, her chin began to tremble.

Erom had witnessed seven thousand passengers at the end of their crossings. He had seen fear. What Zeranna was exuding was not fear. It was resolve. Whatever endeavor had caused her to be condemned, whatever transgression she may have committed, justice was still possible, and she would pursue it.

The wharf was unattended except by a pair of ravens at a gibbet, picking at the remains of a hanged man's face. Erom was heartened to see it so forsaken. After all, why would folk want to linger at a charnel gallery? As for Zeranna, she seemed relieved to have no observers of her homecoming.

He eased the gondola to the end of the pier and took hold of a dangling rope.

"Go quickly," he urged.

She did precisely that, clambering up the ladder. From what he could guess, it was only after she reached the deck of the pier that she believed the river would in fact restore her to Allistoya.

She beckoned. "Will you not come with me?"

The invitation was a lance through the heart. "The river needs its ferryman."

"Does that have to be *you*?"

"The ferryman before me was…lacking. For as long as I can manage, I will serve. The river always knows where a traveller should go, but it can't always get them there without help." He flexed his left arm; his elbow had started to throb. "As you saw, sometimes the way is fraught."

Zeranna blinked away tears, but a smile blossomed on her face. "There once was a silly girl who thought the worst thing that could ever happen to her was to hear a good man say he would not go with her."

A good man. He tried to be.

"I will not say good-by," she added. "I think perhaps we will meet again."

"I would like that," Erom said. "But I think they will hang you before they let you ride with me again, given how ineffective a banishment it was this time."

"Then we will count on the river running dry."

She laughed. And with a spritely step, she marched up the pier and onto the ramp toward whatever destiny awaited in the land of olive trees and bleating goats and a dynasty that had ruled for too many generations.

He laughed, too, and with new vigor suffusing his wracked body, he poled out into the regathering mists.

Even when Zeranna and her homeland were lost to sight, Erom's smile lingered. Long years he had endured. Every once in a while it was worth it.

Memories Traced in Snow

COMMUNITIES WERE SMALL in the loftiness of the Peaks. Flat land was scarce, the growing season short. In the hamlet of Cascade Dell, the chimney smoke of each homestead rose within sight of every neighbor. When snows grew deep, the families gathered to spend four and sometimes five months housed within the great lodge, their dogs at their feet, their livestock in the vast barn across the yard.

Of all the people of the Dell, only the Seekers of Truth lived apart. That bleak fact plagued Scholar Radiance as she emerged onto the balcony of the contemplation hall. A stone's throw to her right, the waterfalls for which Cascade Dell was named thundered into a great pool. The noise failed to drown out her thoughts. She gazed down the terraced slope. The distance from abbey to lodge never shrank. But today, the weather fair and her fortnight's quota of scrolls already copied, Radiance had dispensation to enjoy the refuge of those log-and-mud walls again, if only for a few hours.

Her feet collapsed newly fallen snow as she set out along a trench path deeper, in shady areas, than she was tall. The scholar inhaled the tang of the fresh powder, a rarified, scentless scent she doubted she would know again this spring. Much as she loved the white purity that cloaked the peaks, she welcomed the melt. The winter's storminess, sheer cold, and extended darkness often pre-cluded visits such as this, even when her monastic duties did not.

Numbness was clutching at her toes by the time she raised the flap of the scullery entrance and descended upon her usual stool by the kitchen hearth. A cornucopia of aromas washed over her. Rising bread. Hot clay. Cooked bacon. Welcome smells of home — even the whiff of ripe swaddling clothes as Metirha suckled her new baby by the butter churn.

"Mulled cider for you, Scholar?" asked Metirha's older daughter. The eight-year-old, looking very pleased that she was no longer the youngest of her family, filled a dipper at the steaming pot.

"Thank you, child." Radiance let the first swallow percolate downward, quelling the residual shiver in her bones. She smacked her lips.

Metirha grinned. Shifting the baby to her other breast, she commented, "Your near-brother was asking if you had come down the mountain today."

"Where is he now?" the scholar asked.

"Splitting logs, I believe."

Radiance sipped more cider, fortifying herself against the renewed embrace of the snow.

She found the day already much milder. Perhaps it was that her stockings had been warmed by the fire. Probably it was the company.

Axil looked as handsome as ever as he swung his maul onto a wedge. His upper body was clothed in only a shirt, its laces undone. The hair curling out of his collar was going grey, but the chest itself was supple and toned, the battle scars no longer vivid.

In her young womanhood, his comeliness had made her ache in a way that could not be assuaged. He was the son of her mother's sister, as well as the son of her father's brother. A first cousin twice over, and therefore too intimate a relative to marry even by the standards of the Dell. All he could do was spoil her for any man less fine. At eighteen, she had sworn the oath of the Seekers. That same summer he had accepted the king's service and gone on to soldier for nine long years in the lowlands. For all that circumstances and choices had pulled them apart, still she could sit down on a log near him and be immediately at ease.

He tossed the firewood he had split onto the pile near the lodge wall. To her disappointment, he did not tender his usual smile of welcome.

"I need your help."

"You have it always," she replied.

At that, his smile flashed. Suddenly she was conscious of herself, wondering if he would note the new skein of grey in her hair, the ink smudges on her fingers.

He turned solemn again. "I do not ask you as my near-sister or as my friend. I ask you as a scholar."

She tilted her head. "Go on."

"I need the assistance of someone who can read and write."

"I see. What troubles you so?"

He set down the maul. In the distance, a hawk plunged toward some unseen prey behind the trees to the west. He paused to watch it. Stalling.

"This morning I went to fetch my wife a reed basket," he began. "When I pulled an old one from the north storeroom, my mind took a fey turn. I was sure I had seen the basket many times, with a woman's comb laid atop it."

"And?"

"And that is all. A memory of a comb on the basket lid, laid there by habit. It was not Vittra's comb, nor that of any woman I know. Wooden, one side adorned with a carving of a creek lily, the other side inlaid with a bit of polished mussel shell."

"A detailed impression."

"Yes. I would have dismissed it as a sunlight dream save that when I was milking the goat this dawn, I recalled a time when I had been milking that very doe and heard a child sing, 'The Girl Who Made the Avalanche.' But what girl, I don't know, even though I remember that the child altered the lyric so that the avalanche girl's mischief was ultimately the fault of her brother."

"Have you had such turns before?" Radiance asked with concern.

"No. Or so I thought." Axil gestured at the large stump he was using to brace the logs for splitting. "You see these marks here? I made them to start a tally of the recollections, see how often they might afflict me. As soon as I finished the cuts, I noticed these."

Radiance followed his finger a third of the way around the stump. Two other marks lay in the wood. The cuts had yellowed; they were perhaps a week old. Her mouth popped open.

Axil nodded. "After I dug away snow from the stump, I found these." He revealed yet another pair of marks, blackened by months of winter.

"Are you sure you made them?"

"See for yourself. They are identical. The extra pairs must mean I had unexplained recollections in days and months past. Were I to have two even in a matter of hours, it is in my nature to begin a tally. Yet now I have no memory of *having remembered*. To my knowledge, today was the first time I tapped the corner of my hatchet into this stump."

"Sorcery," Radiance murmured. "Is that your fear?"

At once she understood his earlier hesitation. "Surely there can be no enchantments afflicting the Dell," he said fervently. "Perhaps I should not have broached the matter with you."

"No, you are correct. It may be nothing, but we should take measures. What do you want me to do?"

"I may succumb to forgetfulness again. I need a record that mentions details. Will you write one?"

"Of course."

He sighed, but did not entirely relax. The poor man. She knew he fretted that he was acting too much the warrior here amid the peace of the Dell. His wife, Vittra, had once described how his swordhand would twitch in his dreams if he slept out of easy reach of the weapon. He must have been truly unsettled to have been willing to discuss his qualms. To do so was to reveal the stirring of the soldier within.

She rose from the log, touched his cheek. She let her hand linger, pleased that he allowed it. "I revere your trust in me. Take comfort. We *will* find the answer."

By sunrise, Radiance had completed her morning rituals—a bath in the hotsprings at the heart of the abbey, porridge with her novices in the dining hall, meditation in the contemplation hall, where the waterfall's roar was intended to overcome all distraction. Now that sufficient light poured in through glazed panes to make possible the meticulous copying of Old Empire records — the chief duty of all scholars of the Seekers of Truth — she stoked her workroom fire and, breathing on her hands to warm them, reached for her quills.

She stopped, puzzled by the layer of slate leaning against her spare bench.

She knelt beside the object. The surface of the slate gleamed. In a corner lay the mother slab, one layer thinner than she recalled. Someone had tapped loose a new piece — chalk on slate being the medium of choice for temporary, mundane writings, preserving ink and precious vellum for work meant for the ages. Had one of her novices chosen to leave her a message?

No. The glyphs inscribed on the slate were in her own hand!

Heart beginning to race, she pored over the sentences, recognizing her own diction and style. By the time she was done, she was shivering so badly she feared she must return to the hotspring and immerse herself head and all.

She stumbled in the direction of the abbess's sanctum, to beg dispensation to visit the hamlet again.

Axil was a changed man when he received the news. No longer a shepherd and mountaineer struggling to cast off a youth spent in war, he brimmed with a veteran's readiness to act. As soon as he had heard her recount what she had read, he marched from his family's alcove in the lodge hall outside to the woodpile. Radiance had to scamper to match the pace of his strides.

He halted on the woodchip-littered snow and regarded the stump. The tally marks were there, just as her journal entry had described.

"How many other times have I forgotten?" He nearly spat out the words. "Am I haunted by a memory every day, and fail to note them here because I only have one between each sleep?"

"Do not dwell on that," Radiance said. "It is vile enough to distill sorcery as the cause. Come, let us tell the others."

Axil did not step with her toward the lodge. Instead he rubbed the marks on the stump, frowning.

"You believe we should keep counsel among ourselves?" Radiance guessed.

He nodded. "For now. I cannot imagine that anyone within the clan is in league with an enchanter, but it is a fact that an enchantment stole our memories as we slept. It is best that we tell no one of our discovery, for fear the knowledge will reach the one who forged the spell."

"Does he or she not already know?"

"I think not, or my tally marks would be obscured, and your slate would have been wiped clean. If we act in secret, perhaps we can flank the enchanter. In the near term, it is the enchantment itself that is our foe."

"How do you suggest we defeat it?"

"First, we must ensure we do not lose the gains we have made. Sorcery that affects the mind must be borne by a living emissary, true?"

"So say the scrolls. A minor spell of persuasion can be carried by a gnat or a flea."

"And magic that makes one utterly forget?"

"That would something larger. At least a mouse, a bat, a bird. Perhaps one of the frogs that live in the well."

Radiance pictured the well that ran into the earth from the main hall of the lodge, unfrozen even in the depths of winter. Many a night as a girl had she fallen asleep on her pallet, listening to the croaking beneath the wooden lid of the hole.

"Dogs? Livestock?"

"Possible. The owners would notice changes in their beasts' behavior. A mage would prefer not to leave such clues."

Axil pulled out his knife and began tossing it into the stump top, as if imagining the wood housed his enemy. "There is no way to make the lodge secure."

"I fear not."

Axil pointed his blade up the slope. "The abbey is not so vulnerable. Take me there."

"But—"

"Men can visit in daylight, with cause."

She did not disagree. She was merely startled by the idea. Her near-brother had been to the abbey only once in his lifetime, and then only as a member of the funeral party come to collect the body of the old abbess to be given to the eagles. "Come, then."

Once Radiance heard Axil's plan, she saw its merit. The abbey had been built in the old tradition. It was warded from familiars who might carry spells. Such minions, be they ticks or bears, could not cross the building's thresholds of their own accord. They could only enter if assisted, wittingly or not. The lodge might be infested, but the abbey should be lean of invaders.

"This is manageable," Axil said, gazing about her cubicle. "Surely we can root out any creature that may be hiding here."

Radiance burned with embarrassment to have him see her living quarters, much less inspect them. No male had been within its confines in her lifetime.

To his credit, he behaved as if blind to any feature save those he had come to seek. Though stripped of weapons and awash in the purification anointment the abbess had dabbed on his face in the main vestibule, he was fierce with the demeanor of combat.

"I don't know where it might lurk," she said. The cell contained little beyond the bed, a few neatly folded garments, and a manuscript she was reviewing. Axil raised her blankets and saw for himself that she had no straw tick in which a mouse might nest, only a frame laced with strap. But to have stolen her memories, something must have brushed her skin during the night.

He reached for the manuscript. She bit back an admonition to be careful. It was unnecessary. He caressed the leaves delicately, revealing to her what he had spied. She now perceived a minute gap amid the stacked sheets. Two pages did not quite rest upon one another.

He left it to her to nudge open the volume. She found a pressed flower, a meadow kiss.

"Easily explained," she said. "You know that Xivhia, Morzei's daughter, has been my novice these past three years?"

"Yes. I saw her at midsummer, when her brother Borto left for the king's army."

"Borto picked her a bouquet of these flowers. I have found others preserved thus. I fear she will be long worrying over him. Fate allow that he will come back to the Dell, as you did."

Axil looked straight at her. Suddenly he seemed very near, though he had not moved. "Not a night will go by that he will not dream of that homecoming," he murmured.

He knelt down to examine her fireplace. That, she was proud to display. Her status as prioress had won her little luxury beyond a cell of her own and the ability to command novices, but the hearth was a marvel. Built generations past according to a design in a scroll now lost, it did not pilfer warm air from the room as did a normal fire. Doors of iron separated the room from the burning logs, letting in heat, but permitting no drafts to form. The air that fed the flames and vanished up the chimney originated outdoors, drawn through a duct in the stone walls.

Did Axil suspect the duct to be a means of entry for a familiar? The wards should prevent even such furtive access as that.

Axil turned his attention upon the small pile of unburnt cordwood in the nearest corner. Opening the metal doors, he seized a log with a large amount of loose bark and placed it on the blaze.

The piece was wet and moss-flecked, the sort best used when retiring to bed, when one wants wood that will take all night to be consumed. It hissed and steamed. Axil waited, leaving the doors open. Firelight danced across his features.

Abruptly, a salamander burst from a crack and raced to the part of the log farthest from the flames. Axil's hand struck like a viper, catching the amphibian on the first attempt.

He held it up in a grip so snug Radiance blurted, "Remember the law." Residents and visitors alike were abjured from killing any living thing within the grounds of the abbey.

"Fear not," he said. Carefully he turned his hand over and began to study the small beast.

A salamander was a likely familiar. Radiance knew that sorcerer-healers used them to swallow the nightmares of people whose sleep was chronically troubled. For an enchantment requiring subterfuge, what better carrier than one that seldom needed to reveal itself in order to forage, one that could ride across warded thresholds concealed in ordinary firewood?

"I will need to take care," Radiance commented. "My novice might bring in another infested log."

"Best if you carry your own wood from now on, inspecting each piece before you come in."

The salamander wriggled. Axil ignored the movement. Its magic would not influence him while he was awake. He turned it this way and that. Abruptly, he grunted.

"See the way the red and black combine? Does it not appear as though a troop of ants were crossing its back?"

Radiance studied the pattern, imagining the black portions were insect silhouettes. "Yes."

"The markings tell me this is native to a particular stream over the pass to the east." Eyes narrowing, he rubbed his empty knife sheath. "We have done more today than secure your den. We have learned where our enemy can be found."

The snows melted, the wildflowers bloomed. Life in the Dell went on, the families dispersing to their homesteads to raise their annual crops of grain, hay, and flax. The summer closely resembled those of the previous few years, with no exceptions of any apparent consequence: Some rejoiced at the number of births after a barren spell, and wagging tongues commented upon the frequency of Scholar Radiance's visits to the home of her near-brother.

Radiance was sitting near the entrance of Axil's root cellar one afternoon when Axil returned from his tenth journey to the uninhabited valley to the east. As he approached, she sighed and set down the mallet she had been using to shell walnuts. She had been enjoying the warm, brink-of-autumn sunshine, but now the day was marred.

Axil was carrying a gutted-and-dressed deer over his shoulders. Hunting was the public reason why he had gone over the mountain pass. Her mood had soured because the arrows in his quiver were all feathers up. According to their code, if he retained his memory of the real reason for his trip, he would have left two or three arrows points up.

He had forgotten. Again.

Radiance gnawed her lip, busying herself with cleaning up walnut shells and storing the nuts in the cellar while Vittra and Axil's three boys, ages nine, seven, and one, greeted their father. Only when the returning hunter had indulged fully in the reunion did she approach him, finding a private moment while he was hanging the carcass from a pole.

His face clouded as she recounted to him the phenomenon of the missing memories. It was an oft-repeated tale.

Nearly every morning in the lodge or his house he woke up as unaware as ever. Up in the abbey, she had thrice been ensorcelled, discovering what had occurred by reading her journal. Mice or salamanders had breached her cell a dozen times, but usually she found them before she went to sleep.

"Everyone has lost memories?" he asked.

"All who live in the Dell, it seems. Metirha or Vittra or Morzei will describe an odd recollection. The next day they will know nothing of it."

"And the nature of the glimpses is the same?"

"Yes. Just snatches of experience. They add up to nothing decipherable, except that many have to do with small children. I myself noticed the way Coiz's toddler's blond locks resemble the hair of some other, unremembered boy."

Axil studied the unturned arrows in his quiver. "On my other trips to the east, I kept my memories?"

"Usually," she confirmed. "You would sleep under the stars, and apparently the enchanter's familiars did not find you. This is the second time you have come home unknowing."

He paced restlessly around the suspended deer. "Some trap of the mage may have snared me."

"You expressed this fear the last time this happened, near midsummer."

"If I failed twice, I may fail again. We must do more."

"Should we enlist others?"

"Perhaps." He tugged his beard. "But as before, we know not who may be the ears of the magician. Let us try once more unaided. This time, you must accompany me."

Abbess Tranquility gazed at Radiance with brows furrowed. They were sitting in the abbess's chamber, a room barely half again as large as Radiance's own and nearly as spare, save for the desk and visitor's chair. Radiance had just finished making her petition.

"The journey to the valley and back requires the larger part of a day," the abbess said. "Do you intend to be gone overnight?"

"Yes. Two nights, perhaps."

The older woman pursed her lips. Radiance was all too aware of what went unspoken. Couples who slipped away into the forest sometimes did so to engage in a dalliance. Radiance's official reason for the journey was believable. She would go in order to catalog wild medicinal plants, making maps of their locations, drawing them in their native terrain, gathering samples. Axil's knowledge of the mountains would speed her task, and he could also serve as her protector.

Still…

The abbess tapped her fingers on the desk. The calluses, thick from years of labor with stylus and quill, resounded loudly against the wood. Finally she spoke.

"If your near-brother's wife has no objection, then neither do I."

Radiance stumbled over her thanks.

"Child," the old woman added when her petitioner rose to go. "One day I expect you to succeed me. Now would be an unfortunate time to become entangled in the distractions of the hearthfires."

"Have no fear," Radiance replied, wishing she sounded more convincing.

Radiance hated lying to her superior. How much easier it would have been to take Tranquility into her confidence. The same applied to Axil's wife.

Vittra listened silently to the request. Radiance had never been anything but kind to her, had tended Vittra as a child in the years before departing up the mountain to become a novice. Still, it came as a relief when Vittra agreed.

"Axil has been so unsettled lately," she said. "Perhaps the task will distract him."

Vittra gave her the same measured glance that Tranquility had used. Both women trusted her, but both entertained the possibility that their faith might be shaken. Radiance left the cottage ill at ease with the price she had paid to make the excursion. Elsewhere in the Dell, gossip would flow. It was like the cascade. Once it poured down the mountain, it would not go back uphill.

One thing was certain: Had the sole purpose of the trek been to create the treatise on plants that Radiance was now obliged to compose, Axil would have been an ideal guide. By the time they reached the valley, he had already pointed out dozens of useful herbs, seeds, and fungi. He knew varieties of mushroom at a glance, and easily recited which were toxic, glorious to the palate, and/or capable of prompting visions. The latter were prized by the Seekers of Truth in certain rituals.

They came to a stream that tumbled over boulders and through pools toward a lake. The valley was starkly beautiful, the sort of place that would long have been settled had it contained flat land or were it closer to the trade routes.

"The salamanders can be found along this brook," Axil said.

They hiked up the gentle canyon until they came to an expanse of bracken grown thick and high over the summer. They tucked themselves into a bower of lacy fronds. A deer had smoothed a bed in the shadows. From this refuge Radiance and Axil could observe a long stretch upstream and down without being seen in return.

Radiance, her scholar's legs unused to long travel, was grateful for the respite, but Axil remained strung hunter-tight, eyes roving the land.

Twilight soon claimed the forest, for most of the first day had been devoted to the journey and the need to attend to the treatise. They ate dried meat and nutmealcakes. At last, when the darkness precluded any hope of glimpsing their prey, Axil lay back with a sigh.

He did not converse. Radiance had grown used to that these recent years, but here, alone, with no wife or kin or neighbor within sight, she thought of the times in their youth when, hidden behind a haystack or in a loft, they had talked long into the night. At that age he had bubbled like a hotspring, chattering of dreams and new discoveries, his words weaving such a rapturous spell that she would have lain with him were it not for taboo and her younger self's smug faith that opportunities repeated themselves.

She would lay with him now, if it would cause him to open himself as he once had. She had never asked him what had happened in those long nine years in the king's army. There would never be a better time than this. All it required to broach the matter was that she rekindle the boldness that had led her to announce, long ago, that she would go up the mountain to learn and copy ancient lore rather than stay in lodge and homestead as her parents expected and be bred to a ram less worthy than her near-brother.

Her calves throbbed from the hiking. The thin air over the pass had left her throat raw and her mouth tasting of metal. The more she readied herself to speak, the more she felt like an old woman. Lying in the gloom a mere arm's-reach from him, smelling his musk, united in a great task, only now with her excuses stripped away did she know the choice to alter her life's course to be a thing entirely surrendered to the past.

They spent the night in silence.

The deer had chosen its bed well; the overhang of bracken fronds fended off the dew. Radiance awoke without the stiffness that so often earmarked a night's exposure to the elements, though her legs had lost none of their ache.

Axil was wrapped around her, his front to her back. His warmth staved off the chill and prompted her to linger beneath the blanket, savoring this token intimacy. It did not change their roles, but it was a balm.

The moment lasted as long as her bladder would allow. All too soon they were folding their packs, downing a cold breakfast, and resuming their station.

"Are you troubled?" Axil asked as the last of the dew evaporated.

"Some. It will pass," she replied. *All things do.*

They waited hours longer. Once, she suggested another location, but he shook his head. "I have hiked the length of this creek from lake to source on visits past. Our best chance is to remain hidden in one spot."

Waiting further tested her composure, but she could see the sense of it. Salamanders, magical or not, had limited lifespans. This day or another, the magician was sure to pass by while collecting new specimens.

"I cannot come here with you again," she said.

"No. Not without blighting your reputation, and that I will not ask of you."

Radiance was surprised to hear him state the case so succinctly. She hadn't been certain he perceived all she risked. After all, no one would dare accuse Axil to his face of impropriety. She had misjudged him. Strong as his limbs were, he could be wounded by the disapproval of the clan, even that which occurred behind his back. The Dell was not a place where any resident could hide from the judgment and opinion of the community.

As she contemplated that fact, a face briefly drifted into her mind's eye. She saw a narrow-chinned woman, her dark red hair streaked with one lock of white. The woman was thin in the shoulders and wide in the hips, with a pock mark beside the corner of her mouth. The pox had visited her as a child, that same winter that Radiance herself had been taken abed with it.

Radiance had possessed no memory of the woman's face until that moment.

Her breath caught. "Axil..." she murmured.

He motioned suddenly for silence.

A cloaked figure was meandering along the stream.

Radiance's pulse thundered in her temples. The stranger was thin, well wrapped even on this temperate day. Beneath her hood her face was deeply wrought with wrinkles.

Someone of her age had no good reason to be so far from the nearest hamlet with no younger person to escort her.

Every few steps, the newcomer bent down and turned over a stone. Despite her age she was nimble. At last a salamander scurried from a niche she had uncovered. She caught it deftly and thrust it into a moistened sack. The fabric rippled with the movement of other captives.

Axil strung his bow, but he left his arrows in his quiver. When the crone was on the verge of vanishing downstream, he began to follow. Radiance kept silently at his heels.

Following so quietly proved itself unnecessary. When a woodpecker rattled in a tree, when a pine cone thudded to the earth just behind the cloaked stranger, she did not react. Deaf or just hard of hearing? In any case, she concentrated on harvesting salamanders, catching two more before she headed back upstream. Axil and Radiance hid themselves while she passed.

By midday, they reached a gently sloping meadow. The old woman abandoned the stream and set out across the treeless area. The pursuers had to hang back lest they be revealed.

Halfway across the meadow, the crone disappeared.

Radiance hissed softly. Axil grunted.

"Did you see her step down?" the scholar asked.

"No," her near-brother replied. "One instant she was walking; the next she was gone from our view."

They hesitated to emerge from the clump of doe-brush that concealed them, but they dared not let the trail grow cold. They crept to the verge of the meadow.

Axil scowled. "Do you feel it?"

"Yes. I am seized by an urge to skirt the meadow's edge to avoid the boggy places."

It was true the meadow appeared boggy, especially at the center where the stranger had vanished. Had they encountered the site by chance, they would surely have surrendered to the inclination to go around.

Instead, Axil strode forward with determination. The compulsion increased. Radiance found herself revolted by the cold, squishy clutch of the mud sucking at her feet. Only her high level of suspicion ensured that she recall that her feet were encased in fur-lined boots that would never be penetrated so quickly and thoroughly as they seemed to have been.

The compulsion vanished as if they had snapped a weaving of spiderweb. They found themselves on solid, grassy earth. Not a boggy meadow at all, but a pleasant sward gone yellow and firm with summer's end, and their feet quite untouched by mud.

In front of them stood a handsome cottage, its roof pitched sharp against the snow of this elevation, its walls of stone and log thick enough to withstand winters for generations.

"I have passed this way a dozen times in my life, and never saw this dwelling before," Axil murmured.

Radiance was still sloughing off the tremor that comes with confronting powerful magic when her near-brother glided up to the thick door, bent down, and peered into the crack where it was latched. He returned and whispered, "It is barred. We will have to create a welcome."

He quickly explained his plan. Setting down his bow, he boosted Radiance up the stacked stones that made up the chimney. The footholds proved worthy. She reached the top and covered the smoke hole with her pack blanket.

Smoke soon began to trickle out the tops of the shutters. On the ground near the entrance, Axil unhooked his axe and raised it one-handed.

The sound of coughing grew louder. Next came the noise of a bar being raised. Axil stepped forward, slipping out of Radiance's view. He reappeared dragging the old woman into the open, holding his blade so that one stroke would end her life.

Radiance removed the blanket, tossed it to the ground, and clambered down without injury.

The old woman's wide eyes darted from Axil to Radiance and back. She crumpled to her knees.

"He will not harm you," Radiance said, hoping the woman was not, indeed, deaf. "As long as you supply answers."

The hand that held the axe twitched. Radiance swallowed hard. She had never seen Axil confronting an adversary before, except in play. He was not quick to step back, and then only two steps.

The woman's trembling lessened when she spied the tiny tattoo upon Radiance's cheek. "Seeker," she said.

"I am Radiance, prioress of Cascade Dell abbey."

The old woman reached to her own cheek and smoothed out the wrinkles beneath her eyes. Her skin was marked by an identical tattoo, its blue tint gone to grey.

Radiance gasped. "Who are you?"

"A scholar."

"And an enchantress."

The old woman blinked. "Yes. My studies include the lore of sorcery."

"Then why are you not in a city, serving the king or his governors?"

"I would be, should my interests have lain in the areas of spying or war. I came here long ago, in order to pursue charms of a gentler sort."

Axil drew air through his teeth. "Gentler? You are the one who steals away the memories among my clan."

The mage looked down. "Yes."

"Why?"

"I could explain, but you will believe me only if I return your memories to you."

Axil lowered his weapon. Radiance knew he had not expected such a reply, nor had she.

"That is true," he said, "but how can I trust you to do so without treachery?"

"When last you came, you bound me in such a way that I could not escape without your help." She smiled humorlessly when she saw the reaction to her statement. "Since you have a companion this time, she can stand guard. The process is swift. Shielding a person from one's own spell is trivial compared to weaving the lace of it around him."

He studied her for five heartbeats. Radiance would have needed the rest of the day to decide, but her near-brother was not given to vacillation. He handed the axe to her.

Radiance hefted the weapon, hoping she projected the impression she could use it.

The old woman climbed to her feet and dusted off her skirt. "Come with me," she said. Her voice was overly loud, in the way of a crone with bad hearing, but her smooth tread as she reentered her abode demonstrated her profound health. Radiance no longer wondered how the woman had survived the wilderness alone.

The enchantress waved away the pall of smoke. She filled a small brazier with coals from her hearth and set it upon a worn table littered with earthenware bowls and beakers of glass and metal, including one of gold.

She tipped a splash of liquid from a pewter cup onto the coals, which shifted from orange to azure in color. She lifted the lid of a small barrel to reach inside. Axil stopped her long enough to inspect the contents. He nodded, and she withdrew a salamander.

She uttered a sentence in a language Radiance recognized from Old Empire writings. The scholar had never heard the tongue spoken aloud, and could not decipher the words on the spot.

To Radiance's shock, the old woman hefted the amphibian onto the coals. The creature did not burn. It huddled as if in confusion. When it had taken on a halo of the same color as the coals, the woman lifted it toward Axil.

"Breathe its breath, and your memory will be as if I had never cast my spell."

Axil leaned in, placed his nose a finger-width from the salamander's mouth, and inhaled forcefully.

His eyes widened. He cried out in anguish. "Take them away! Take them away again!"

"You recall now how it was when last you came here," the old woman said. "You know how many hours it will take to repair the weave. Do you wish to sleep?"

"Yes!" Axil cried. Radiance had never once heard him sound so plaintive, not even when he had broken his wrist when he was nine years old.

The enchantress uncorked a bottle and filled a thimble cup with a dark, odoriferous liquid. She waved it toward Radiance in explanation. The younger woman recognized the aroma as that of a powerful soporific. The amount she was offering Axil would make him sleep profoundly, but was not enough to endanger his life.

Axil seized the cup and quaffed the dose. Holding his head and stifling whimpers, he tumbled onto the bed in the corner and closed his eyes. The potion took effect in moments, but even then his breathing snagged and sharpened unpredictably.

"By the time he awakens, I will have restored his forgetfulness," the crone said gently.

Radiance realized she was still holding the axe aloft. Her grip had grown slick with sweat.

The sorceress continued calmly, "So you are the reason he has come again. I feared he must have an accomplice, but he would tell me nothing."

"He has truly been here before?"

"Yes. I sent him home without his memory, hoping that would make an end."

"How can I be assured this is not some sort of trick?" Radiance asked.

"I can give you back your memories," the crone said.

"My escort is asleep. I fear to let down my guard."

"That is wise." The woman settled onto a stool. "How may I gain your trust?"

"Give me a reason for the enchantment upon Cascade Dell that I can believe."

"I wove the spell at the request of my closest friend, whom you knew as Insight, your late abbess. It settled a debt I owed her from the time we were novices at the Seeker's Retreat at High Cliff. But in truth, mercy alone demanded that I undertake the task. I have willingly maintained and refined it these past three years. It will be a few years more until I can leave it untended."

"Why did Insight ask this of you?"

"To forget an atrocity. To heal the Dell."

"What could have happened in the Dell that we would want to forget it had occurred?"

"You find it near impossible to conceive of it. That is as it should be, according to my enchantment. Even the roots of the tragedy are obscured."

"You have not answered my question."

The crone reached down and picked up the salamander where it had fallen. It still gave off a slight blue radiance, and did not scurry away as would an untouched specimen. She set it gently in the barrel with its kin.

"Well?" Radiance insisted.

"You love the Dell, and see it through loving eyes. But consider its long winters. Imagine how they might be to someone who does not wish to be there, whose presence is looked upon as a blight."

"There is no one who—"

"Not anymore," the old woman said.

Radiance's throat tightened. She recalled the image of the red-headed woman with the pockmark. "She is dead?"

"Beyond dead. So dead that, until a moment ago, I was the only person in the world who recalled she had ever existed, and I had no occasion to meet her in life. The wolves took her bones, and should I live long enough, the pain and loss and guilt she caused will have vanished with them. It was Insight's wish, and I granted it."

Radiance shook her head, wishing not to believe, but feeling her resistance ebbing. "Surely there must be some sign left, one that enchantment cannot erase."

"Alas, yes." The magician wilted. "Tell me, Scholar, how many children are there in the Dell between the ages of three and seven?"

"Eight or so."

"Half as many as one would expect, save in a year of pox or the fevers."

"There was a barren time." Radiance choked on her words. "Oh, no…"

"I would spare you the recollection," the enchantress said solemnly.

Radiance set down the axe. "No. Now I must know. Answer me a final question or two, that I may be sure of you. If you truly knew my late abbess in her youth, you will recall her name before she became Scholar Insight."

"Yes. She was Ophille."

"Do you recall the name of the abbess's older sister?"

"You speak of the one who died young, inspiring Ophille to take the vows in place of her? That was Lireth."

Radiance nodded. "Restore the past to me," she said.

"As you wish." The sorceress drew a fresh salamander from the barrel and repeated the incantation. Radiance inhaled.

The images hurled into her. They cut her more deeply than had the original experiences by virtue of arriving all at once. The blood. The horror and sorrow and rage and vengefulness on faces she knew well — it all flared to the point of blinding her.

But she was blessed with a cushion Axil had not possessed — she had been in the abbey when the event occurred that winter night in the lodge. She had observed the aftermath, but she had not seen Axil strike, saving the remaining children from a kinswoman claimed by snow-madness. She had seen the bodies of the victims only after they had been covered.

The worst part, for her, had been to witness the broken spirit of her near-brother, bent over the shrouded remains of his only daughter.

"How could she? How could she?" Radiance moaned.

"You know the answer to that," the crone said.

The truth was bitter. No one in the Dell — aside, ironically, from the youngest generation, the group that had become the victims — was truly innocent. All had done their part, in their own way, to create the conditions that led to the tragedy. The Dell could speak in one voice. In most matters, that was its greatest strength. But not when one kind word, one mitigating caress of approval, might have kept a lodge dweller from the brink of insanity.

Radiance turned toward the bed. Axil was twitching in his sleep. "After all the things he must have seen in the wars. I know he had comrades die in his arms. I know enemies died so near he smelled their last breath. He weathered that."

The crone bowed her head. "He had a lodgepole. He was able to endure what he endured because he had faith he would one day retreat to a place untouched by such evils."

"What am I to do?" Radiance murmured.

She had spoken too quietly for the crone to hear, but eventually the other said, "Peace, child. I will take the pain from you again."

"No."

"Eh?"

"It won't work." Radiance explained how she and Axil had solved the mystery of the enchantment. "Even if the journal I have already made is destroyed, the same inclinations will lead us to repeat our efforts. Ultimately we would return here."

"No doubt you are correct. That is why Insight chose to recall the past entire, so that she might keep others from stumbling across it. Her death unravelled that part of the scheme."

"I must take her place. When Axil is troubled by minor remembrances, I will purchase the time to allow him to forget his suspicions. I will erase his tallies, and keep no record of my own."

"I could not ask this service, but if you offer it, I will accept. Are you certain?"

"I am a Seeker of Truth," Radiance replied. Never before had she suspected how much truth she would have to know.

A weight lifted from the old woman's shoulders. She went to a shelf on which sat a dozen books—the most Radiance had ever seen one person own—and opened a volume. She withdrew an eagle feather from between its pages.

"I wish you to take this. Do you know what it is?"

"It is from the funeral bower of the children," Radiance said. "A token left by one of the birds who ate their flesh and ferried their souls to the afterlife."

"Do you know why I ask you to hold it?"

"For the same reason I must stand outside the enchantment. Someone must remember the little ones, now that Insight is gone to the eagles." Someone had to remember her little cousin, who loved to sing of the Avalanche Girl.

"Indeed." The crone handed over the feather. "I can only imagine that this is why you were given the life path you took. You show by this demonstration of your character that you were always meant to be a Seeker."

Radiance frowned. It would take more time before she could believe this herself.

"Let us make our plans," the sorceress declared.

In Cascade Dell, harmony ruled. The long winters were treasured for their role in binding the families closer. Axil grew old raising fine sons and eventually daughters as well. The abbey absorbed those members of the community who craved to know the written mysteries, or who needed to retreat from other destinies. The edifice weathered the years on its perch beside the waterfall, apart. Radiance never spent another night outside its walls, but she was not contained.

Conceiving Kings

STALKS OF FLAX BRUSHED Verra's lower legs as she hurried across the field. Blue flowers fluttered to the ground in her wake. The un-reaped hectare should have sweetened her mood with the prospects of harvest, but it stood now as a hindrance, retarding her progress to the woodland beyond. Lifting her skirt higher, she quickened her pace, heedless of trampled plants.

"Pertto!" she called again. No answer.

The tightness inside rooted more deeply, seizing her belly in an echo of the pangs she had suffered birthing the boy, thirteen summers gone. He could not, would not, be worrying her for the sake of mischief. He was not that sort of son.

The sun puddled behind the treetops to the west. Pertto should have long since been home, measuring out the dyer's-weed she had sent him out to find, helping determine how much more they would need to color her most recent batch of cloth. By nature he would be entreating his Aunt Linna for a taste of the coney stew she was preparing for supper. He was never late for meals.

Trees enveloped her as the tilled area gave way to native forest. While her eyes adjusted to shadow, she carefully examined the verge.

There. Footprints.

That much was as it should have been. The tracks were still plain in the dust, obscured only by the recent passage of a stoat on its way to the brook. A few of the impressions revealed the dimple in his left heel, what the clan healer had called the moon's kiss because its crescent shape mirrored that visible in the sky the night Pertto — only five years old then — had gashed the foot falling from a tree.

Verra worked her way deeper beneath the boughs. Her son had come along the edge of the flax, taking the long way around in respect of the crop, and had turned in by the deer trail that led to the patch of greenweed that would have been his prime destination.

The signs led on without detour to the nearest cluster of the shrubs. Disrupted, fragrant soil revealed where he must have yanked plants loose to stuff into his sack.

Her breath caught. The sack itself lay ahead beside the trail, unlaced, contents scattered. The loam was scarred by the divots and fantails of abrupt struggle.

Ambush.

Twilight muddied the details as Verra hurried on, but she saw enough to confirm the worst. Footprints made by large men in shoes led away from the patch of greenweed, the traces overlaid by a double channel of disturbed soil, such as would be made by a pair of dragging heels. On the far side of the nearest knoll, the signs were replaced by the hoofprints of burdened horses, one set pressed noticeably deeper than the others.

In Verra's small hamlet and the adjacent farms, only the headman was rich enough to own a horse. He had only one. It was a big-footed beast that pulled a plow willingly enough, but would not tolerate a rider.

Strangers had kidnapped her child.

As suspicion became certainty, her anguish nearly seized control of her. Hurrying twenty paces to the brook, she flung water on her face. Three, four, five scoopings. The bracing splashes quelled the feverishness, drove the beeswax softness from her knees and from her spine.

With a clarity that rivalled the droplets trickling off her chin, she banished the temptation to run back to her hut to enlist the aid of her sister and nieces. Her home was in the wrong direction. She had to run onward, in the wake of the kidnappers. Help was needed, but it had to be found along the way, where it might be near enough to give

Pertto a chance to be rescued.

She picked herself up and raced into the forest.

The farmer grabbed his splitting axe as Verra burst from the darkness beyond his woodpile. He had the tool raised over his head by the time he recognized her.

"Goddess preserve me, Weaver," he cried, rubbing his instep where, in his haste, he had dropped the log he had been raising to the chopping block. "You nearly turned the rest of my beard grey."

"My apologies, Vollo," she blurted between inward scoops of air. "Riders have stolen my son."

It soothed her heart that he did not hesitate, did not question her assessment. Surely she must look the part of a madwoman—her face and arms bleeding from her dash through the night-shrouded woods, her braid unravelled, sweat darkening her blouse from neck to waist. She and Vollo saw one another at most twice per year, and those brief exchanges at market fairs when he and his wife stopped by her racks to gossip or to purchase cloth from her. He ran immediately to his shack and reappeared with his three eldest sons, axes and clubs in hand.

"Be they Romans?" the farmer asked.

"I don't know," Verra replied, voice steadier now that she had her breath back. She explained all that she had seen. "I did not try to follow their trail in the poor light. I came straight here."

"Haste was fitting," Vollo agreed. He ran a hand through the thinning hair atop his head. "If the riders continued this way, they'll be seeking the Roman road. It's but a league that way." He waved west toward the narrow cart path that served his holdings. Behind him, a newly risen gibbous moon tempered the darkness. To the weak-willed, the shadows might have seemed sharper and more ominous, but to Verra, it meant the Goddess's light was with her, guiding her toward her child.

Vollo sent one of his boys north to reconnoiter the woods should the riders be avoiding the trails. Another son scampered away south-ward. The eldest, brawniest of his offspring ran ahead down the cart track, soon disappearing into the gloom on the way to the next neighbor's cottage.

Verra knew that after her long run she couldn't keep up with a healthy youth with fresh legs, but she pushed on so fervently that Vollo was soon wheezing and staggering to keep pace.

"All those years at the loom haven't worn you down," the farmer puffed. "Rane was always going on about his robust wife. I see he did not lie."

"Rane never lied," Verra replied. As far as husbands went, hers had been all she could have wished for. Now the one thing she had left of him had been taken.

Her companion appeared too winded to say more. Better that way. "I will not think less of you if you drop back," she said.

"Nay. Braddo's holding is just over this rise here. I can keep up."

True to Vollo's word, the cottage, hog pens, and grain fields soon appeared in the moonglow. A watchfire had been lit in the summer cooking hearth near the pond. Folk were gathering there.

Vollo kept up, but only just barely. Verra rushed straight to Braddo, another customer of her wares at festivals, even less known to her than Vollo, but just as quick to greet her with seriousness and belief. They were all Iceni. They protected their own.

"My kinsmen are already inspecting the Roman road," he said, pointing west. "The route passes along the edge of my land. In the meantime, you may want to hear what my youngest boy has to say."

With a curt wave from his father, the child, a gangly lad of eight or nine, timidly emerged from the shelter of his female relatives. Verra squatted, making her height less than his, and ultimately he ventured within arm's reach.

"What is it?" Verra asked, trying to sound calm but unable to eliminate the warble from her voice.

"This morning, I saw three men on horses turn off of the Roman road and ride east."

Verra leaned in. "Romans?"

"No. Not legionnaires. Their clothes looked like ours."

"But they were not Iceni?"

"No. The tattoos were not like ours." The boy gestured at the tribal decorations along his father's arms.

"Were you not alarmed? Did you not tell your parents?"

"I…"

"He did not," his mother interrupted sharply. "He was sampling honey from a hive on the far side of the stream, instead of fetching rocks to expand the hog pen. He did not want to reveal his transgression."

"He ought to be punished," his father said. The boy paled. "Yet I think I will spare him. His testimony brings us closer to knowing whose clan must pay the blood debt, if such payment becomes necessary."

A passionate murmur of agreement travelled from Braddo's wife to Vollo to Braddo's aged grandsire. Vollo tested the edge of his axe.

Verra patted the child's hand. "It took courage to speak up tonight. I thank you."

The boy smiled, but soon retreated from the firelight, no doubt relieved at the preoccupation of the adults. By the time Verra glanced his way again, he was out of sight. All those assembled turned to greet Braddo's nephew, returning from scouting the road.

"We found hoofprints and droppings laid down early in the day," the youth reported. "No sign that riders have used the road since then." He waved his burned-out torch back and forth, mimicking a search of the ground.

"They may very well be hiding in a thicket until dawn," Vollo suggested.

"It seems likely they will return to the road at some point. Our best hope is to lie in ambush until they appear," Braddo said.

The men immersed themselves in planning, assigning some of their number to gather further help, others to scout, and a group to lie in wait. Verra nodded her acquiescence, taking comfort in the energetic response to her crisis. Braddo's wife brought her bread, wine, and cheese, and insisted that she eat.

A consensus was reached. The men gathered weapons and small

quantities of provisions, and departed. Braddo's eldest was assigned to alert the Roman garrison. The locals put little trust in the legionnaires—the crones and greybeards of their families had, in their childhoods, personally witnessed the defeat of their great queen by Suetonius Paulinus—but the foreigners did enforce the laws from time to time, at least on those occasions when they were not themselves guilty of the crimes. Regrettably, it would take the youth the rest of the night and half the day to reach the outpost.

Braddo, one of the most capable warriors, went with the ambushers. Verra was soon left with the women and children of the household, whom Vollo had stayed to guard.

"Now, we wait," Vollo said.

Already Verra was shifting restlessly. She rose from the stump where she had sat to eat, setting down her bread half eaten. Until now, the search had consumed her, kept her mind partially clear of the images of what might be happening to her child. Now all manner of unwelcome thoughts rose up, including one which, she realized with a start, she should have considered earlier.

"Suppose the abductors are not going to the road at all. What other sites lie near to which they might take him?"

The shadows beneath Vollo's brows deepened. "Between your land and the road? Save for my holding and Braddo's, there is naught but forest and swamp."

"There is the old barrow," she said in a whisper.

Vollo sucked in air sharply. "No one goes to the barrow."

"All the more reason to fear Pertto was taken there."

"It is not the sort of refuge any group of men would select. Certainly it is no place to go near at night. Bury this notion, Weaver. It will only gnaw at your heart."

The food Verra had just eaten became a cobblestone in her middle. The notion would not go away.

"If the men did take Pertto there, they didn't want him for a slave," she said urgently. "Their designs are more horrid than that. We have to find him *now*. He will not survive the night."

Vollo turned, his grimace revealed by the embers of the outdoor hearth. "No one has ever entered the barrow and come away unblighted."

"But Vollo…"

"I will not go there with you, Weaver," persisted the old farmer. "Nor will I allow any of the women and younglings here to be tainted by such a visit. If you insist, if the abductors do not appear along the Roman road in the morning, a party of us will go and survey the barrow and learn what we can. At *midday*, and from a distance."

Verra stepped back, shocked. Her friend, who had proven so true these past few hours, had transformed himself. "I must go. If not with you, then alone."

Vollo sighed. "I see that you must. Mark me as a coward if you will. I have fought battles, and I have seen some of the wonders of the old realm. I will face either one again if need be. Not this. The barrow reaches to a part of Otherworld better sundered from us forever. You do not remember my uncle. You are too young…."

"No. I did not know your uncle."

"He survived the crush of Boudicca's army. Thought himself blessed with fortune. On a dare, he visited the barrow. He returned to us changed. Two seasons later, he took his own life. When he died, my father wept not with despair, but with relief. It is best you think of your boy as already dead, and concern yourself with marking those who must pay our people the blood debt."

Verra saw that she could no more persuade him than haul one of Braddo's full-grown sows up an oak tree, greased. Braddo's wife, who had listened to it all, avoided her gaze, holding tightly to one of her half-grown daughters.

No time. No time. Verra's legs—and the stamina that Vollo had praised earlier in the night—were Pertto's last pillars of hope. She sprinted eastward, seeking a path little used for generations.

The moon rode higher and higher in the sky, cleaning away some of the sylvan dimness along her route. Not enough. Her haste still led her to stumble over the serpentine ankles of oak trees. Twice her footing gave way as she stepped on rodent burrows. She rose, spitting grit, limping, and forged onward until her breath came in wheezes and her hair was limp with sweat.

She moaned when the stars began to wink out, and the blackness of the void condensed into the deep violet of the world's roof. Birds stirred, their twitters heralding the new day. A diffused, dew-heavy haziness flowed into the gaps between the trees.

Suddenly a peculiar flash cut through the woods, a glimpse of bluish, eldritch light that vanished as soon as it came, as if a door flap had been raised and immediately dropped.

Verra choked down the scream that threatened to sprout from her throat.

Until then, despite weariness, she had managed a trace of speed. Now it was all she could do to raise her heels off the carpet of dead leaves and twigs. She crept on in blind determination, dreading what she would find.

A misty dawn absent of sun had claimed the landscape by the time she emerged into the clearing around a small marsh and found herself in front of a low cairn of stone. The rock was not hewn. The lichen and scrub of thousands of years cloaked it, yet the pile still wore the aura of having been placed there by sentient design. How slabs so large could have been transported was beyond Verra's knowledge. There were no outcroppings of its type anywhere else in the region's expanses of fen and woodland.

A low opening yawned at its base, seemingly no more than a fox hollow, and barely broad enough to allow a human to enter. Approaching cautiously, Verra noted piles of horse dung and an array of hoofprints and footprints, all fresh. The incoming trail showed that one horse was heavily burdened, as she had seen in the spoor near her flax fields the previous evening. The departing trail, heading around the far side of the marsh, indicated all three mounts now carried normal loads.

The aroma of horse still clung to the air. The shrews and toads in the leaf litter were as yet motionless and silent, in the way of wild creatures that have been recently intruded upon.

She gave no thought to pursuit. Much as it chafed her to let the perpetrators go, she had not come for them. She had come for Pertto.

Body trembling, she lowered herself to her hands and knees and inched into the low cave. The spider webs were broken by recent passage, the dirt scarred by dragging knees, feet, and burdens.

Once she was fully into the passageway, but before her eyes could fully adjust, a wave of chill air rolled over her. Light leaped at her from every direction.

As before, the flash lasted no longer than a beat of her heart. Blinking, teary-eyed, she glanced back the way she had come. The clearing and woods at first appeared not to have changed, but something was eerily wrong. Finally she perceived what it was: No dewdrops fell from high places to low, no branches swayed in the wind, no birds fluttered. The view was an imprisoned moment of time, as lifeless as a carving.

Licking dry lips, trying not to let her breathing turn to panting, Verra crawled onward, descending. The walls, strangely, seeped only a little moisture, despite the proximity of the marsh. Within a few bodylengths the passageway expanded. She brushed a pair of long objects. More by touch than sight, she identified them as unburnt torches made of tightly bound wicker.

She drew out her tinder pouch and flint and lit a flame. In another moment, she succeeded in igniting one of the bundles, which appeared to have been steeped in oil. Acrid smoke swept over her, but when it rose away from her face, she could see a large chamber of the type of stone that formed the above-ground portions of the barrow.

"Ah! Oh, no!" she cried, and fell to her knees, ripping her skirt, bruising her kneecaps.

Bones littered the floor. Freshly gnawed, streaked with lingering blood, marrow still seeping. A few gory shreds of cloth—fabric she had woven—clung to the grisly remains.

How long she remained there, tears blinding her and convulsive sobs racking her body, she didn't know. Eventually she grew aware that something else shared the cavern.

She picked up the torch she had dropped. The flame revived, casting at the dimness with lively strokes of orange and yellow, enough to delineate the mica and fungi of the walls, but for some reason, insufficient to reveal the…being…directly in front of her, ten paces away.

She didn't wish to speak to it. She wanted only to get away. It was as if someone else were using her lips and tongue as she asked, with a forcefulness that surprised her, "What are you?"

"Not even I know the answer to that," the thing replied. Its voice settled on her ears from all directions. "Those who come to this place usually know what form they wish me to take."

"Then take the form you showed to the men who left moments ago, the ones who brought my baby to die in this foul place."

"As you wish." The creature's form coalesced. It became large, reptilian. Great, leathery, folded wings jutted up behind its head. Its mouth was as wide as Verra was tall. The shortest of its teeth could have skewered her head from crown to mandible. Its skin phosphoresced from pus-yellow to maggot-white, as if the creature had lived all its life in this subterranean haunt.

A dry bubble of air caught in Verra's throat.

"You are impressed? *They* were. They wanted to petition the guardian of the soul of the White Isle. In this form, I hold within my claws all the strands of destiny that affect this land. Naught has happened, or will happen, within its shores that I have not seen, that I cannot touch."

"You control fate?"

"Control is not my function. It is one thing to have power. It is another to use it."

"I see."

The dragon gestured at its form. "I have granted your request to see me thus. What will you do for me?" It leaned closer, inundating her with the earthly aroma of fens, low hills, chalk cliffs — all the scents of Britain at once. It licked its stained, fissured teeth. "You might be tasty."

"I might be, but you are not hungry," she said, again wondering at her bold tone. The longer she remained in the barrow, the more she recalled all the anger she had ever felt—the unfairness of her spouse's untimely death, the disdain with which the legionnaires regarded her tribe, the unceasing toil of her daily life. Always strong-willed, she was hardening beyond any former capacity.

"True, I have feasted," the entity admitted. "Perhaps I will let you leave this grotto alive, if you prove an entertaining visitor."

"What occurred here this night? Who were those men, and why did they offer you my son?"

"In olden times, your family ruled the Iceni?" the dragon asked.

She nodded. "Boudicca was my mother's aunt."

"Your son's blood was necessary to the enchantment my supplicants asked for. It was the ichor of chieftains, full of youth's vigor, within a vessel untouched by either battle or carnal indulgences. In centuries to come, your clan might have produced another leader of the caliber of your aunt. Now, that potential rests with another line."

"They wanted a queen, and you gave them one?"

"A king," the dragon said. Its scaly lips twitched, as if it were suppressing laughter. "Your son's death catalyzed magic that allowed me to tweak the strands of fate. In three or four hundred years—an eyeblink—after the Romans have retreated from this island, a man bearing the standard of the white dragon will be high king of all the Celts."

"This, at the price of murder."

"Great things come with a price. I am bound by my nature to do what I can to grant the desires of those willing to offer the appropriate tribute. Given such reward, I might even be persuaded to help *you*."

"Undo the spell," she demanded. "Let no one benefit from my son's death. That is the help I desire."

The apparition's smile became a chuckle. "Weaver, you should know that once the garment is woven, the skein cannot be pulled out.

I told you I can touch all the strands of destiny. It takes power beyond mine to *alter* what I touch. My recent visitors gave me what was necessary to accomplish such an act, but now that corner of the tapestry is done."

Verra's chin fell. Her shoulders sagged. "Then, I am in truth too late. Even if my people find the abductors and I take their lives myself, my son's death will have served them. I cannot take my vengeance in the manner that would grieve them most."

She dragged herself to her feet, dabbing her bloody kneecaps with the hem of her torn skirt. She turned toward the exit, but did not step that way. She was unsure she would be allowed to go. If not — if the beast took her life — so be it.

"Good widow," the dragon said with the geniality of a co-conspirator, "a high king there will be. The crowning is foreordained. But the pact did not address the question of that high king's progeny. Across the history of this isle, dynasties have not always endured the transition from founder to heir. Inasmuch as you have lost a son..."

Verra raised her face and locked gazes with the dragon. "What bribe will it take to gain your cooperation? Have I the means to tempt you?"

"That depends on what you are willing to do. But I am sure, goaded as you have been, that you will find a means. May I suggest possibilities?"

Verra knelt down again to listen, and she listened very, very well.

Knives

LEDDA WAS TENDING HER GARDEN when she heard familiar voices calling her. She rose, a cluster of weeds in her hand, and stared across fields of barley and flax. Bello the Bald and his son were leading their hay cart down the lane that led to her cottage.

She waved to them and shaded her eyes, catching sight of the man in the cart. He was clinging desperately to the slats, obviously unable to sit upright, though the ride was not rough: A stranger.

Now she knew what it had meant to find the sprig on her great-grandmother's rowan tree that morning, budding out despite the approach of autumn. She went inside, filled her basin, and washed her hands. She would need to perform a Touching.

She emerged as Bello and his son were setting down the yokes. They started to wipe the sweat from their brows, then sprang to action as Ledda cried out. Their passenger was falling off the open end of the cart. They caught him and lowered him to the packed earth.

Ledda had never seen a man display such pain. The stranger's lips were pulled back in a rictus, teeth bared. No sooner had the other men laid him out flat than he folded up, rolling onto his side. Drool stained the dirt.

He was a Roman. A soldier, judging by the armor and greaves. He was tall, with curly dark hair and hints of a muscular build, though he fit his garments poorly. Hollows pocked his cheeks and his movements spoke of bulk suddenly lost. His eyes contained a wounded-animal glassiness.

"Julia Ledicca?" the man croaked, peering up at her.

Bello answered. Ledda supposed he was saying, "Yes, this is she. The healer," but her command of Latin was meager at best. The stranger turned to her, his expression filled with pleading, his mouth opening and closing as if ready to pour out an epic if only he had the gift of her language.

"Bring him inside," she said. She held up the flap while the village men deposited the Roman on the pallet reserved for the ill. She brought her new patient a dipper of water, which he gulped down eagerly.

"The legion physicians don't know what to do for him," Bello explained. "He says it is the curse of the forest folk."

"Mother preserve us," Ledda whispered. Aloud, she added, "Tell him I'm going to lay hands upon him. He should lie as still as he can."

Ledda had heard tales that Roman soldiers shied away from the touches of wise women, or any woman at all save those they took to their beds, but the stranger complied meekly, gratefully. Ledda loosened his armor and let her palms roam. In less time than it would take to recite the healer's oath, she had located five areas where his flesh quivered unnaturally. They were hot, like wounds. Yet he had no fever. Elsewhere his skin was cool.

No snake-bite marks. No insect stings. No gathered pus beneath the skin. He had scars here and there and one knee was swollen, but the injuries were old and did not seem related to his main affliction. It was only at the five mysterious spots that his muscles did not loosen as she massaged them. On occasion the mere rubbing and manipulation involved in a Touching was enough to relieve symptoms. Not this time. She had hoped Bello's reference to the curse might be a figure of speech — every sickness, some said, could be blamed on the fairy folk. But there was no doubt. This was indeed the product of elven magic.

She paused over his left ribs, holding her hands beside one of the loci of his agony. She stared and stared. As the details of her hut dimmed and the aura of the legionnaire revealed itself to her, she perceived a shape woven of the fabric of spirit: A knife.

Its bone hilt ornately carved, its flint blade sharper than steel, the weapon hovered above the ribs, point almost nicking the skin. As if eager to perform for Ledda, it plunged inward. The soldier screamed and clutched his side. Ledda jerked back, losing the Sight.

No visible cut appeared on the man's body. No blood flowed. But Ledda knew he was feeling the blade as if it physically existed.

The soldier gasped. Ledda guessed the phantom flint had withdrawn, leaving the slightly less agonizing discomfort of a fresh wound.

"How often do they stab you?" Ledda asked via Bello.

It varied. At least once a day for each of the five spots, usually just as he was beginning to gain control of the suffering, often when he had just managed to fall asleep. The dark rings beneath the soldier's eyes hinted at many nights when he had not managed to sleep at all.

Ledda rose and paced the room, rubbing her palms and fingers. A Touching often numbed her hands, but never more than this time. "He should stay here until tomorrow," Ledda told the two village men. To the farmer's son she added, "Go fetch my brother from the mill."

The youth departed, nodding respectfully. Ledda uncovered the embers of her cookfire and added two logs. She filled her tea kettle from the stream that cut across the corner of her main room — the healer's houses of her people were always built over water — and set it to heat.

Ledda sat beside the pallet again and indicated that Bello resume duty as translator. "Have him tell me his story."

He was Lucius Arpagius, a cavalryman until recently with Agricola, governor of Britain, helping to pacify the Brigantes and other tribes of the north. As a reward for good service and because his knee was healing poorly after a horse had fallen upon him, he had been sent south to areas long since brought under Roman jurisdiction. He was to report to the commander of the garrison at the *civitas* in Canterbury to be assigned to some duty in which his leg would not be an undue handicap.

Well short of his destination, riding alone through the extended twilight of midsummer night, he was drawn from the road by the sound of boisterous laughter and the music of reed pipes and some sort of harp. It seemed to be a mere stone's throw away, but he journeyed nearly half a league, oddly giving no thought to turning back, before he gazed between two remarkably large rowan trees at a fantastical banquet.

A group of some fifty men and women feasted around a sprawling table carved from a fallen oak. The wood was lovingly polished, the pedestals graven with laughing faces and the exposed roots hung with skins of wine. High stanchions held candles that smelled of bayberry and beeswax, but their flames were cold and blue, lacking any of the normal warm golds and oranges. It reminded Lucius of moonlight, somehow captured until the burning wicks released it.

By this spectral light, he saw that these were no ordinary folk. Their faces were abnormally lean and angular, their skin as pale as milk, and their joints seemed to bend in either direction.

That should have been enough to make him turn and speed away. Instead, he dismounted and limped forward, and only the stiffness of his knee reminded him of where he was. He paused at the line between the rowans, thinking that he should tether his horse, then suddenly he was across the threshold.

The diners caught sight of him and waved, holding up strips of venison and portions of bread. They guided him to a seat and placed in his hands an earthenware cup filled with mead. He lifted the fermented honey to his lips, uncertain that he should drink, but then the harpist resumed playing. Without a conscious decision, Lucius poured the brew down his gullet.

A warmth greater than that of alcohol radiated outward from his stomach. His companions laughed at him, jabbering in a lyrical tongue only faintly similar to the Celtic dialects of the great island. They hovered about him, peering at the mole on his cheek — they seemed to have no such blemishes—at the hirsuteness of his arms. They leaned nearer than was polite, yet inexplicably he did not push them back. Simply keeping his balance on his stool seemed labor enough.

His hosts avoided his sword, knife, and anything else on his person made of metal. Their own lack of metalware became blatantly obvious. Their clothes were fastened with laces or cords. Their jewelry consisted of stones or crystals hung on leather thongs. Their weapons were without so much as an inlaid filigree.

The sudden urge to be accommodating overwhelmed him. He stood and removed his weapons, his belt. In due course he was completely naked, yet this did not disturb him, despite the many close examinations of his body. He willingly let himself be led away from the small pile of his possessions.

A figure in long flowing hair and ankle-length robes came forward. Lucius assumed at first glance that it was one of the women, but the more he looked, the less sure he was of the person's gender. For that matter, all these sylvan folk had smooth skin, hairless faces, narrow limbs—they possessed the androgynousness of children, though they were adult-sized, with mature calculation in their eyes.

The elf's face grew larger and larger until it totally blurred Lucius's vision. Something stirred inside his head, unleashing a torrent of scenes of his life, his past. He felt the elf smile....

As the soldier was finishing his account, Ledda rose and strained the leaves from the mug of tea she had brewed.

"He cannot remember the visions clearly," Bello relayed. "He does not think he fell asleep while he was there, but the rest of his memory of the night is gone, save one thing: Every image contained a knife, and after a time, knives seemed to float about him like gnats. The next he knew, he woke in the forest with his clothes and articles beside him. It was morning. No sign remained of the forest folk or their banquet, though the rowan trees were only a few paces away."

"How many days had passed?" Ledda asked.

When Bello repeated the question in Latin, the Roman blinked, clearly impressed. "Three. But he didn't know that until he found his horse and reached the nearest village," Bello said. "By then, all he could think about were the knives."

Lucius added that he had once been stabbed in a battle, and cut on other occasions. He knew what knife wounds felt like. The first of the elven blades attacked before he returned to the road. It struck the spot between his ribs, and the shock left him barely able to stay on his horse. Since then, the torment had not ceased. He reached an outpost where a physician examined him, but neither that man nor any other Roman healer could help him. After two months Lucius had leaped at word of a native wise woman who might know how to lift an elven curse. And here he was.

"And here I am." Ledda pressed his hand soothingly and held the tea to his lips. "Drink this. You will sleep."

Lucius did not even wait for the translation. He gulped, pausing only to draw in enough air to keep the brew from scalding his throat.

The soporific acted quickly, aided by his deep exhaustion. Yet even after he had fallen unconscious, he twitched. Soft moans often escaped his lips.

"Nothing is as cruel as what the forest folk can do," Bello muttered.

Ledda nodded. Lucius had been their plaything, and as the legends said, they relished exploring ways to make people suffer. How different their world must be, and thanks be that it overlapped human Britain in only a few spots, usually only on nights of power, and did so less often as the centuries passed. "Any native would have known not to be abroad on such a night," she said, "and would have recognized the warnings."

The door flap lifted and in stepped Bello's son, followed by Votto, Ledda's brother. The latter nodded at Bello, blinked a few times at the soldier, and began to hone his hatchet to split kindling. Votto had been a halfwit ever since a milk cow had kicked him in the head as a child. He never spoke in sentences. Whenever he was unsettled, he would retreat to some mundane task, such as sharpening his tools or tending the livestock. Ledda could tell he was full of questions about the Roman he could not manage to give form.

"You have fields to tend," Ledda gently reminded her neighbor. "Thank you for your help. Come again in the morning. I will need you to speak with our visitor again."

Bello tipped his head. "At your service. I don't envy you your choices, Ledicca."

"I would not wish them on an enemy," Ledda confirmed. She watched father and son rattle away with their cart, then pensively remained standing beneath the lintel of her home.

Votto's presence soothed her. He might be a poor conversationalist, but he was fiercely loyal and his size intimidated even the boldest of men. Not that the legionnaire was a threat in his condition, but Ledda would have been troubled to be left alone with him. She lived opposite the tilled areas from the rest of her village, first so that her cottage could straddle the creek, but also to be within easy access of the medicinal plants of the wild wood and out where others would not have to breathe the fumes when she made potions. At times such as this, the isolation did not suit her nature.

"Stay with him," Ledda told her brother.

She slipped outside, passed through the rows of herbs she had been tending that day, and followed the stream into the wood. The third tree she passed was her ancestor's rowan, from which she took the rogue sprig of blossoms. The twitter of finches and rustle of shrews among the leaves above and below calmed her with their familiarity, assisting her to meditate.

The Roman presented her with a problem beyond any she had known in her thirty years of life. He had done the right thing to come to her, however. Assuming the mother goddess extended her blessing, she was one of the few people in the province who might be able to help him.

The question was, should she try? He was not of her people. She owed him no debt. If anything, he verged on being an enemy. His nation had subjugated hers.

She pressed her fingers to her temples. How could she even think such thoughts? Her duty was plain. She could not pretend enmity where there was none. The conquest had occurred well before her birth. Even the revolt of Boudicca was no more than a faint childhood memory. A few of the village men had participated, and two had died, but the conflict had never touched Ledda and her family directly. To her, the Roman presence meant no raids by other tribes, new trade goods at market fairs, better roads between the major towns. Lucius was a human being in need. If she did not try to help him, she did not deserve to call herself a healer.

Yet what he asked of her made her legs shake. She inhaled the aroma of the blossoms and dropped the sprig carefully into the pocket of her apron. Unsteady, she bent to a stream and splashed her face. She shivered, but it was not from the chill of the water. To deal with the creatures of faery, she would need to find a new source of courage. She knew the rituals that her task required, but that did not mean that she had ever expected to put them into practice.

She knelt upon the yellow leaves, the first debris of the season, and bowed her head in prayer.

"I will help you," Ledda told the soldier. She said it directly, having been coached by Bello in the Latin. That way the oath became real, less subject to vacillation. Then, via translation, she explained her plan.

Lucius, wincing and breathing thinly, listened with total fidelity and agreed immediately to his part. He pointed to the saddle bags that Bello had delivered with him, and had her remove a small purse.

For the rest of the morning, Ledda ventured from house to house, speaking with neighbors. Some refused her request. Most said yes, and were rewarded with coins from the soldier's purse. When she had as many permissions as she felt she needed, she returned to her cottage, went to the far end of her garden, and dug up patches of soil marked by tiny circles of cobblestones.

To visit elves with any hope of safe passage, she needed an offering. The dirt contained the decomposed remains of human afterbirths. All came from children who had been stillborn—the afterbirths of live, healthy babies were kept by the families to bury near their houses, to add vigor to saplings planted in honor of the newborns. As midwife, one of Ledda's less pleasant duties was to till this soil of sorrow, so that perhaps the gods would not curse the same mother twice.

She sighed as she finished filling a pair of bags, carefully tying the laces. She did not like making use of such sacred material, but it contained the most powerful magic she knew, and the elves craved it—so much so that they were known to steal the babies from women's wombs to have it. They would pay attention to such a bribe.

She wished there were some way to avoid negotiating with the fairy folk. They were not to be trusted. They might blight her for her trouble, or steal her away for a decade, or simply refuse to give her audience. They were capricious and seldom merciful. But visit them she must. They had laid the curse. They alone could remove it.

That afternoon, as Votto gathered provisions and arranged riding mounts for Ledda and himself, the healer sat down and with Bello's help had the legionnaire repeat over and over directions to the site of the elven banquet. Ledda worked the turns and distances into a rhyme to aid her memory.

There was little time for false trails. If the legends were true, the portal between worlds would open next on the autumnal equinox. Getting to the site in time would be a challenge, but she would have to make the attempt. "We can't wait as late as samhain," she explained to Lucius. "I don't know if you will survive the additional weeks." And by samhain, the winter storms would be rolling through, not only making travel difficult, but prompting seasonal illnesses among the villagers which were her duty to treat.

The soldier did not try to refute her assessment. The distant look in his eyes showed that he understood how few reserves he had left. Meekly, he let Bello load him onto the cart. He would stay within the household of Ledda's sister, who would continue to administer herbs to help him sleep and to deaden the pain.

"Try to eat as much as you can," Ledda commanded. He had vomited his porridge that morning.

As the cart bounced over the ruts toward the village, Votto arrived with the horses and provisions. The sun was dipping into the foliage of the oaks to the west, but the pair set out anyway, riding until the dusk grew too deep to continue.

Votto, like most villagers, had never been farther than a day's walk from his birthplace. His gaze was full of wonder at the new hills and dells, at towns twice or thrice the size of the village. He marvelled at the width of the first river they came to, and at the ferry barge required to cross it. When learning her healing crafts, Ledda had travelled throughout the south and east of Britain, and still made treks to gather rare plants, but her brother's childlike presence allowed her to see the land in a new, radiant light. That was a much-needed balm, because more often than not she was lost in thought, brooding about her quest.

Once, a pair of men appeared from the woods between villages. One had a scar running down his cheek. Both were muscular and quite dirty. But they took one hard look at Votto's broad shoulders and simply waved and turned back, as if they were respectable locals hunting deer. Ledda rode with eyes in the back of her head the rest of that day, but there were no other incidents. She found herself imagining that they had been ambushed and robbed and that it would be impossible to reach their destination in time — a daydream that held a certain degree of appeal.

But reach it they did, at noon on the day of the equinox. The rowan trees that the soldier had described stood in front of them, separated by perhaps twenty paces. They were indeed peculiarly large. Rowans were typically slender and willowy. Nor did they grow in this region naturally. They could be found only where deliberately planted, as Ledda's great-grandmother's tree had been. These trees were guardians. Not only did they mark the threshold into faery, but legend hinted they might actually prevent the inhabitants from crossing into the world of humankind. Ledda was not sure she believed it, but she saw no point in ignoring the old tales. She carried a staff of rowan, and before nightfall she would don a cloak stained red with the juice of rowan berries. In addition, she wore a necklace of iron links, iron bracelets, iron anklets. Votto was arrayed with his own accoutrements of red cloth and iron.

Such precautions would probably be enough to save Votto from the elven glamour, for he would remain on this side of the gateway. Ledda doubted it would fully protect anyone so foolish as to cross of their own volition.

Nothing else about the spot seemed out of the ordinary, though the overcast sky lent the forest an air of brooding. She ordered her brother to retreat and make camp well out of sight, warning him not to come after her. He was to wait for her until the food supplies ran low, and if she did not return, he was to go home alone. She knew that his concern for her would prompt him to disobey, but he would not think to do so for at least a night or two, and by then he would be safe. At times such as these, his halfwittedness was a comfort.

As the hours dwindled, the creatures of the forest grew unusually silent. An owl, awake far earlier than usual, took up a perch on a high branch and surveyed the area intently. Ledda was able to determine the exact moment of sunset in spite of the cloud blanket: The gap between the guardian trees flickered, and as the gloam deepened, the trees of the true forest grew indistinct. In their place new trees, some of species Ledda did not recognize, gained substance and depth. The foreground was dominated by a banquet table carved of a fallen oak.

True night fell before the elves appeared. One moment they were absent, the next they sat at the table, eating, drinking, and laughing, as if they had been there all along, but invisible to Ledda's eyes.

Deciding that waiting would only make the task more fearsome, Ledda drew in a deep breath and stepped across the threshold.

The fairies turned as one, greeting her boisterously. They held up fruit, bread, venison, cups of mead, skins of wine. She shook her head, and with that refusal she thought she detected glints of anger, of surprise, of intrigue in their glances. They were wondering why she was not yielding to their spell.

All pretense of revelry vanished. Four of the handsomest elves shifted to the forefront, each seeming tall and stately, in clothes finer than any seamstress of the Roman Empire could hope to copy. The four were, in fact, as short as she, and before she could be lured to think otherwise, she cast her gaze downward, denying them the potency of their stares.

"I have a boon to ask," she stated quickly, before they tempted her toward some other course. "I offer this as my token." She set the bags of soil on the table and backed away.

They seemed more interested in her than in the bags, but they remained an armlength from her, frowning at her iron ornamentation. She began to worry they could not understand her language. She did not understand theirs.

The slimmest elf, oddly the one who seemed most imposing, tugged open the sack and idly dipped his fingers within. He raised a few particles to his nostrils. He smiled and at a single chirped command, a gnarled, wizened man leaped from beneath the table and disappeared with the offering. Ledda gasped—the servant had unquestionably been human; he bore tattoos of the Iceni.

The fairy leader—Ledda thought of him as a lord, though lady was a possibility—waved his arm toward her, and though he seemed not to speak, his meaning formed inside her head: *Ask your boon, and we will consider it.*

She began to shiver. The fact that she heard the "voice" proved that her body and mind were not immune to intrusion. As if she were Touching, she could feel the hearts of the fairies, and they were cold. To make contact with them was like plunging into a pond at midwinter.

She described the Roman legionnaire and his affliction. She asked them to remove the curse.

The four elven nobles murmured among themselves. The leader gave a high, cackling laugh. He gestured Ledda forward, insistently, making it obvious that he would brook no disobedience. Nervously rubbing her bracelets, she inched forward until she stood in the center of the quartet. Suddenly they shifted, and she was face to face with an elf with long, flaxen tresses — the most masculine of all, save for that hair. He reached out, not quite grasping her head.

Ledda gasped. She was barely aware of the grove, the banquet, the elves. She was suddenly elsewhere. Around her were the walls of the mill house near her home. But not the mill house of the present day. It was the old one, the one that had burned down a few seasons ago. Naked, she was sprawled indulgently atop a blanket behind sacks of newly ground flour. Sarro, the miller's son, was lowering his body between her legs, which she was spreading in welcome.

Disoriented, Ledda cried out. To no effect. Her mouth emitted only sighs. Sarro breached her, was engulfed by her wet warmth, and began to rhythmically move his hips.

Ledda knew this scene. She had been fifteen, and Sarro had evolved from childhood companion to likely husband, though they imagined this was a secret known only to them. Two months before they had given each other their virginity. By now they had passed the awkwardness and discomfort of the first few times. Their bodies knew each other. The younger Ledda smiled, limbs taut, wondering how anything could be so good. She was almost afraid of the emotions claiming her — ashamed that her body would rule her faculties so profoundly. She would have done anything for Sarro.

But Sarro died that winter of the pox. That tryst in the mill house had been the pinnacle of their time together. It was the older Ledda's most cherished memory.

And now the elf had taken it, gutted it, laid it out on the table for all to see. As the vision faded, the healer collapsed to the ground, weeping.

The elf stroked his chin, considering her, as if measuring her by the nature of what she considered most private. She realized she was not the first human he had evaluated this way. It was said that his kind were immortal. Lucius had been only the latest victim of dozens, perhaps hundreds.

The process…amused them.

A second elf, this one with braided hair and green, catlike eyes, loomed over her. She/he extended hands, and Ledda grew dizzy. Images floated to her mind like the hypnagogic stream seen each night as she drifted to sleep. The elf murmured, debating which memory to investigate.

Ledda had no clue how to resist. They would open her. The iron and the rowan protected her body, but now that she had let herself venture within their circle, her inner self was theirs to toy with. She retained control in only one respect—she was aware of every facet of the violation, and knew her recollection would not fade, whereas Lucius, like most humans the fairy folk played with, had enjoyed the blessing of forgetfulness.

"No," she said abruptly. She could not simply submit. If her magicks had proven feeble, her great-grandmother had spoken of one other way to spar with elves, though it was the least dependable method: she had to appeal to their principles.

"You dishonor me," she stated forcefully. "I remain on this spot of my own will." And this, she realized suddenly, was true. If she were willing to forsake the boon, she could crawl back across the threshold, out of their reach, leaving them hissing and impotent as they tried to tug at her metal-laden body. "I brought you tribute. You will give me what I ask, and leave my soul to me."

The elf with braided hair stepped back, turning to the leader. They spoke. The other pair of nobles joined in, provoking a sharp, four-way argument. Finally the leader raised a hand. He knelt beside Ledda.

Very well, he said. *We will show you what we did.* And he held up a knife of bone and flint.

Birds, celebrating an unusually warm autumn morning, twittered in the branches as Ledda staggered through the trees to

Votto's camp. Her brother rushed to her side and steadied her as she sat on a log.

She had never before realized how intense the colors of her world were. Especially red, she thought, clasping at the edges of her cloak. She opened her eyes wider, trying to take the scenery in, claim it.

Votto stared at her with narrowed brows. She patted his hand. "I am well," she said. "Well enough. How long was I gone?"

He held up three fingers.

Three days. Like the soldier. There was still ample food in the saddlebags. The hint of guilt in Votto's posture indicated that he had indeed come looking for her, and was still distressed that he had not found her where she should have been.

"Worry not," she told him. She lifted her fist and opened it, revealing a silvery grey acorn. "We have only to take this to the soldier, and our task will be done."

Votto grunted, and they headed back to the road.

It seemed every man, woman, and older child of the village was out in the fields as Ledda and her brother returned. The harvest was abundant, making up for the poor crops of the past two years. Ledda acknowledged greetings, but she did not stop to talk.

Her sister greeted her at the door of her home. Ledda ordered a nephew to fetch Bello, then she knelt down beside the pallet where Lucius lay.

He was shaking and sweating. His body was almost skeletal in its gauntness, his face drawn and haggard. The herbal remedies had left his eyes a little less rheumy, but clearly he was wasting away.

She knew what he was experiencing. The elves had shown her with deliberate vividness. Ethereal knives had prodded her, cut her, sliced parts away, until she could not contain it all, could think of nothing but pain. But then it had ended. Lucius, however, had been allowed no escape. The knives had been with him for three months. She was certain that by now, on many levels, he had already gone insane, kept from total dissolution only by a stubborn faith in a cure.

As a Roman, perhaps part of him refused to acknowledge the reality of faery and its denizens, nor their power to affect him.

Her arrival helped him rally. He sat up abruptly, calling to her in Latin. She showed him the acorn. He caressed it timidly, obviously unsure exactly how it might help him, but certain that it would. Then he clutched his leg, groaning as a knife pierced him.

Ledda located a small mortar and pestle. She hulled the acorn, placed the meat in the bowl, and began to grind it. Meanwhile, per her instructions, her sister brought fresh water from the well and set it to boil. Bello arrived as Ledda poured the acorn flour onto a cutting board, dribbled hot water, and formed a tiny morsel of dough.

With Bello translating, Ledda explained, "I will cook this into a biscuit. It has not been leached, so it will be bitter."

He nodded.

"He says to hurry," Bello said.

She removed the flatstone from the fire's edge, anointed it with a smear of butter, and placed the disk of dough upon it. The biscuit gradually stiffened and began to steam. She flipped it onto a cloth and held it toward him.

"Eat it as soon as it is cool enough not to burn your tongue."

The soldier blew air to speed the cooling, nibbled first along the edges, then as the steam dissipated, he wolfed down the remainder.

Ledda folded her hands in her lap, and seemed to lapse into meditation.

Suddenly the Roman fell to the floor, spasming. "No!" he cried and burst out with a torrent of Latin.

"He says there is another knife, cutting him behind the knee!" repeated Bello, eyes wide.

"One for the Brigante child he hamstrung because the boy would not lick his saddle clean," she intoned.

Bello hesitated. "Tell him!" Ledda hissed.

Hardly had the farmer done so than the soldier screamed and clutched his face, as if an eye was being gouged out.

"One for the old warrior you blinded when he looked at you

defiantly with his one good eye," Ledda said, this time speaking directly at Lucius, who surely understood all too well. He screamed again and cupped his groin.

"And that for the black-haired girl you raped, and for forcing her mother to watch."

The soldier writhed on the floor, tongue rolling over the packed earth, joints straining to their limits, sweat exploding from every pore. Votto, Bello, and the others cringed back. They cast nervous glances at Ledda. Her sister still had hands over her ears, as if she could not believe the words that had come from the throat of her own kin.

Ledda opened her mouth to announce the crimes behind the original five knives, but all at once, the ice inside her broke. She sobbed and lowered her forehead to her palm. "A pox upon all elves!" she choked, shaking with the knowledge of what she had done. The fairies had known she was too compassionate to levy such a sentence of her own will, however much she might agree that the legionnaire deserved it. They had laid a compulsion upon her.

She flung the empty acorn hull into the fire, spitting on the coals. "Send him back to his people," she whimpered. To her relief, her brother and Bello, their faces black with outrage at what she had been forced to endure for so unworthy a person, had already begun to drag the Roman away.

Whimsical were the elves, and seldom merciful. But never would she accuse them of lacking a sense of justice.

Foam

CORAL SWAM SLOWLY, with trepidation, into the reception hall of her father, the Sea King. The lord of the ocean, clad in the visage of a giant turtle, rested on the sands, quiet save for the pensive shifting of a flipper.

Gone were the dolphins who had swum and sung across the vaulted chamber. Gone were the crabs who danced on the tables of rock, leaving behind their gifts of shells and jade. Gone were Coral's brothers and sisters, come to congratulate her on the anniversary of her birth.

There was only the Sea King, dimming the sanctuary with cold green melancholy.

"Father?" she asked, setting her fluke timidly upon the sand beside his beak, wishing she could cure his mood.

"Today you are fifteen years old," he said. "Today you venture into the world for the first time."

Her brows drew together. Hours earlier, he had celebrated this same fact.

"I feel her," he said. "She is waiting for you."

The current streaming off his shell carried the sting of an Arctic floe. Coral shuddered in the chill. "The Sea Witch?" she asked.

"She has always thwarted me. I am Life. She is Death. I tell the amoeba to divide, I make fertile the eggs of the marlin, I anchor the roots of the kelp. She brings to them age, rot, and dissipation. She and I may never share the same place and moment, but I feel her presence. I know her desires."

The Sea King turned his turtle eyes toward his offspring. Massive and opaque, the pupils dwarfed her, capturing her reflection like an insect in amber. Her long red tresses flowed rich and full around her human half, down to the dorsal fin on her long, whalelike fluke.

"She hates you most of all," the king said. "You are beautiful, you brim with young life, and because you are made from my essence, you will not succumb to the decay she has loosed upon the rest of my world. To kill you, she must actively break the magic which formed you, with your consent."

Coral lay a hand gently on her sire's beak. "Why would I give her my consent?"

The turtle closed his eyes, as if in pain, shutting out the reflected vision of her. "I cannot protect you, once you leave these walls. You must dare Death alone, if you are to overcome her. If you are my true child, and if you make the right choices, you will prevail. If not..."

One of his fins moved, spawning a surge of water that sent Coral back, into the central portion of the grotto. The quivering of his great eyelids betrayed that he would rather have cupped her form beneath him, and guarded her forever.

"Go, my daughter. Show the world your beauty. Be all that you can."

The currents lifted her up, gently buoying her through the long passageway to the open ocean. Her father's grief followed her, as he wept for older children who had never returned to his side.

Twilight silvered the ocean as Coral emerged from the depths. Vestiges of the day blessed the clouds with hues of rose and gold, and up in the pale pink sky the evening star held court. A large three-masted ship idled in the calm sea, sails hoisted as offerings to a fickle tradewind. Sailors hung like monkeys from the rigging and from the yards. They sang, made music, and lit hundreds of lanterns that, with their different colors, looked as if the flags of all nations had been borrowed for display.

Coral floated just beyond the range of the lantern light, drawn by the jubilation frothing in the hearts of the crew. They were near the end of a long voyage; the coast of their country had come in sight as the sun had set. Holds full of trade goods, they anticipated the wealth and welcome awaiting them in the morning.

All this the mermaid gleaned from their minds, but the facts meant little to her compared to the feelings associated with them. Such fire, such a cacophony of hope, schemes, and relief.

Her father had often told her of humanity, of how the Earth Mother had sent him the ape, and how he had stripped the creature's hair from its skin and aligned its pelvis with its spine until, stream-lined, it could swim and dive with ease. He had heightened its sense of hearing, prompting its first use of vocal language. He taught it to use tools, with which it battered open shellfish to eat.

But the Earth Mother, seeing what he had fashioned, called her gift back. The new species took its language, tools, and erect posture back to the land, forsaking the Sea King.

At last, Coral understood why her father spoke of man with such wistfulness, and why he had shaped her upper body like them. Never had she encountered so many consciousnesses, gathered so closely together, burbling with such keenly felt desires. Their passions tugged her like spawning beds drew the salmon.

One human stood out. Dark-haired and tall, he seemed quite young, and yet every other man on the ship deferred to him. Was he a prince? Yes. A prince of merchants. Within his awareness flashed images of lively negotiations, careful intimidation, and a paternal concern for his crew. She saw why they looked to him with loyalty and respect.

Yet overriding his satisfaction at a job well done, he brimmed with another urge. He gazed toward the night-shrouded coast. A woman waited for him there. Body aching, he dreamed of their reunion.

Coral surged up, until she rose waist high in a wreath of foam. Eyes closed, she drank in the prince's hunger. Her skin, exposed to the air, rose with fine prickles.

Her eyes came open. She had wandered into the lantern light. At the gunwale, the prince stared. He lifted his flagon, as if to accuse its contents of addling his senses, but he never looked away from her.

His dream woman transformed. Her plain brown hair became Coral's luxuriant scarlet tresses. Her breasts rode higher, her waist shrank, and the bones of her clavicle grew more distinct. Like Coral.

Her exclamation rode across the water. The prince blinked. He called to his companions.

Coral submerged. The other sailors glimpsed her white skin so briefly that, moments later, they joked at being so foolish as to mistake sea foam for a mermaid. The prince scowled, laughing only to give them less to tease him about. Agitated, he scanned the waves.

Coral remained below. But not from fright. She could not banish the image she had seen in the prince's mind, an instant before her cry shattered it. It was she, reenvisioned by the prince's fervor.

Her face, her arms — and below that, her legs.

When Coral finally nudged above the surface, she was far from the lantern light. She could still distinguish the silhouettes of the men — and of the prince — but a gulf yawned between her and the ship, as awesome as the deepest trench of her father's domain.

She floated listlessly, drifting away from the ship. The scales of her lower extremity flashed in the moonlight, and the glare hurt her eyes as it had never done before.

The moonlight faded. Swells deepened and the wind rose. Coral scarcely noticed. Storms were no threat to her. But at some point she realized that the sounds of revelry had died out, replaced by harsh, barked orders to furl the sails and secure the ship.

Weather's fury arrived in a wall of turbulence and hard rain. Waves loomed black and mountainous. The ship dived like a swan into the troughs of the swells and rode up again on their towering crests, masts creaking. The young mermaid might have enjoyed the spectacle, but she was still attuned to the humans, and felt their fear.

The vessel groaned, the stout planks yielding to the heavy pounding. A spur of reef suddenly appeared in the trough ahead. As sailors screamed, the craft struck.

The mainmast snapped. The ship gave a lurch to one side. Water gushed through the ruptured hull.

Coral plunged forward. Wreckage threatened to slam into her at the whim of the gale. She sought and found the familiar essence of the prince. He was underwater, caught in a morass of rigging, losing consciousness.

She dived, reaching the man as his lungs gave out. The ropes and tackle clutched him like a lover. She yanked and bit at the hemp. No good. Deprived of quicker choices, she worked a knot free and fed the line through the pulley that held it. Success. She rushed the prince to the surface.

As her father had taught her, the mermaid created an islet of calm within the tempest. Floating on her back, she cradled the prince on her belly. She squeezed his midsection. Salt water burbled from his mouth. He coughed, heaved, and collapsed against her. His breath returned, ragged but continuous.

The depths took three, five, then seven of the prince's sailors. Coral resolved that he would not join them. She kept the storm's violence at bay, ferrying him gently to the shore.

She swam so carefully that, by the time sand brushed against her back, the worst of the gale had passed. Though awkward on land, she dragged herself and her charge high above the reach of the breakers, into the lee of a grassy dune.

He shivered. She removed and wrung out his drenched garments, curled around him, and draped them both with the fabric. He stopped shaking, though he still twisted restlessly.

The sensation of his body against her brought a puzzling weakness to her muscles. Pleased and curious, she huddled closer.

He moaned. She wiped beads of feverish sudor from his forehead and the bridge of his nose. He rolled over, facing her. His eyes opened.

Even with thick clouds and rain shrouding the moon, he recognized her. He caressed her cheek. Coral read his confusion. He believed himself delirious. He trembled to find warm, tangible flesh beneath his fingers.

In answer to his unspoken question, Coral leaned in and placed her mouth against his. He pressed up, into her kiss.

She played with the hairs on his chest. His lips teased the lobes of her ears. She wallowed in the sensations like a fish suddenly given the gift of breathing air. His hand found one of her breasts, cupped it, treasured it.

Coral writhed, tingles crawling over her skin. Was it this way for humans all the time? No, it couldn't be. A human woman could not look within the prince's mind and see how much he cared that his touch give her pleasure. He gave himself to her, totally.

Coral absorbed his love, and was claimed.

His hand drifted lower, brushing past her skin and onto the scales of her lower body.

He jerked. He stared down with wide, disbelieving eyes, willing the night's gloom to vanish and show him that she was not half-fish after all.

She reached for him. He retreated. She cast back the passion he had sent into her, hoping that he could sense it.

He shook his head, as if in pain. But as she stroked his shoulder, and massaged the firm muscles of his belly, he sighed, tears welling, and sagged back on the sand.

At last she could read through the tangle of his thoughts. Her mermaid features were proof to him that he was dreaming. He cried because he did not want her to be a dream.

He draped his arms around her. "Stay with me," he murmured.

She answered him as best she could. She snuggled close and held him tightly.

But he, believing himself asleep, gave into the fever and exhaustion, and sank into true slumber.

She left him in the morning, lingering in the shallows as search parties from the town arrived on the debris-ridden beach. The prince babbled feverish sentences as they placed him on the litter.

Coral swam away with the listlessness of a minnow who has met with the nettles of a jellyfish.

She wished she possessed the human ability to sleep. She wanted desperately to purge the stream of thought and emotion from her consciousness. Below, life on the sea bottom continued as ever — anemones captured their diminutive prey, a hermit crab hunted for a new shell, a manta ray patrolled its territory — but not one aspect of that drama mattered. She knew the cycle too well; none of it could surprise her.

What she had felt when the merchant prince had touched her was new. It was outside the knowledge passed down to her as a daughter of the Sea King. Suddenly this food she had never tasted before had become the only thing she could eat.

Coral wandered. For three days, she fluttered through the currents. She was not aware of choosing a direction, but in the end she arrived at the harbor of the port where the young merchant lived.

She could sense him. The connection remained. She wriggled along the shallows of the coast until she reached a small beach past the edge of the town. A cottage rose atop the dunes. He was there.

She glided back into deep water. The few yards of sand that separated her from him might as well have been an entire continent.

As Coral drifted out to sea, the water turned brown and murky. Dead fish hung before her eyes. Strange polyps wriggled on the sea floor, feeding on the sewage carried from the port by the river.

Coral turned to avoid the zone of putrescence, only to be stopped by a voice.

Why are you sad?

In front of Coral loomed a horrific creature. A crab carapace supported a humanlike head. Its legs writhed like those of an octopus, suckers withered and discolored, the extremities tipped with pincers. Its hair was made of thin eels whose jaws snapped incessantly.

Who are you? asked the little mermaid.

I am the Sea Witch, said the apparition.

Coral darted backward. *Be gone,* she demanded. *You will not have me.*

I can give the prince to you.

The water suddenly chilled her. *No one can do that,* Coral responded. *We belong to different worlds.* She stopped short of asking how the goddess knew of him.

I can.

Coral swam in a slow, tight circuit, eyebrows drawn together. She knew she should leave, but she could not keep from listening further.

How? Coral demanded.

I cannot bring him to the sea, but I can send you to the land. I can give you legs.

Coral touched her scaled hips, on the very spot the prince had touched. *Many of my brothers and sisters have died at your hand. Why should I trust you?*

I am the embodiment of Death, said the Sea Witch. *I have no need to lie — I always win, given time. I will help you because it will serve my ends.* She raised a pincer toward her heart, as if to say, here I am, my nature undisguised. Coral knew that the witch could have worn the beauty of a siren had she chosen it.

How?

I can create nothing. My tools are death and decay. If I change you from an immortal mermaid into a mortal human, I will have moved you in the direction of death. The act is its own reward.

Coral tensed her fluke, trying to imagine what it would be like to have two limbs there instead of one. Vividly she recalled the soft, tapered legs of the woman in the young merchant's vision, and his pleasure at the consideration of them.

It cannot be so simple, Coral stated. *There must be other prices to be paid. Tell me, and leave nothing out.*

The Sea Witch laughed. *Indeed there are. And I am happy to tell you, for they please me.* Her tentacles stroked the sea floor, stirring up decayed polyps and fermenting sediment.

First, it will be painful, as if I had cut your fluke down the middle with my claws. This suffering will fade as the legs dry, but then, whenever you walk, your feet will feel as if you are treading on knives or pricking gimlets. Given time, this too will ease, but time is the thing you may not have.

Why not?

My powers have their limits. I can only make you human for three days. In order to complete the spell, and achieve a normal human lifespan, your prince must lie with you. Only his love, given in passion, will finish the transformation.

Only three days. The little mermaid knew she should be frightened, but the prince's desire had been unmistakable. Were she to don legs, and come to him in the light of day, would it truly be so difficult to consummate their attraction?

If you do not succeed, continued the death goddess, *you will wither to dust. And there is no turning back. Should you enter the sea during the three days, you will dissolve into foam. Only if your man proves his love will you have the years a human normally has. You will also regain the ability to visit the ocean, but you will swim only as people do. The water will tire you out as it does them. You can never be a mermaid again. Even if I should wish it, my power cannot restore a being to immortality.*

My prince will want me, Coral asserted. *I have seen his soul's longing. Yet you wear the smile of one who owns the better side of a wager. What have you not told me? Why would this man not help me, should I ask it of him?*

The Sea Witch laughed until her crustacean belly disintegrated into a spongy, gelatinous mass. A foul, inky substance extruded from her pores.

How will you tell him? Unless you can learn human speech in three days, you will be mute among them. But 'tis true, you have your pretty form, your graceful movements, your desire. Perhaps these will be enough. But I think you will fail, and that gives me great joy.

The little mermaid refused to let so foul a creature taunt her. What she had seen in the prince's mind was a pure and true emotion, and she knew her own heart. To reach the fulfillment of that bond, she would risk anything.

Very well, said Coral. *If you speak the truth, my fluke will split. If you lie, the magic of my blood will know it, and preserve me.*

I speak the truth, stated the witch. She raked the front of her bilious form, opening a gash. Black, viscous blood spumed out and snaked languorously toward Coral like strands of molten tar. *Drink of my essence. One draught, no more. Then flee to the shore, for soon your father's realm will spurn you.*

Coral grimaced, drawing her hands and body away from the fluid. Arching her neck, she sucked in a mouthful. It tasted as evil as it looked. She swallowed, if only to drive it away from her teeth and tongue. It seared her throat and tore at her stomach as if she had swallowed a harpoon.

Coral surged up, broke into the air, and raced along the surface, barely within the water. Even the laughter of the Sea Witch could not keep up with her. The beach reached for her. She struck it at a frightening velocity and skidded up the embankment onto dry sand.

The impact grated skin off her arms and breasts, but she hardly noticed. That discomfort was lost within the agony welling up from her lower body. Phantom pincers closed, snipping her fluke down the center.

She cried out. Salt tears streamed from her eyes. She grasped handfuls of sand and tightened her fists until the knuckles threatened to explode. Far too slowly, skin closed in around the exposed tissue. Knees, ankles, and toes took vague shape.

She endured until she could sense the bones hardening and joints meshing, then mercifully, consciousness failed her.

Coral felt eyes upon her as she woke.

She lay on the sand beside a jumble of driftwood. A gull perched there, gazing at her intently. Its dark eyes sparkled with intelligence. It opened its pure white wings and hissed softly, as if to tell her something. Groggy, Coral could only shake her head.

Abruptly the gull took flight. Coral turned to see what had

startled it.

Two boys stood a few steps away. If she had been a giant kraken, they could not have stared with more awe.

She tried to move. Her body squirmed strangely, and abruptly, she was gazing at herself with as much astonishment as the children. Two shapely legs, as fine as the pair in the prince's dream, extended from her equally human pelvis.

She rolled over. The boys, startled, pranced backward. Suddenly they burst into a run, straight toward the cottage on the dune. She ignored them, mesmerized by the sensation of knees bending and toes wriggling.

When she looked up, the boys were leading two men down from the cottage.

One of the men carried a blanket. She recognized him instantly as her merchant prince. Her eyes locked upon his, and did not shift until he leaned over her. She reached up, not quite believing it as her fingers brushed the firm, warm flesh of his neck.

He spoke to her. In his mind, she read the meaning of his words, but when she tried to reply, only a meaningless squeak emerged from her throat.

"It's her, Tane," he told the other adult. "I told you there was a girl on the beach with me the night of the gale."

"She's real enough," Tane replied. "But if you think a little thing like her could have pulled you from the waves, your fever must have returned. She's nothing but a cast-off waif herself. Cover her, Adan, before she withers away."

Adan wrapped her carefully, yet his hands betrayed a certain reluctance to hide her beauty. "It's her, I tell you. I couldn't forget a face like this."

Coral smiled.

"Then where's she been the past three days?" Tane argued. "Where was she when we salvaged the wreck and scoured the coast for the dead? You've never seen this man before, have you, girl?"

As Tane spoke, doubt took root in Adan's mind. He remembered the touch of fish scales against his hips.

Coral shook her head, willing him to believe his instincts, but to her dismay, both men took her gesture as a reply to Tane's question.

"There's your answer, Adan. Here, let's help this poor lass inside and send the boys to fetch Lara. You know, it's just as well your new ship will have that bridal cabin. You're too young a trader to ply this strait without a wife aboard. It leaves your imagination without an anchor."

Coral struggled to think of a way to communicate. The more Adan analyzed his memories, the more he attributed the night on the beach to delirium. Tane was his mother's brother, his mentor and financier. Adan had obeyed the man's advice all his life.

While the men lifted her upright, Coral started to gesture — anything to get their attention. But as weight settled onto her feet, pain blotted out her attempt. She doubled over, gasping.

"She's ill, Adan, or hurt. Perhaps we'd better take her to the healer."

Thinking quickly, Coral shook her head again. She wouldn't let herself be shut up some place away from her prince, now that she'd found him. She steadied herself, and stepped forward.

Her innate grace maintained her for the first two paces. By then, she was reading in the minds of Adan, Tane, and the boys how she should walk. She forced her legs to obey that mental model, though each grain of sand beneath her soles seemed to penetrate to the bone.

The men shrugged and followed her, dispatching the boys to a nearby cluster of houses.

"Lara will see to you," Adan said as he helped Coral into a chair. "Perhaps some of her younger sister's clothing would fit you."

He hovered near her. Coral gazed at him longingly, resentful of Tane's presence.

"Don't you speak at all?" Adan asked.

She touched her lips, and shook her head. Then she pulled his hand within the blanket to the center of her chest, and let her heart beat against it. She nodded.

Once again, the connection was made. She could tell he was reliving the vision that had first drawn her near his ship. But to her frustration, the recollection only made him recall the ridicule of his crew, and he retreated from it.

Tane cleared his throat. Adan pulled his hand back.

"Mute as a fish," Tane said.

"She's obviously had a terrible experience," Adan replied. "Do not be so harsh."

Coral beamed at his defense of her. He smiled back. Just then, the door opened.

A young woman entered, with the boys. She looked at Coral and smiled. The Sea King's daughter read concern and empathy in the newcomer's mind, but she ignored it. What she saw in Adan's mind consumed her full attention.

Betrothed. This woman was his intended mate. And he was devoted to her.

This could not be, Coral insisted to herself. Lara's prettiness was quiet, unimposing—and yet the affection in the prince's heart could not be denied. Coral began to shake, caught in a wave of betrayal mitigated only by her sudden fear for her existence.

A sudden, warm wetness drenched the blanket beneath her. She glanced down, startled. The liquid spread darkly across the cloth, heading for the floor.

"Oh, you poor dear," Lara said, hurrying forward. "Out, all of you. She needs privacy."

Coral had only to glance in the mind of anyone present to understand why she was suddenly being treated like an invalid. In the sea, she'd never had to be concerned about when her bladder emptied. She watched forlornly as her prince exited with the others, leaving her with a nurse she could not have resented more.

"Let me take this," Lara murmured soothingly as she tugged at the blanket. "Some broth will warm you up. Do you have a fever, child?"

Coral resisted the urge to fling Lara's hand from her brow. She wanted to rise, to follow her prince. But as she placed a foot on the floor, the knife-sharp twinges stunned her back into place.

By the time Lara had returned with a fresh blanket and a washcloth, Coral's anger at the woman had faded. Her body prickled with so many strange needs. Lara seemed to understand what she required, though she herself did not. Broth, what was that? She looked in Lara's mind, and all at once understood the meaning of the pangs in her abdomen.

Mer did not eat. They drank only salt water. The Sea King had made his children so that they would not need to take life in order to preserve their own. But Coral's new body had no such magic. She had much to learn.

Coral had already lost half the first day lying unconscious on the beach. She would not waste the rest of it. As Lara mothered her, the former mermaid gleaned the information necessary to behave as a human being.

Eating, walking, bodily functions, customs of attire, roles of parent and child, male and female — all the mundane aspects of living that any resident of the kingdom took for granted were prey to Coral's thirst for knowledge. When at last Adan appeared out of the darkness of early evening, she was well-prepared for him.

She stood in front of him in a plain but well-fitting singlet. She had chosen a sash that emphasized the sea green of her eyes.

"Our little piece of driftwood has become a lady," Lara said cordially.

"You work miracles," Adan said. Coral would have resented the way he credited her transformation to Lara, had she not been able to read behind the words. When his glance lingered on her hair, it was its natural sheen that captured his approval, not how well Lara had combed it. When he looked lower, the way she filled the weave mattered far more to him than the choice of garment.

He gave no sign to Lara, but Coral knew Adan regretted that his betrothed was not equally lovely.

Coral tried her best to keep his attention that evening, using the wiles she had stolen from Lara. She held her implements with dainty finesse, she smiled and made eye contact at carefully selected moments, and most of all, she hid her jealousy of Lara. The latter proved difficult, for she saw that Lara, as was often the custom in this realm between promised mates, intended to stay the night.

As the moon, in its waning quarter, slipped below the horizon, Lara set up a bed on a divan in the common room for Coral. As Lara allowed her privacy to disrobe, and Adan was busy outside splitting a few extra pieces of firewood, Coral sensed an opportunity. She hurried beneath the covers and feigned immediate sleep.

Lara soon checked on her and, believing the ruse, tiptoed back into Adan's bedroom. Moments later, Adan passed through on his way to join her. He paused to gaze in the direction of the divan.

Coral sat up, peeling the blankets off her naked body. She rose with a sinuous motion. Ignoring the agony in her feet, she crossed over to Adan and nudged against him before he could gather his wits.

Reluctantly, he pressed her back to arm's length. "Lord of the sea, what I wouldn't have done to have met you a year ago."

From the deep recesses of his being, she read the scroll of confession that he kept sealed to all but his view. He did not love Lara. Fondness, yes. Devotion, yes. But not love.

Coral tugged his wrist urgently.

He loosened her grip. "I cannot. My lady awaits."

He turned away from her silent protests, and vanished into the bedroom. Coral sank back on her pillow, stricken.

He wanted her. His heart said it, no matter that his spoken words declared. That promise alone gave her the strength of will to remain where she was.

She lay there, tossing, feeling death swimming nearer. What was she to do? Oh, how smug the Sea Witch's laugh seemed now.

Until the Sea Witch had split her legs, Coral had never known unconsciousness. She understood that humans slept, but she also knew that they often went without it for a night or more. She remained awake until the pre-dawn, and was caught unaware when her body asserted its needs. As a result, she then did not rouse until the sun broke through the fog late in the morning.

Crusts on her eyelashes, she stumbled to the window, disbelieving her senses. She willed the sunshine away, back to the previous night. Her three days were nearly half gone.

Wooden clogs scuffed the floor. Coral turned to see a matronly woman emerge from the pantry. Her memories of Adan's mind told her this was Lara's mother, Netta.

"Here, now, you can't run around the house naked," the woman scolded. "Didn't my daughter provide you with night clothes?"

Coral let herself be led back to the divan, too distracted by the shooting pain in her feet to protest, and too amazed that she had not felt the pain until then. Netta introduced herself, adding, "Adan and my daughter went sailing in his ketch. They'll be back at dusk. Are you hungry?"

Coral blinked until tears came. There was no way she dared follow Adan. The sea was death to her. And to her annoyance, this human body of hers *was* hungry.

At least that was one need she could assuage.

While she ate, Coral tried to think of a plan—anything to keep the panic at bay. Netta was a resource, just as Lara had been. Among other things, in her youth, Netta had been a dancer.

To use legs so fully—it was so human an activity that Coral immediately claimed a section of porch, extracted the choreography from Netta's mind, and attempted the movements. Phantom slivers sprang up from the planks into her heels, but she did not stop.

The matron laughed with delight. Memories bubbled into her consciousness, where Coral could read them all the better, and use them to refine her cadence, posture, and tension.

"You've got the gift, child," Netta declared. "Show it to Adan. He so loves dancing."

When Coral heard this, her practice could not be stopped,

especially when Netta's reminiscences shifted toward her long-held disappointment that her daughter had proven so uncoordinated in the art. The pain never left, but Coral endured it. She would take advantage of any avenue she could find into the prince's heart.

Finally, legs wobbling, she rested. She wanted to be steady when the time came to perform for Adan. As afternoon waned, she sequestered herself on a dune and worked on the greatest obstacle to her goal—her lack of human speech.

She could not glean the knowledge of how to speak from Netta or any other human. Use of their voices came so naturally to them that they gave the process no conscious thought. Trial and error was the only way Coral could teach her throat, tongue, and lips what they had to know.

Toward sunset, she could grunt and hum. "Nnnnnn," she said as she observed the prince's ketch approach its dock. She could not even correctly transfer her excitement into the utterance.

She sighed. Given a few weeks, she might manage a sentence. But left with only two nights and a day, she would be fortunate to form a single word.

She brushed the sand off her skirts and hobbled toward the docks.

"You should see how she dances!" Netta chirped as soon as her prospective son-in-law appeared.

Adan glanced at Coral, intrigued. To her delight, it was arranged that, as soon as the evening meal ended, the Sea King's daughter would demonstrate what she had learned.

Adan's eyes gleamed as he watched. His mouth hung open, until Lara, annoyed, closed it for him.

Coral could not have danced better had she been born a human. She raised her arms above her head and spun on the tips of her toes, she pranced, she swam through the air. She continued until the throb in her feet overwhelmed her. Her audience applauded as she swayed into a chair.

"Our little foundling seems to have completed her recovery,"

Adan said.

"Perhaps tomorrow we can arrange a permanent home for her," Lara suggested.

Adan pursed his lips. "Perhaps we can," he said equably.

His annoyance at Lara was matched only by his approval of Coral. The former mermaid smiled into her cup. Dizzy and exhausted from the dancing, Coral bided her time for the rest of the evening, until at last, as Lara and her mother talked, she saw a chance to act. Grasping Adan, she tugged him out to the porch.

"What are you doing?" he whispered.

Her lips came up to meet his. He kissed her back fiercely.

But he pulled away much too soon. "We must go back. Lara must not find us here."

She pulled him toward the steps, toward the beach. When he anchored himself, she brushed her thigh along his.

"No," he said.

His interest in her coursed through him like a rushing mountain stream, fueled by an unstoppable snow melt. But as she watched, he placed a dam across it.

"I'm promised, and that's all there is to it," he said. He turned toward the door.

She clutched at him, dragging him back. Just then, Lara called for Adan. Bitterly, he flung himself free. Coral, poised awkwardly on her tender, exhausted legs, nearly tumbled over. Adan disappeared without looking back.

Coral blinked through tears. She couldn't go back in. She didn't understand how any human could sequester his feelings as Adan had. He wanted Coral, more than any woman he'd ever seen, certainly more than the plain bride he'd settled for. But his determination was undeniable. He had come to his harbor, and would not weigh anchor.

A flutter of wings startled her out of her despair. A white gull perched on the porch rail beside her.

She knew instinctively that it was the same bird that had kept watch over her on the beach the previous day. It opened its wings and held them wide. Its sentient eyes gazed at her.

Impulsively she reached out to contact its mind. Blue fog retreated from her probe. The gull dwelled in the realm of the air, and its language rested just across the border of her understanding.

The bird flew off. Coral turned and stared forlornly at the door. Head down, she left the porch and vanished into the dunes.

The third day passed swiftly, as time does when a person wants it to linger. Coral wandered the heath and the dunes just outside of the town, avoiding passersby, sharing the thoughts of the populace during those rare times when she could block out the image of Adan. The richness of those thoughts told her she would have liked living in that town, among its people, until she grew old.

As the lamplighters strolled down the streets on their rounds, Coral inevitably turned in the direction of the cottage.

The Sea Witch's magic seemed to be weakening already. Coral's bones creaked. Every joint in her new legs and hips gave her pain. She was stumbling by the time she arrived at Adan's dwelling.

Dark windows confronted her. He was not there.

She sank to her knees on the porch. She did not know why it should matter whether she saw him again or not. Best merely to stay and die, on the very spot where she had first acknowledged the Sea Witch's victory.

But there was little enough to do with what remained of her life. Finding Adan was a goal to stave off the bleakness of her reveries.

She probed randomly until she detected the pattern of Adan's consciousness. It came from the direction of the docks. She dragged herself toward the source.

Adan was on his ketch. Coral glimpsed him through a porthole, just before a forgotten candle guttered out in its holder. He and Lara were wrapped around each other, asleep in the bunk of the tiny master cabin.

Coral walked unsteadily out to the end of the pier. Deadly as the water might be, it was no more threatening now than the land.

She had not been there long when shapes appeared beneath her dangling legs.

Her sisters.

We have learned of your pact with the Sea Witch, announced the eldest. *We have made a new pact. Your life may be saved.*

How? asked Coral.

Our father has agreed that if you live out your proper mortal span, he will not fashion a new mermaid for a thousand years after your death.

But the Sea Witch said her power could only grant me three days and nights.

Not if you give her a death. She can give you a human lifetime if it is taken from another. The eldest threw a coral spike onto the end of the pier. *Kill your prince's lover. Cast her body into the ocean. Her lifeless blood will fuel the magic.*

Coral shrank away from the spike in horror. *I cannot do this!*

You must, or your own life is forfeit.

Her sisters submerged, leaving Coral to stare at the weapon they had left.

Entering the cabin proved surprisingly easy. Coral's natural grace served the cause of stealth well. A few long minutes after her sisters had departed, she held the spike over Lara's heart.

Coral dreamed that she was in the woman's place, there beside her sleeping Adan. In her vision, he did not wake during the murder. He and Coral met months later, when she had learned human speech, and he had overcome his grief. Unimpeded by a rival, Coral won his love.

At their marriage ceremony, he reached for her hand. He held it up and turned it over, ready to place a ring on her finger.

A pool of blood, lying in her palm, rolled out of her hand and splattered her wedding gown.

Coral lowered the weapon without striking.

She could not kill. However close to human she might be,

however desperate, she was still the daughter of the Sea King, and the Sea King acted only in the interests of life.

She crept out as stealthily as she had entered. She stood at the gunwale and frowned down at the spike.

At once, a glamour lifted from her. She understood how she had been duped. Her sisters had never come to the pier. They had been an illusion. Greedy for one more death, the Sea Witch had tried to trick her. Spilling another's blood would not save her life; it would merely increase the witch's victory.

All that remained was for dawn to come and change her to dust. So be it.

With a subtle whisper of wings, the white gull landed on the deck beside her.

Impulsively, she reached out. It nodded three times. As her eyes widened in surprise, the bird launched off and skimmed the waves beside the boat, webbed feet grazing a strangely thick layer of sea foam.

Suddenly sure of herself, Coral leaped overboard, into the foam. Her body popped to the surface, boiling. She began to dissolve.

Yet, strangely, no sense of death overtook her, no lapse of consciousness. She heard the raucous screeching of the gull as it dived toward her. The bird caught a wisp of the froth that had been her heart and ascended.

And suddenly, Coral was high over the ketch. Adan and Lara, awakened by the loud splash, rushed on deck.

Coral looked beside her, and found herself in the midst of hundreds of ethereal creatures, winged and garbed in every shade of the rainbow, even in the starlight. The brightest and most beautiful of all sailed forward, forsaking the gull's shape, and smiled at her.

Who are you? asked Coral.

I am the Queen of the Air, said the entity. I am to the sky what your father is to the sea and the Earth Mother is to the land. Welcome.

How did I come here? I thought I would die.

You are the child of a god, replied the Queen of the Air. *You cannot die, unless you betray your nature. By remaining true, you have merely transformed yourself. Your father dared not reveal this ability to you earlier, for fear the Sea Witch would steal the knowledge from you. She does not realize the joke we play on her. She thinks me powerless, because no life is born of me. She does not realize her own magic is the catalyst that sends me offspring.*

The goddess glided upward. *Come, daughter. Let us travel over the world and celebrate its life, and provide solace to the mortals in our care.*

Coral nodded eagerly, but spared one last glance below. In the ketch, her prince and his lady gazed out at the foam on the water with solemn faces, as if comprehending her sacrifice, and mourning her.

Coral descended. With her breathy, invisible form, she touched Lara on the cheek, and kissed Adan on the lips. They looked up, startled, and confused smiles brightened their faces.

And the merchant prince, until the end of his long life, was known as the captain who the wind treated with unusual kindness. Always, his sails were filled.

Dust and Sand

DABRIA FOUND THE STRANGER on her way back from the cliffs, where she had gone to gather chalk for her next dust painting. The man lay unconscious on the wet sand left by the retreating tide.

Dabria had never seen anything like him. He wore clothing even though it was not a holiday, along with a type of sandal that completely enveloped his feet. The hair she brushed from his eyes was black as the charcoal she used in her artwork. If he had been standing, he would have towered half a head higher than Old Krelall, the tallest man in her village.

She rolled him onto his back, checking for wounds, confirming that his breath flowed regularly. Despite his location, he seemed not to have come from the sea. His clothes were wet only where a far-reaching wave had just lapped against him, and his skin was free of crusted salt and seaweed. It was as if he had emerged from the sand like a newly hatched turtle.

He murmured without opening his eyes. For a moment Dabria thought he might speak, but he merely flopped his gaunt head listlessly from side to side. Pressing her hands to his temples, she found him blazing with fever.

Dragging him higher, she left him in the shadow of a clump of salt grass and hurried around the promontory to the shoals. As she expected, three of her brothers were there hunting tidecrawlers. They returned with her.

"Looks like he hasn't eaten in a year," quipped Brem, the eldest. "What do we do with him?"

"Take him to my hut," Dabria said. It was the closest building. "The healer can look at him there."

The brothers nodded. The youngest ran ahead, and by the time the bearers arrived, Neuann the healer was waiting along with Hemar, Dabria's father.

"Remove these wet garments," the healer commanded. The brothers stripped the stranger and placed him on Dabria's spare mat.

Neuann examined the stranger's mouth, ears, and glands. Her narrowed brow implied she saw no obvious cause for his condition. Though he was bony, he did not seem malnourished as Brem had implied. Forsaking common measures, the healer lay hands on his chest and slipped into a light trance. She emerged from it frowning.

"This illness is unlike anything I've seen or heard of. It is not catching, however. Provide him with rest, warmth, and water. He will recover or not on his own. This is something he has brought upon himself." Covering the patient with a blanket, Neuann hurried off, for it was nine months after the Rain Festival and two of the village women were in labor.

The brothers, needing more tidecrawlers for their feast, left soon after.

The stranger lay as if drained of life. He gave off the aura of an old man, though Dabria guessed he was no more than forty or so.

"What's this in his belt pouch?" Hemar asked. He pulled out a wooden slipcase. It opened to reveal a set of carving tools. "I've never seen metal like this in the Five Islands."

"Where could he have come from?" Dabria asked. "The Land Beyond the Ocean?"

Hemar grunted. "Even if that land supports life again, the people there would look like us." Hemar lifted a strand of the unconscious man's dark hair.

"He is a mystery, then." The thought appealed to her.

"Are you sure you want to leave him in your hut?" asked Hemar. "We don't know his character. Perhaps it would be better if he stayed in the men's lodge."

Hemar was Dabria's true-father. Of all her womb-mother's lovers, he was the one who had visited most often when Dabria and her siblings were small, bringing gifts and joining in the children's games when the women of the household were too busy. Not that Dabria was ever neglected—for most of her girlhood she had been fortunate to have five breast-mothers—but she enjoyed the paternal attention. Now that she was an unattached adult, she appreciated Hemar's undemanding presence even more. This courtship hut, for all its appeal and tradition, was a lonely place for someone accustomed to a communal household.

"And how many men stay in the lodge when they are sick?" Dabria asked. "I seem to recall you wearing out Rallea's spare mat that time you broke your leg." Rallea, one of Dabria's breast-mothers, always made room in her portion of the hut when a relative, male or female, faced an extended convalescence.

"That is different."

"Look at him," Dabria said, pointing at the pallid body of the stranger. "Even if he intended to harm me, I would be in no danger."

Hemar had to nod. Dabria had held her own for two decades against the impish harassment of five strong brothers. "I will come by every day anyway."

"I would welcome it," Dabria said, and meant it. She touched him affectionately on the wrist. He smiled at her, frowned at the sleeping man, and ambled down the path toward the lodge.

While the stranger slept on, Dabria pulled out one of her design trays. Festival week was nearing, and it was her task to coordinate the decoration of the village grounds for the Dance of the Blossom Moon. This was the third year she had won the honor, and perhaps she had become too complacent. If the elders rejected her initial design, she would scarcely have time to submit another.

She poured several handfuls of the chalk she'd gathered that morning into the tray and smoothed it into a thin layer. For her festival paintings she always used a white foundation; that helped preserve brightness and flair. Next she dipped into her urn of island soil, working it between her fingers until the tiny lumps of clay turned to fine powder. This she carefully poured into a spiral atop the chalk base.

Rust over cream. Those colors would work both in the sunlight during the children's part of the festival, and beneath the moonlight as the adults danced. Also, the chalk and clay were plentiful — Dabria had not forgotten her first festival painting, which required far too much crumbling of dried acanth leaves. Acanth leaves were the only source of the radiant brown Dabria had wanted for that design; these days she limited such indulgent choices of color to paintings that didn't have to be re-created at a scale large enough for the entire village to dance upon.

As she added accents of this pigment or that, the painting began to come alive. The hint of blue — that would sparkle in the children's eyes. The little circles of moss green — that would inspire fertile thoughts among the young women. A smile grew on Dabria's face. To create a painting was akin to creating life. A good one would make her forget to eat, or leave her young men waiting in vain for a promised rendezvous.

While she worked, visitor after visitor came to her hut, all wanting a glimpse of the stranger. After the sixth interruption she pointed out that the man needed rest and she needed concentration. With the characteristic politeness of the islands, the callers took their speculations and advice down the valley to the village tea house.

She worked well into the evening. Finally she could think of nothing more to add to the design. The colors burst out in undiluted celebration. Any who danced the pattern of whorls and circles would be caught in its joy. Elderly men would prance, and the shyest women be bold.

After her dinner, she fetched the elders, who viewed and approved her work. Just after their visit the stranger stirred. His fever, which had eased earlier, was again forcing sweat out of him. He moaned and rolled on his side. Dabria bathed his face and chest with a damp cloth. He was still twisting restlessly when she retired for the night.

Dabria spent much of the morning down by the pools with Limron, swimming and making love. Though Abrel was the young man she suspected she'd choose when the time came for childmaking, Limron excited her more. Whenever life grew challenging, as the day before had been, Limron's playful attentions massaged away her cares.

When she entered her hut, she found signs that the stranger had awakened. His chest was once again rising and falling in the rhythm of deep slumber, but he had drunk a great deal of the water in the pitcher beside his mat, used the urine pot, and in his hands he clutched a piece of driftwood and one of his carving knives.

As Dabria eased the items from his grip, she saw that the wood contained marks. With a few deft strokes he had carved an image of an island.

Strangely, the island seemed familiar, though she had never seen that bay, and the mountain showed no sign that human inhabitants had ever thinned its jungle. She could only recall one other example of art that had ever evoked such a sense of presence — her own.

Yet this was so different from her work. A dust painting was always susceptible to the adjustment of a finger or a puff from puckered lips. Malleable, alive. The image in the wood was permanent. And it was so literal. The island resembled one she might see on the horizon of an ocean somewhere, whereas her designs were chiefly like that she had made the night before — abstract, meant to evoke moods. The carving offered no emotions; it simply recorded a view.

The carving fascinated her, though it disturbed her as well. Out of respect for his obvious talent, she took care as she set it aside. From time to time as she prepared her midday meal, she glanced at it. And at him. Despite her relaxing morning, she had to struggle to keep tension from stiffening her shoulders.

After the meal, she visited the village and set her assistants to reproducing the festival design upon the grounds. This first day, the main task was hauling more chalk from the cliffs, for which her presence was not needed, so after marking the perimeter of the design, she accepted her friend Melanya's invitation to stroll along the beach.

As they reached the shore not far from where she'd found the stranger, she almost tripped over her own feet. The formerly open sea to the west was now a narrow strait. A large island took up most of the horizon. Uncut jungle cloaked its hillsides. A bay faced the strait.

"How long has that been there?" Dabria asked.

Melanya stared at her quizzically. "Are you feeling well?"

"Perhaps not. I don't remember that island being there yesterday."

"It's been there forever. Why do you think we call our home the Six Islands? That is Robos."

Dabria stifled a wave of dizziness. As if a hand had reached into her and plucked at the threads of her memory, she could now recall an entire history of the island. Robos was uninhabited, reserved for the dead, visited only by funeral parties. It was, as Melanya said, one of the six main islands of their archipelago.

But that could not be. Robos was the name of a canyon on the island of Timmila. In ancient times its caves were used as crypts, but that had been when the people were few in number — long ago, before the custom arose that limited women to three children of the womb.

Five Islands. Her land was the Five Islands. What was happening?

Melanya gazed back with a furrowed brow.

"My mind played a trick on me," Dabria said quickly. "I'm fine now."

Melanya did not press the issue, but Dabria felt no relief. There should not be secrets between them. Melanya was to be her breast-sister. As soon as Dabria became a mother, she would join the household that Melanya and her true-sister Veya had founded. Melanya was already pregnant, and it was Dabria's fondest wish that her own motherhood would arrive soon enough that she could help suckle this first child of the family. Her falsehood troubled her all the way back to the village.

At her hut, the first thing she did was grab the stick of driftwood the stranger had carved. The image was just as she remembered — a representation of what she had seen in the ocean to the west. The "new" Robos.

She was debating whether to try to awaken the stranger when he thrashed and opened his eyes. At first he gazed blankly at the thatch overhead, but as she loomed over him, he focussed on her.

"Hee makabbi olo retmei," he said. *"Aki sliff gammon?"*

She had no idea what his words meant. "My name is Dabria," she replied, merely to say something in return. "Where do you come from?"

He spouted more gibberish, growing more frantic as it became clear she did not understand. He tried sitting up, but fell back immediately. His voice trailed off, his eyelids fluttered closed, and his breathing became rhythmic.

Dabria paced around the room, feeling hemmed in by the walls, overly aware of the scent of her own perspiration. She took fresh round-nut butter and smeared it over her body until all she could smell was its rich musk. Yet that merely dulled the edge of her uneasiness.

She snatched a tray from the stack. Briskly she poured in a layer of sand, then crumpled a stick of puckerspice and threw on a dash of round-nut flour. Almost as if she were preparing a recipe to eat, she stirred the mixture in the tray until the ingredients merged into a uniform beige, not so much a design as a layer of incense.

As she achieved the exact color she was trying for, calm pervaded the room. Her nascent headache faded. The effect extended not just to her, but to everything. The stranger ceased squirming and rested peacefully.

She had resorted to such measures many times in the past. Yet abruptly she stopped stirring. The calm remained.

The calm remained. And she had brought it. Dabria set down

her implement and stared at her hands as if they belonged to someone else.

Evening found Dabria sitting with Hemar outside the men's lodge. Though women were welcome at the lodge at any time, in practice they seldom visited — they could count on the men to circulate among the smaller domiciles of the women and children. Dabria, as one of the village's most eligible unpledged women, was a particular attraction. Predictably many of the young men were managing to contrive reasons to be outside — some demonstrating their agility and speed in a game of long shells, others merely strutting.

This night, Dabria ignored the show. Her father's doorstep was the place that, all her life, she had come whenever she had a problem she didn't wish to share with her mother's household — for that was the same as sharing it with everyone.

"You are not acting like yourself," Hemar commented. "Is it the stranger? Shall we move him after all?"

"Not yet. Tell me, Father — you have visited all the islands. In all the festivals you've seen, were there any as…moving…as the ones for which I've painted the grounds?"

"Of course not." He laughed. "Those are the best."

"Answer as if I were not your daughter."

He grew serious. "No, child. The festivals that you decorate are something special. You've always had talent, but since you've become an adult your paintings have gained an added quality. They never fail to engage the senses. This is not just my opinion; it is there for anyone to see. Is this not what you want?"

She gazed skyward, hardly noticing the inspired acrobatics of a pair of glow moths scant inches from her face. "Yes. I suppose it is. I just never realized before how unusual it was."

Dabria woke long before dawn. One thing after another conspired to keep her awake — first a full bladder, then thirst, then the noise of a frog near her door. The painting of calmness she had made the night before no longer soothed her whatsoever.

When sunlight peeked through the cracks in the thatch, she abandoned her mat. To occupy herself, she made several trips to the stream in order to fill the water barrel outside her hut.

When she went back inside, the stranger had thrown his coverings back. She was reminded of mornings when she had sat and admired the body of a lover in the early light. This man had a certain handsomeness—take twenty years off his age and he would be the type that Melanya favored from time to time. But whatever small amount of sexual attraction Dabria might have felt for him was buried beneath the pity evoked by his lined brow, meatless ribs, and ragged beard.

The man opened his eyes. He turned immediately to his host and said, quite distinctly, "I need your help."

Dabria blinked. He spoke the language of the Five Islands as if he had been raised in her village. "How did you learn to talk?"

He gestured feebly at a scrap of driftwood sitting beside the one on which he had carved the island. Dabria raised it up and saw it contained the image of a mouth pointed toward an ear. Though the piece was tiny and the detail scant, she recognized the characteristic lopsidedness of his mouth. The ear would be hers, judging from the gold hoops, one small, one large.

"I have no knowledge of your tongue, but from now on when I speak, you will understand."

"You carve things and they come to pass?" she asked, more for confirmation than out of surprise.

"Yes."

A shiver ran down Dabria's spine. "Are you a god?"

"Like a god, perhaps. Call me a sorcerer."

"Yet you're sick. Can't your magic heal you?"

He paused. "My magic is the cause of my ailment. The more I use it, the worse I become. But I had to risk it to find you."

Then as she had suspected, it had been no accident that she had found him on the beach. He must have arranged it from the start. "Why am I so important to you?"

He smiled faintly. "You are like me. You, too, create things that come to pass. I with my carvings. You with your dust and sand. We are a very special kind of magician."

"So it seems." She would have liked to deny it.

"You've realized it. Good." He coughed, and looked as if he might fall unconscious once more. "Will you help, then?"

Slowly she nodded. That much was clear. She had to follow this through.

"Good." He licked his chapped lips. "Listen carefully, while I still have the strength to speak. First, do you see the waterfall in the first carving?"

Dabria looked closely at the image of the island. On the face of the nearest mountain, she saw a faint notch. Though it was a single knifestroke, it did look amazingly like a cascade.

"Hidden behind the water, in a cave, you will find what I need. Here is what you should do...."

She went alone, as requested. The trip across the channel was not difficult. She had learned to sail at age six, and the early morning breeze propelled her catamaran across the waves as fast as a gull could fly. She made landfall at the base of the mountain, secured the boat, and began to climb.

The thick growth, unlike the well-maintained paths on her home island, lashed her bare flanks and regularly tried to trip her, but she was young and nimble-footed, and the destination was barely two thousand paces uphill. She reached the falls before the coolness of morning had dissipated.

The passageway behind the falling torrent lay hidden within the spray, and she nearly lost her footing on the slick rock. But soon the cave opened up, its floor nearly level and lined with soft sand. She drifted inward. Right where the filtered sunlight grew almost too faint to illuminate the chamber, she saw a wall of fog.

The grey barrier was not mist; it was dry to her touch. Her hand could press no farther than the length of a finger joint, though there did not seem to be anything truly solid in the way. She wasn't quite sure why she tried; the stranger had told her she wouldn't be able to pass through in so mundane a fashion.

As instructed, she smoothed the cave floor and set about crafting a painting. Aside from the sand itself, her only working material was a small bag of dirt she had scooped up as she approached the waterfall. Within a short time, the sand began to resemble the wall of fog. The dirt became a hole within the fog.

She looked up. An opening took shape within the barrier. A dim chamber lay beyond — featureless, reeking of still air, with only a single distinct item. On the ground lay a slab of wood.

Tentatively, Dabria reached into the opening. Her hand breached the threshold. From there it felt as though she were thrusting through honey. The air clung, resisting her. Swallowing hard, she stepped in.

Everything around her swirled. The cave and waterfall appeared distant, the opening no more than a rathole. Fighting off the dizziness, she seized the board at her feet and pressed back the way she had come. The opening seemed to dodge and hop, but she did as she had been advised and never stopped walking. Suddenly she was across. The hole in the wall snapped closed, and then the wall itself dissolved, leaving a view of ordinary rock.

The wood she'd retrieved contained a scene of a beach near a set of chalk cliffs. The figure of a man stood on the sand at the edge of the surf. Dabria tucked the carving under her arm and headed home.

When she returned to her hut, the stranger was up and dressed. He had the dazed, tousled look of a man whose fever has just broken, but he was steady on his feet, and his voice was almost robust as he greeted her. He reached out for the carving.

She kept the board close to her body. The time had come for answers. "You made this?"

"Of course," he replied, lowering his hand. "It should have remained with me, but my powers were even weaker than I had supposed. When I realized it was not on my person, the best I could do was create a gateway, and send another shaper — you — to pull it across the threshold."

"Before you made this, you did not exist in my world."

"That is true. I have a world of my own."

She nodded. "This thing you have done to me — is it permanent?"

He frowned. "I have done nothing. You've simply become aware of abilities you already possessed. Yes, it is permanent." Again he reached out. "May I have my talisman?"

She surrendered it. Smiling, he sat down on the mat. She paced. "Tell me your story. Tell me how these things can be."

"My name is Evad. I was born a woodcutter's son, and inherited a hobby of carving from my father. When I was twenty, a woman called Birhea visited my small cabin. She could take a small piece of cloth and whatever scene she embroidered would come to be. She proved it first by fashioning a large tree near my home, a rare variety prized by my family because the furniture makers always paid us good silver for its hard, dark wood. The strangest part was, my father insisted that tree had been there all along. He explained that his grandfather had planted it to benefit his descendants."

"No one but shapers realize when a world is altered?"

"No one." Evad spoke with such pain that Dabria edged away from him. "For decades, I have been alone."

"What happened to Birhea?"

"She guided me through my first creations, showing me that my knives and chisels would work as well as her needle and yarn, then she left, saying she would one day return and see what I had made of my world.

"The years went on. I shaped my surroundings until they contained every spectacle, every pleasure, every facet of beauty conceivable. Still she did not come. Can you imagine what it is like, being the only real person in a land of marionettes? I craved someone of my own level, someone not created from or altered by a whim of my mind.

"Finally I learned the means Birhea had used to travel between worlds. It requires more than simply carving an image of myself into a landscape. You experienced only a taste of it today. A full crossing is much harder.

"Alas, though I visited world after world, I never found Birhea. Nor any other shapers. All those places lay unguided. Some were no more than flat plains with a single building. Some had oceans that poured off the edges, destroying the sailors who ventured too far from the coasts. Some contained only beasts, no people at all.

"I thought to myself that if I embellished these lands, perhaps Birhea would stumble across my work, be pleased, and seek me out. Nor, in truth, could I resist such a venture. Picture whole continents and peoples left to their own random fates. How could I not help them find their destinies? In a few cases I started with black void and left behind valleys and seas, nations and cultures.

"And then, my powers began to sour. Each new carving left me fatigued. Travel across the thresholds was especially taxing. Eventually my gift would work fully only when I was home. Leaving became so painful that I knew if I tried even one more time, I would die."

"Yet you're here, and alive," Dabria said. She found it hard to interrupt the narrative. When Evad spoke, his passions and experiences came across as if they were her own. It was so potent an effect that she had difficulty sorting out her own reactions to his account. It was as if he were shaping her word by word.

His voice faltered as he continued. "Yes. I am here. But at great cost. I had to destroy one of my carvings. Do you know what that means? Though I memorized every knife cut and will re-create the piece when I return, for the moment, an entire land has ceased to exist. It was the only way I could free up enough of my power to search for another shaper."

"Couldn't you have simply *made* another shaper?"

"No. I tried. I could no more succeed at that than halt my own aging. No, the only answer was to find whatever shapers might exist spontaneously. I had always focussed upon the search for Birhea, but she was either dead or deliberately blocking me. I had to widen my efforts."

Evad waved the piece of wood Dabria had fetched from the cave. "I placed this board in front of me every day, eyes closed. After many weeks, an image appeared on the backs of my eyelids. Somewhere a shaper was scooping chalk from a cliff near a beach, dreaming of other worlds, meditating on her next work of art. My hands, without conscious guidance, carved what she saw — and placed me in the scene. And there I went. Here I am."

Dabria recalled vividly the moment at the cliffs. The feeling of being watched had been intense.

"What now?" Dabria asked. "Will you live here?"

"No," he answered quickly. "I would die if I stayed. I must go immediately, while my strength is high."

Suddenly Dabria knew what Evad would say next. "You want me to follow you."

"Yes." Evad grinned at Dabria like a child beaming at its mother. He set down the board and picked up still another carving from his mat — a new one. "After you have matured into your powers, you will be able to travel as I used to. This will guide you to me."

Dabria gazed at the carving. Her lower jaw dropped, amazed at the artistry. He'd had scarcely two hours to fashion it, yet the detail was fabulous. A cottage lay in a forest clearing. Sweet sunshine poured through the branches of the trees, brightening the lane that passed by the front stoop. To the side was a garden and an ornamental pond.

"This is my home. When the time comes, create a dust painting of this scene. Paint yourself into a spot — let us say the bench by the pond. You will be transported there."

"And then?" she asked.

"Then, with my guidance, you can resume the work I have had to abandon. You will be able to travel all the lands, setting them to rights. By the time your own powers are exhausted, we will have located other shapers and enlisted them to our cause. The universe need never lie unattended again."

Dabria touched the carving tentatively. The trees had the texture of leaves and needles, not carved wood. The cottage walls felt like sanded lumber, the chimney like stone and mortar. Evad urged the piece into her grip.

"Say you will come. It may be a year, perhaps five, before you master the means, but I will wait. Could any other goal promise so much?"

Dabria struggled to keep herself afloat within the tidal wave of his plans and desires. Standing here in the same room, his influence was overwhelming. "No, none other could," she heard herself say. "Of course I will come. In one year or five, as my talent allows."

Evad kissed Dabria on the forehead. Then, as if gaining her acquiescence had used up his last reserves, he swayed and sat down abruptly.

"I have to go now," he said. "But no matter. Eventually we will have all the time we need."

He took the carving she had brought from the waterfall. Aiming his largest chisel, raising his hammer, he struck several times with grand expertise. When he raised his hands away, the beach and cliffs remained, but the image of Evad himself was missing.

"Until we are together," he said, smiling. He was already ghostly transparent. When he had faded entirely, Dabria reached out and touched the mat. The thatch was cool, as if Evad had never been there generating body heat.

Dabria began to shake. Crawling to her bowl of wash water, she made as if to clean the spot on her forehead that he had kissed. But she stopped. No matter how much she scrubbed, the imprint of his lips would remain.

Her reflection stared back from the water. She hardly knew herself. His offer had seemed so reasonable as he uttered it. She had been right to say she would follow. The promise had sent him on his way, and only in his absence would she know her true feelings.

Now, and only now, could she decide whether or not that promise was a true one.

Sitting down, she placed all four carvings in front of her, and stared at them for a long time. The wood was firm beneath her fingers. It did not yield. How many carvings must lay within Evad's cottage? Thousands? Tens of thousands? Each affecting reality in tremendous ways. He was probably already beginning to restore the one he'd sacrificed to make the journey to the Five Islands.

What would she be like in twenty years, if she took his path?

Keeping that thought uppermost in her mind, she stepped outside and threw kindling and tinder into her cooking brazier and struck the flints. When the fire was hot, she placed the carving of Robos on the coals. As it burned, she climbed the ridge to the west, where she gained a view of the ocean.

Robos hovered like a mirage on the waves, grey as smoke. As the brazier did its work, the isle faded entirely, taking with it the nagging false history of its crypts and funerals. Dabria waved, half in regret, half in relief.

Back at the brazier, she immediately added the piece of driftwood with the mouth and ear. The board containing the portrait of Evad's home clung to hands slightly longer — not because of the fabulous craftsmanship, but because Dabria was reminded of the passion Evad must have put into its creation. Ultimately she gave it to the fire, turning it upside down to prevent herself from memorizing its features.

She kept the remaining piece, the one from the cave. With the figure removed, the scene was nothing more or less than a bit of coastline she had known and enjoyed all her life. This she hung on her wall.

The brazier was cold by the time Dabria returned that night. She dumped the ash into a clay pot and set it aside. Many days passed before she retrieved it — days filled with good company, with dance and celebration, and with the satisfaction of knowing she had contributed in important ways to another festival. Never had her way of life seemed so precious.

Finally, one peaceful morning, she took one of her trays — she owned only five — and poured the ash into it, using it as the foundation for a painting. Then, dipping into her urns of collected pigments and sands, Dabria crafted an image of the rocky hillside across the valley from her hut, complete with its lush hanging vines and ledges of exuberant tropical growth. A few bits of charcoal from the brazier served to deepen the shadows and lend depth.

She rarely painted landscapes. Her hands wanted to burst free, craft a design, but she forced herself to be disciplined. Her skill was such that by late afternoon she had a rendering as lifelike as Evad's carving of his home had been.

And then she added to it. She took one of her rarest pigments — pollen harvested from the stamens of the shade lily — and sprinkled the rock face with dabs of bright yellow.

She went outside. There, across the valley, yellow flowers never before known on her island grew in the cracks of the rocks.

She hadn't doubted that she could do it. The sorcery begged to emerge. Yet there was only one way she could wield it and remain true to her nature.

The evening winds were picking up. Dabria placed her tray on the ground, where the riffling of the breeze would gently erase the work she had done, and sat down to admire the flowers while they lasted.

The Heart of the Forest

THOUGH THE RAIN had passed hours ago, the trees dripped, creating an ominous whisper among the freshly fallen autumn leaves. The loam gave up a fecund aroma—a primal breath as old as the land itself. In his fifty-three years, Oxal had intruded beneath these boughs only twice. This time felt no more familiar or welcome. The Forest of the Old Ones did not lightly tolerate the presence of humans, certainly not a company of fifty armed soldiers, some with axes.

The rider ahead tugged his beard, nervously eyeing a raven that watched from a tall, leafless spar. Saddle leather creaked as he reined back and leaned close to Oxal.

"This is a fool's quest," he murmured.

Oxal raised an eyebrow. "Yet here you are, Yram. Are you calling yourself a fool?"

Yram scowled and nudged his mount back into formation.

Oxal regretted his curtness. Yram's skepticism was warranted. Other men—good men—had failed at this search. Yet the pikeman should not have spoken so. It was disrespectful of the lord who led the quest. Oxal would not be party to such criticisms. He considered it vital to behave as a proper soldier, playing the role right down to the ancient practice of going beardless so that an enemy would have less to seize during combat—though Ayana teased him with spousal goodwill that he shaved only to hide the grey in his whiskers.

The company halted as they came to a large meadow. Here the woodland presented a choice of obvious paths—either along the stream that fed the expanse of peat, or over a hill strewn with rock outcroppings.

Oxal favored the former for its flatness, its proximity to water, its promise of fresh game for the night's cookfires. The scree draping the hill could slide underhoof.

At the head of the procession, a tall figure in blue and gold dismounted. Oxal had never been one to admire the physiques of other males, but he did so now. Prince Rahnnic radiated the lithe, angular beauty of the Arith. In an ordinary human, his aspect might be called delicate, but in him the smooth complexion and subdued musculature somehow conveyed the impression of virility and strength.

Yet this prince was a stranger, unproven in many ways. Handsomeness mattered little here. If Rahnnic could not determine which route to take from the meadow, he had no business leading a mission into the forest.

Oxal watched keenly as Rahnnic knelt and lifted a handful of soil. Sniffing it deeply, the Arith royal scanned the treetops. He tilted his head, as if listening. Finally he began to walk. Stopping periodically, he repeated his odd ceremony until he had wound past both the stream and the hill and come to stand across the meadow next to a dense thicket. Three pikemen and the standard bearer clung to his heels, guarding him vigilantly.

With sudden confidence the prince waved for the remainder of the column to join him.

The main knot of riders started forward, tracing their lord's route along the fringe of the clearing. But the rider just ahead of Yram chose to cut straight across the meadow. Yram, Oxal, and the rest turned as well.

Halfway across, the hair on the nape of Oxal's neck began to stiffen. The grass, toughened by a long dry summer, gave good purchase for the horses' hooves, yet as a mass it seemed to wobble, as if the layer of turf were suspended over liquid.

Prince Rahnnic turned from his examination of the forest and saw his riders in the open. Shock blanked his features. "Go back!" he shouted.

The echo had not yet faded as the ground gave way beneath five of the horses.

Oxal's mount dropped from under him. Boggy soil poured in from every side, submerging the animal and burying Oxal to his shoulders. Caught like the victim of an avalanche, only a desperate surge of strength freed his arms. From the waist down, his body was trapped.

Enveloped in the muck, his mount thrashed frantically. Just in front of Oxal's the ground trembled. Oxal dug quickly, uncovering the gelding's face. The beast snorted, eyes rolling in terror.

"Easy, easy," Oxal murmured, knowing that if the horse struggled too much, it would die. Broad, gentle swimming motions would keep them from sinking further, but rapid wiggling would draw them under.

Oxal had cared for his roan since it had been a day-old colt. Though terrified, it obeyed him and grew calm. Only then did Oxal have the chance to look about him.

Yram and his mount were nowhere to be seen. Of the other victims, the head of one companion remained above the surface.

Ropes landed among the stricken warriors. Oxal grabbed one. Meanwhile from the periphery of the meadow unmounted men, their armor and heavy gear shucked, crawled across the uncollapsed area with digging implements. Valiantly they dug where their comrades had vanished, trying to create breathing funnels.

Prince Rahnnic sat cross-legged, entering into a spellcaster's trance. Oxal wasn't certain what sort of magic could help — perhaps an enchantment to harden the ground — but he did know it would be too late. Sorcery was a sluggish affair; otherwise soldiers would be obsolete.

Before the spell took effect, the diggers uncovered Yram's upper body. He had suffocated.

"This is how the Forest of the Old Ones greets intruders," muttered a veteran sourly as the last body was pulled onto solid ground. Three men were dead. That it could have been worse did not lessen the sense of gloom.

Oxal, brooding over his last words to Yram, occupied himself brushing the mud from his gelding's coat. His was the only animal saved. Four mounts and a pack mule would remain part of the bog forever.

For the dead riders there would be a pyre. The captain raised an axe toward a sapling, glaring defiantly at the forest as he did so.

"No," declared Prince Rahnnic. "Killing trees will not bring him back, and it will only anger the guardians of this place. Gather fallen limbs."

Reluctantly the captain nodded, though he made it a point to have the pyre built at the very edge of the woods, where the flames would lick at the tips of extended branches.

The company watched with tightly pressed lips as the fire burned. Many faces turned back toward Irithel, toward home.

"Do any of you wish to leave?" asked the prince.

The company stirred. Here and there, a man muttered under his breath. Yet Oxal knew that no archer, pikeman, or horse soldier would wish to return to the capital wearing the badge of cowardice.

However, it was a good strategic move of Rahnnic to ask.

"For those who would come, this is the way," Prince Rahnnic said, pointing into the thickets at the meadow's edge. His statement was unequivocal. As the prince threaded between the close-set trees, a narrow trail appeared where no passage had seemed to exist. Everyone followed.

Perhaps, thought Oxal, the quest could succeed after all.

As dusk neared they came to a spot where a year earlier a brushfire had cleared the terrain. The prince announced they would camp there, beyond the reach of living trees.

When his chores were done, Oxal declined to join his comrades at the cookfires, preferring a few moments alone to mull over his narrow escape from death. He found a granite slab worn smooth by untold seasons of rainwater and sat, regarding the forest. An old oak, its trunk charred from the fire, drew his attention. Had the tree shifted closer to its neighbor since the company had camped?

"Sprites are moving the trees with their songs. They will play such music all night."

Oxal stood abruptly, bowing to Prince Rahnnic.

The Arith lord waved his soldier back down, and joined him on the slab. "You are Oxal, are you not? You were cool-headed in the meadow. I would not have cared to lose another man."

Oxal inclined his head, acknowledging the sincerity in Rahnnic's tone. "You did what you could, Your Highness."

"I could have sensed the trap earlier had my attention been on the meadow, rather than on the route away from it."

"Hindsight," Oxal said.

The prince shrugged, unwilling as yet to let himself off so easily.

Oxal nodded at the trees. "How far can they move?"

"No farther than their major roots can stretch. They are trees, after all, and are moored to the earth. But they will strain far enough by morning to disguise the existing trail, leaving a new path to lead us astray. I have to be vigilant to keep ahead of such tricks, if we are to find Lady Arameth." Rahnnic's gaze seemed to penetrate deep into the woods, as if he were already fathoming which way to travel in the morning.

He had finally mentioned her name aloud. "They say she was the most beautiful princess of her generation," Oxal said.

Rahnnic smiled in a melancholy way. "It would please her to hear such words. A hundred years ago, it was her voice that folk complimented. To hear her sing to our children—every father should have such an experience."

Oxal found it odd to hear someone talk of bygone days with such immediacy. Odder still to sit next to a legend. For all Oxal's life, the story of Rahnnic and his bride had been told at the hearthfires: How Theron raiders had attacked the capital without warning, hidden until then by the most simple of illusions—fog. How Rahnnic's defense of the palace allowed his grandfather, the king, to escape and, with reinforcements, recapture the city that same year. Such tales of valor had been what drew Oxal to a martial career. He would often visit the shrine in the old throne room of the palace, where Rahnnic stood like a statue, frozen in time within the ward he had formed in the last desperate moments of battle. Everyone knew that someday the ward would burst and Rahnnic would rejoin the world, but when it happened at last, Oxal was not the only one who had to make a pilgrimage to the shrine and see it empty before he would believe the hero lived and breathed once more.

The prince's voice fell to a whisper. Oxal averted his glance. Obviously, it pained Rahnnic to speak of children gone to the grave. After ninety-seven years suspended in time, the prince had lost nearly everyone he had known. His grandson now ruled Irithel, and for the sake of political stability Rahnnic had agreed not to seek the throne, accepting an honorary role as advisor to the crown.

But the story was not yet over. There was a chance that Arameth, wife of Rahnnic, still lived. She had not been able to bear living out her life without her prince. She waited ten years, until her children were of an independent age, and then she vanished into the forest to give herself to the dryads. As a dryad, she would be nigh immortal, and survive until Rahnnic's release.

The talespinners always spoke of how Rahnnic and Arameth would one day be happily reunited. But in truth, no one knew if that could happen.

"Your Highness..."

"Yes?"

"How can you be sure the lady is alive? The search parties her father sent found no sign of her. How is it you know where to look?"

To Oxal's relief, Rahnnic took no offense at the question. "In truth, I have no way of knowing if she lives. But if the sylvan folk accepted her pledge to become one of them, they would have taken her to dwell in only one place — the Heart of the Forest."

"But no one knows where that is," Oxal protested. "Some say it does not exist."

"It exists. I can find it."

Rahnnic seemed to glow in the numinous way of the Arith as he spoke. Oxal was reminded of passions he had felt at one glorious moment of his youth when, in the span of three seasons, he won the city wrestling tourney, was accepted into the palace guard, and came to know the favors of the potter's fine, worldly daughter. Oh, to feel such a fire again.

"Are you married, soldier? Do you have children?" the prince asked.

Oxal shifted uncomfortably. It seemed a sacrilege to speak. His had been a marriage of convenience. His cousin's foster sister had needed a husband; he had needed a companionable woman to make a home. It had been a suitable match, with few arguments over the years, but how could his situation possibly compare to that of legend? "My wife's name is Ayana. Four children. The youngest still lives at home," he mumbled.

Rahnnic nodded respectfully. "I am sure you miss them. With luck, this task of mine will soon be over, and you will soon be with them."

"I think of little else," Oxal lied, and felt relief as the prince returned to his pavilion.

In the morning, the sprites had indeed altered the trail. Rahnnic forged on, leading the column through brambles and around thickets. Often he was forced to meditate in order to divine the correct path. They could have made better time, but the Arith lord refused to allow his men to cut living branches, even when it meant a considerable detour.

The latter courtesy did not seem to temper the forest's animosity. Pines dropped heavy green cones. Twice hornets attacked, forcing Rahnnic to lay a charm to keep them away. The more the men progressed, the more the trees seemed to moan in protest.

Something *was* moaning, Oxal realized. A faint, keening chant drifted on the wind. It was fascinating.

"Hold!" cried Prince Rahnnic.

Oxal stopped. He and several other riders had turned away from the column and were edging toward the lip of a ravine. The prince had to cut off the lead pair of soldiers and drive them back before they would turn away.

"The willows in the ravine are singing a siren melody to make us tumble into the rapids," Rahnnic explained. "Plug your ears. Watch each other carefully. We must leave *now*."

The men obeyed. Eventually the trail turned away from the ravine, and the call faded.

"By the gods," grumbled the old fletcher behind Oxal. "A man can't void his bowels in this forest without fretting that a snake will slither into his undergarments."

Camp was made near a lake in a spot clear of trees. The men preferred to brave the resident hordes of mosquitoes than sleep in the shadows of the wood.

Rahnnic retired early. Oxal noticed bags under the prince's eyes and a stoop to his shoulders. The continual use of magic was taking its toll.

Oxal needed rest, too, yet two hours after bedding down, he woke. Sleeplessness was the bane of his middle age. After another hour of tossing, he gave up the struggle, put on his boots, and relieved one of the sentries.

The frogs had fallen silent. Sibilant whispers seemed to filter from the groves of pine and ash. Oxal shivered. To ease his nervousness, he paced back and forth along the stream bank.

Well after midnight, as the waning moon approached zenith, a scream roused the camp. Oxal whirled. A sentry, who had been perched on a fallen log for most of his watch, was frantically trying to lift his feet from the ground. Oxal rushed over.

Surely, he thought, the moonlight was deceiving him. A mesh of pallid root tendrils poked from the humus and into the leather seams of the sentry's boots.

"They're in my skin!" cried the man as if in the throes of a nightmare. In fact, Oxal was sure that the soldier had been dozing at his post. He sliced through the tendrils with his knife. The man lifted his feet.

Screams were now radiating over the camp. Soldiers struggled in their bedrolls. Oxal saw an archer claw at his feet.

"It has everyone," the sentry moaned.

An hour later, Rahnnic set down the foot of his afflicted captain. A pale nimbus of sorcery faded from the prince's hand.

"I can do nothing," he announced. He dragged his gauntlet across the ground, disturbing the network of vines that had emerged from the soil of the camp. Thin as capillaries, they were tough and sticky, like spider web made of plant matter. At the juncture of each branching lay a thorn as narrow as a mosquito's snout.

Oxal shifted self-consciously from foot to foot, worried that he might yet be stung. He and two of the sentries had escaped because they had stayed mobile while the vines had done their evil. All the other men in the company had been punctured by at least one thorn, save the prince, who would have sensed the encroachment.

"These vines must be woodcutter's bane," the prince added. "Once they poison a man's blood, roots will grow from whatever part of his flesh is closest to the ground. The cure takes weeks to administer. You must return to the city and convalesce in high stone towers. Go quickly. Do not let yourselves become thoroughly rooted or you will never be able to move again."

He pointed to Oxal and the two unafflicted sentries. "You men have charge of their safety. Watch them carefully. Within a few hours, they will begin to *wish* to take root."

"You aren't returning with us?" Oxal asked.

"No."

"Take me with you," Oxal said.

The prince raised his hand to protest.

"You'll need someone to watch your back, someone to share the watch at night. A single attendant is far better than none."

Rahnnic let his hand fall. "You are right. If I wish to succeed, I must not refuse aid."

The captain of the guard spoke. "Your Highness, how are we to find our way out without you?" His tone implied shame at seeming weak.

"Follow our path in reverse. The forest will not hinder you as long as you ride for its borders."

Oxal did not begrudge the captain his fear. Any sensible man would abandon the quest. He found a place away from the patch of woodcutter's bane and waited for the prince.

The next three mornings began at first light after hasty gulpings of cold rations. They rested each midday, making up for nights spent peering anxiously into shadows. Oxal was reminded of a campaign across the Far Dunes. The regiment had risked ambush for days on end crossing the sand. This trek did the same things to his mind. Alert to every mouse scurry and every sigh of the breeze, the soldier lived for the moment, storing little in memory.

Yet they were not attacked. The prince, with only one extra body to protect, managed to keep peril at a distance. Once, Oxal was forced to put an arrow in a rabid wolf that appeared in their wake. Otherwise, the only visible hostility was the forest's continued attempts to lead the men astray.

Rahnnic spoke less and less. Though his gaze remained alert, he slouched in his saddle. He sat listlessly beside the fire each night, leaving the care of the horses and other essentials entirely to Oxal. His cheeks grew gaunt. By late the third afternoon, Oxal was beginning to worry that his lord would fall from the saddle.

Abruptly, Rahnnic straightened up. Oxal followed his gaze. Across the path lay a row of unusually large trees of many types. They seemed to be part of a huge circle.

"We have arrived," the prince stated.

Abruptly the massive walnut directly ahead of them swung its branches, flinging its hard fruit. The horses, stung, reared back. Only quick hands on the reins kept the animals from bolting.

"Dryad trees!" Oxal yelled, cupping a bruise on his forehead.

"Yes," replied the prince. "The greatest of all. We dare not approach. The branches are nigh as supple as our own arms, and nearly as fast."

As if to prove Rahnnic's point, the walnut and a neighboring juniper reached out, shaping their outer branches like great claws. The men were only a few paces from the closest twigs.

"What now?" asked Oxal.

The prince dismounted, shaking a nut from his cuff. He led Oxal and the horses out of the range of more such missiles. "We wait for moonrise."

As twilight arrived, the forest's murmurs grew clearer. Oxal heard the thumping of log drums and the trill of reed pipes. Gone was the oppressive air of enmity. The soldier felt as though he'd sampled a fine ale, sipping just enough to loosen his muscles and dissipate anxiety, but not so much that his senses were dulled.

"Is this a trick?"

"The music is not intended for us," Rahnnic explained. "Have you not heard the tales? This is the anthem of the forest, sung here every night."

The fey symphony grew louder until it was all Oxal could do to resist seeking its origin. This was not like the siren call of the willows. That had been a sinister compulsion. This urge came from within him. He knew he could stifle it, but had no wish to.

Rahnnic stood. He pointed at the moon, which had risen above the treeline. "Now we can proceed."

Leaving the horses tethered, the men approached the guardian ring. The trees swayed menacingly, but Rahnnic raised his arms, palms open to the sky. He caught the moon's light and fashioned cords of glowing silver. When he had accumulated two huge coils, he flung the strands forward. They wrapped two of the trees, pulling their branches to either side, opening a passage.

"Quickly," the prince said.

Oxal sensed the frustration of the trees. The limbs trembled. A single walnut sailed feebly through the air, off target. No sooner had the men sprinted through the gap than the ropes of moonlight snapped, the fragments growing dull and grey as they fell.

The men stood on the lip of an earthen amphitheater. At the center a troupe of women danced around a brightly shimmering pool. They ranged from young to old, from thick to willowy, some as dark-skinned as hill oak, some as fair as aspen. Yet all shared a grace that set them apart from human dancers. When their feet lifted, the grass sprang up as if untrampled, rich with wildflowers and herbs. Each time their soles landed, the ground shook with a vibrant, life-giving pulse that travelled outward into the far reaches of the forest.

Oxal found himself swaying to the rhythm of the instruments — where the musicians were, he couldn't say. He only wanted to partake of the joy and vigor bathing the amphitheater. Here was a treasure barely hinted at in the myths. This could only be the sanctuary where sap was taught the joy of flowing, where antlers learned to sprout from the heads of stags, where the streams learned their babbling. The spirit of the forest reached out from here, giving every sapling and brush finch its purpose.

The forest had not attacked the soldiers out of an evil nature, but out of the need to preserve this nest from which its essence sprang.

The women began to chant. As the melody wafted into the treetops, Oxal was unable to contain the upwelling of celebration inside himself. He cried out.

Instantly the music ceased. The women spun toward the men. Their eyes widened and they fled toward the limits of the amphi-theater. As each reached the bole of one of the great trees, they were swallowed up as if they had melted into the bark.

Oxal's cheeks grew hot with embarrassment. "I...I..." he began, and turned helplessly toward Rahnnic.

The prince's gaze clung to one of the last of the dancers. Oxal saw a glimpse of supple legs in flight, auburn tresses waving behind, and then she was absorbed into a tree unlike any the soldier had ever seen. Only when she was out of sight did Rahnnic turn and face the pool.

"Forgive our trespass," he said. "We mean no harm."

The dryads did not answer him. Waving away Oxal's mutters of apology, the prince skirted the pool and began to approach the tree that had engulfed the auburn-haired woman.

While he was still many paces away, the oldest, hoariest member of the ring contorted and groaned. From its bole emerged an ancient crone. Oxal, who had been moving to join his lord, stopped and retreated. Though the apparition had assumed the general shape of a human, she seemed half made of earth, roots, and grubs, with hair of twigs. The soldier had no doubt she commanded the obedience of every plant and creature of the forest.

"Few of your kind have stood where you now stand, magician," said the goddess.

"I know, Mother," Rahnnic replied. "Few have had such need."

"I know your need. You seek to take the most verdant sapling of my grove. How can you ask me to surrender that which I love so much?"

"Before you had ever seen her, I loved her. Can you tell me that you love her more? Or can you find a place for me here? Show me that either is true, and I will accept it."

The great mother of the forest leaned forward, staring. Off to the side, Oxal shivered. The crone's eyes glazed over, seeing something more than the moonlight could show. Oxal sensed that were she to turn his way, she would peer right into him, uncovering every memory, every quirk of his character, every true emotion he had ever felt. Even the edge of her glance was enough to make the soldier sink to his knees as if reduced to infancy. Yet the prince stood firm.

Gradually the mother's head bowed.

"Yours is a pure soul, Rahnnic of Irithel. Would that there were a place for you here. But you are of fire and air, a rider of the sun's rays and seducer of the moon's light. I cannot alter your nature enough to find you a place here. Nor can I stand against the light blazing in you now. It must be given its moment to shine.

"Take her, then. Take her quickly, while I can keep from reaching to snatch her back. Take her with my blessing. Promise only that if your passion should ever dim for her, you will return her to me."

"I so promise," Rahnnic replied.

The mother turned. Like a baby being born, Arameth emerged from the trunk of her tree. She seemed dazed and almost unconscious, except that when Rahnnic reached for her, she rushed into his arms.

Oxal climbed unsteadily to his feet, almost ashamed to be watching, as if he'd stumbled over a couple making love. Arameth seemed only slightly older than Rahnnic. The gambit had worked. The decades ahead were theirs to share.

It was only as he handed the prince a blanket with which to cover his wife that Oxal realized something was wrong. Rahnnic had already seen it, and the blanket fell nerveless from his fingers.

"She is not as you remember her," the mother of the forest confessed. She held out a round, polished acorn as big as a hen's egg. "Take this. In time you may have need of it."

Rahnnic's hand shook as he accepted the acorn. Stricken, he led his princess from the amphitheater.

The end of the quest was not as Oxal would have imagined. True, hordes of onlookers lined the streets of the capital. Musicians played, clowns distracted impatient children, and decorations hung from shop lintels and street lamps. But the gaiety faded at the first glimpse of Arameth.

The princess frowned at the structures of brick and tile and lumber as if she had never seen them before. The people she ignored altogether. She demonstrated only one sign of intentional thought — occasionally she grasped Rahnnic's hand.

The somber discussions within the palace were the worst ordeal. Since the prince was reluctant to speak, it fell to the soldier to describe the liberation of the princess.

"She seems to know Rahnnic," he said, intimidated to be speaking to so many royals, "but gives no other sign that she remembers her life as Arameth. It's been too long. The human part of her has withered. All the way back she would sit in silence, listening to the babble of streams, raising her face to the sun, swaying as the breeze stroked her. Like a tree."

The royal family could see for themselves the truth of the account. Rahnnic and Arameth retired to private quarters. The king tripled Oxal's pension as a reward for his fealty and granted him permission to leave.

Though he was a palace guard, Oxal seldom saw the prince over the next few seasons. Most of that was at a distance, as Rahnnic guided his mate through the gardens or along the ramparts, viewing the seashore where, in an earlier life, they had shared many walks.

The princess remained wordless, though occasionally she voiced sounds that mimicked the rustling of leaves in the wind. Only a few sights made her smile, chiefly the arrival of birds, who would perch on her and sing. Sometimes on moonlit nights she would dance, and Oxal heard it whispered that it was not such a dance as the proper ladies of the court would dare attempt.

One day in autumn, Rahnnic came to the barracks where Oxal had just completed his round of duty.

"It was a year ago today I took Arameth from the wood," said the prince. "Come. You were my witness then. Be my witness now."

With Arameth at his side, Rahnnic guided Oxal to a secluded area of the royal gardens where a dead tree had recently been removed. Soft soil, wet from that morning's storm, filled the cavity where the stump had been dug out. There the prince planted the acorn given to him by the mother of the forest.

Scarcely had he stepped back than a sprig emerged from the soil. It swelled within moments into a full-sized evergreen bright with waxy leaves and amber flowers. It stopped growing only when its bole was thicker than a man could wrap his arms around. It vaguely resembled a laurel, but its bark was a smooth tan and tiny clusters of acorns hid in the centers of the blossoms.

Arameth stepped forward, smiling radiantly. She slid hastily from her garments, fluttered to the evergreen, and vanished.

Rahnnic sighed, tears hovering on his lashes. He pointed at the ground on which he stood. "She was becoming ill. Though she has left the forest—willingly—the forest will not leave her. This will give her time to remember herself."

"How much time will that be?"

"Who knows? I will have a bench made so that I may sit in her shade. I have memorized her dance, and will perform it with her. Perhaps that is all that I can hope for."

"I am sorry, Your Highness, that things have not gone better."

"Do not be sorry for me, sir. I have her again. That in itself is greater fortune than I had a right to expect. I waited a century for her companionship. I can wait another, if need be, to see her fully restored." A branch of the tree reached downward, stroking his cheek with soft leaves. "You see? She knows that I love her. Surely the rest is worth a bit of patience."

Oxal quietly took his leave. The prince remained, hand tenderly pressing the tree.

The soldier made his way down the familiar cobbled streets to his modest house. Ayana was waiting as he stepped across the threshold. She took one look at him and said, "It is done, then?"

"Yes." Oxal coughed. "Yes."

Over supper he described the scene at the garden. "The legend is fulfilled," Ayana replied. "For better or worse, they are reunited. It makes a mighty tale."

Oxal nodded absently. He was watching his daughter. His baby, Fihelia, now fourteen years old. She was placing the screen in front of the hearth for the night, looking for all the world like a grown woman tending to the duties of her own house.

Gradually his aging, scarred features eased into a smile.

He and Ayana had shared these walls for over thirty years. Quietly, with harmony. Passion had not blazed for them as in legends, but they had grown accustomed to each other in ways that soothed the soul. He had never truly appreciated that fact until he had returned from the forest. And now, more than ever, he wondered how it could have been that once he had been envious of Rahnnic, Prince of Irithel.

It had not been a fool's quest. A prize had been waiting, after all.

The Land of Graves

THE RUNNER, a halfbreed Selanese with the long legs and freckled complexion of his slave mother's people, was puffing hard as he burst from the olive grove and hurried up to the excavation where Tecia and her cousin's crew worked. Hair and loinclout soaked with sweat, the messenger halted at the lip of the trench. "Sorceress, you are needed!" he blurted when he had regained enough wind to speak.

Tecia sighed. "My tasks occupy me." She indicated the inscribed stone walls around her, the men with picks and buckets laboring to carry off the packed silt that had filled the hip-deep space where she stood.

"It is the headman's command. It is most dire. A revenant has been unbound. It has killed two men already."

"One victim the tomb robber, no doubt."

The messenger nodded. "That is correct, Mage Helper. But the other is Gelages, your uncle's strong man."

Tecia tilted her head down and scuffed the debris at her feet, letting the twinge of loss run its course.

"Tell my uncle I will come," she stated.

The runner turned.

"Wait," she called.

He paused, forehead creasing.

"Drink some water. Rest." She pointed up at the sun. "The ghost will not venture out again until twilight. Haste is unnecessary."

The youth hesitated, darting a glance at the broken terrain through which he had to return. She could see him weigh the balance between her advice—sensible, but given by a woman—and his master's command of utmost speed. In compromise, he visited the water wagon, drenched a cloth, and wiped the perspiration from his brow and upper body. After several small careful sips from the dipper, he set off again fast enough to pretend he was hurrying, but nevertheless exploiting some of the respite Tecia had granted.

In the trench, Tecia finished making a rubbing of an inscription in the stone wall, stowed the leaf in her basket, and vaulted nimbly out of the trench.

"Another ten paces should bring us to the drain," she told her cousin Flen, the leader of the workers, as he turned toward her, waving away dust clouds.

He grunted, which she knew meant that if she were correct, they would keep working, but if she were wrong, they would stop and wait for her return, and let her shoulder the blame for the delay.

She slapped the grit from her tunic and took her own turn by the water wagon, cleaning her face and hands and easing her parched throat.

At this arid time of year, it took imagination to recall the point of all this labor was to restore the ancient Ladian water system and reclaim another stretch of swamp. If all went well—if Tecia had translated the old scrolls well enough—when the rains returned, water would no longer linger in pools, nurturing the young of malarial mosquitoes and other vermin of stagnant water. A new generation of farmers could till tracts of fertile alluvial soil unavailable since their great-grandsires' day.

Tecia cursed the luck that forced her to leave. It had taken much persuasion to convince the headman to devote a work crew to the project, and much still had to be done while the dry season lasted. However, a murderous revenant was not an interruption that could be ignored.

She adopted a steady pace toward home. Olive trees closed around her, then scrub brush, relieving some of the sun's glare. By lizard's hour she was up into the hills, following the ancient track. The way was seldom steep, the gravel and vestigial paving stones flat and smooth compared to modern roads, which even in this arid season remained scored by ruts.

A low bluff rose on her left. The necropolis began. Carved columns rose at the entrances, supporting cupolas and lintels still intact in many spots, though wind and rain had worn away the glyphs that had once identified the families buried behind these entrances. The ruins went on and on, covering a parcel many times the size of Quona, the living town supported by this stretch of the Aritis River valley.

Cresting a ridge, Tecia saw Quona itself hugging the upper edge of a shelf of land that extended into the valley beyond. Folk were crowded on the walls, gazing farther out across the plateau. Among the mounds and barrows there she spied another clump of people, their gestures and weapons directed at a house-sized crypt a hundred paces from them. Tecia made out the Selanese runner among them, and recognized the heavy-set man in the center of the group as her uncle. They stood near a pair of limp, supine forms.

As she drew near, her uncle actually dipped his chin in greeting, a deference he had often accorded Tecia's father as clan sorcerer, but which he seldom tendered in her direction, no matter how well versed in the arts she might be.

"This fool violated this tomb here," the headman declared, shaking his bracelet of tiny bronze skulls first toward one of the dead men on the ground and then at the large crypt. "He didn't even try to hex the guardian."

Tecia spared a brief glance at the corpse, that of a wiry, hook-nosed man she thought she might have glimpsed scraping skins at the tannery in seasons past, not the sort of occupation that brought much gain. The wretch must have felt the need, like so many others, to enrich himself with Ladian tomb relics. A desperate hope. While an expert thief or magician sometimes slipped in and out of crypts without consequence, it did not happen often. As her uncle had noted, the perpetrator did not even wear a fetish or talisman to distract the ghost.

She looked longer at Gelages, the strong man. Her family and his tilled neighboring plots out in the valley, and lived only a few houses apart within the walled town. Though the adult Gelages had been too dull to interest her, she grieved for the childhood companion he had been. Always large for his age, he had gladly served his playmates when they needed a strong hand to help them ford the river, and had not minded doing so even for a girl, a scholar's daughter at that.

He had died with eyes wide, his dagger still clenched in his hand. His corpse showed no visible wounds.

"Ambushed," the headman explained.

Tecia nodded. She noted the furrows in the dirt made by the heels of the dead men as they were dragged away from the spots where they had died. Her gaze came to rest on the ornate house of the dead. Unlike the older relics in the necropolis in the hills, the glyphs above the lintel were still deeply etched.

"The resting place of Vicedis, chief wise man of King Tobasi," she read. A great scholar. "The revenant was a warrior?"

"Yes. Tall, armored, carrying a pike."

Not the shade of Vicedis himself, then, nor the kin buried with him. Alas, Vicedis had been so notable among the Ladians that he had been interred with a guard of honor. That ilk were often the restless ones, with grudges to infuriate them, while their masters and mistresses slept peacefully through eternity.

A blistering stream of curses rang out from the crypt, calling for the blood of a certain man. The eerie voice was shrill and inhuman, heard with the mind rather than the ears. Tecia, despite her knowledge of ancient Ladian, could not fully translate the outburst.

The men beside the headman shivered, and Tecia's uncle himself began blinking furiously.

"Put him to sleep, Mage Helper," her uncle commanded.

"Not an ordinary labor," she commented.

One of the headman's eyebrows rose. "Eh?"

"I risk my life to do this," she explained. "I deem this another of the twelve great tasks you asked of me when my father died. The last of them. If I succeed, my boon is due."

Her uncle stared at her hard, then down at the body of his strong man, then back. "This is no time for bargaining."

She folded her hands in front of her, glancing down submissively. "The bargain was made five years ago, and you set the terms. Quelling a revenant has always been counted as a great task of a mage."

The headman glanced up at the sun. Many hours remained until sunset, but days would be required to fetch a mage from another town. In this time and place, none but Tecia could do what must be done.

"Very well," the headman said. "This is the twelfth task. Now lay this ghost down, and be quick about it."

"As you command," Tecia said.

She addressed the headman's servants. "Be ready to seal the tomb."

The group held up pots of mortar dust and water bags, along with a sack of dried flowers for the funerary magic. They would be ready to set the slab back in place and see the ritual completed before sunset.

Tecia crept forward alone. She paused to take a deep breath at the top of the stone ramp leading down to the crypt entrance. The portal, its slab flung aside, yawned ominously wide.

She could make out the outlines of funerary stellae and urns in the antechamber. The mephitis of death wafted out. She squatted down and peered farther inside. She did not venture past the threshold, conscious of the protection of the sun at her back.

The revenant had the capacity to venture into the sunlight. The flattened ground just beyond the top of the ramp where Gelages must have fallen proved it had already sprung out once. But the glare of daylight made ghosts nigh invisible. They did not care for that, because it reminded them they were dead.

The stone couch in the antechamber where the guardian slept was occupied by a skeleton, still bearing a few scraps of gray, desiccated skin, preserved by sorcery and the power of the Ladian embalming arts. Tarnished brass accouterments showed that the deceased had once worn an ornately decorated set of leather armor. Now he was mostly bones. His former wealth and status was proven by the dentures made of gold bands and ox teeth.

Inchoate mumbles directed her attention toward the tomb's main chamber. Here stood the central dais and its sarcophagus — the remains of Vicedis. Pacing in circles around the dais was a tall man — tall in the way of the Ladians, whose flocks and plentiful crops sustained them in a manner unknown to Tecia's people. He was no skeleton, but as his mouth issued its stream of words, she saw that the dentures matched those of the deceased warrior perfectly. The decorations on his armor were the same as the items of metal scattered upon and beside his bones.

The phantom did not seem to notice her. She waited where she was, letting her eyes adjust to the dimness, listening carefully to the ancient dialect. Finally the outbursts became decipherable.

"Where is he? Zaeghus, you child of a she-goat, come forth!"

Tecia had no doubt Zaeghus was the very enemy who had killed this warrior, long ago. Who better to wish vengeance upon? That was all the creature was now — a manifested wish for vengeance. Lethal to any who might get in his way — that being the point of installing him here to guard Vicedis and his family.

Bracing herself, she crept fully into the antechamber. On the vertical face of the stone couch where the warrior had lain all those centuries, she found a carving in relief. The artwork was a portrait of the warrior, his pike held at his side. To judge from the ghost, the image resembled the man with uncanny accuracy. Tecia wished the artisans of her age possessed such skill.

She placed her hand on the effigy and began to murmur words in Ladian. Despite the tension of the moment, she recalled the phrases perfectly. They were inscribed in every Ladian tomb. Other parts of the language were a mystery, but these were not. In as soothing a tone as she could manage, she called the spirit to its rest, to wait for the arrival of the next world, when souls would be given new shrouds and live in the light again.

The specter whirled and glared at Tecia.

"Who is dead?" he cried. "Has Zaeghus killed again?"

Tecia frowned. She was not surprised that the ghost failed to realize the summons was for him, but it should have affected him nonetheless, dampening his anger and lulling him back to the bones on the stone couch.

His phantom eyes glowed as he watched her. She finished the rite. No change. All the tactic had done was call attention to herself.

"Your costume is strange," he grumbled, scanning her up and down. In life, he had probably never seen a woman in warm seasons of the year with her breasts covered, or with a hemline reaching below the knees.

Tecia's circumstances were becoming perilous. She changed tactics. She let go of the carving, stood, and began uttering the chant of exorcism in a raised voice.

The ghost staggered back. He clutched his head and grimaced.

Tecia began speaking faster, as fast as she could without stumbling over the words and having to begin again.

"You may cast out ghosts," he called. "That is no concern of mine. I have sworn to kill Zaeghus. Stand not in my way!"

Tecia did not like her chances. Exorcisms would not work if the subject utterly denied the fact of his non-corporeal state. But having no other means of attack, she began to repeat the chant.

"Fah!" the warrior blurted when she failed to go silent. He levelled his pike and, with the suddenness that had no doubt won him many battles, he charged forward.

The pike skewered her in the heart. She folded around it, unable to deny the illusion. Pain split her. It was as if a shard of ice had plunged inside, and at the same time, heat roared to her extremities. She knew what warriors must feel when the battle goes against them, and they are lost forever.

She collapsed as the ghost withdrew the pike. She thought she heard him laugh at her, even as the world around her faded to black.

She awakened with tomb dust fouling her lips. She groaned and pressed her hands to her sternum. She was as unmarked as Gelages and the thief had been. But she had not emulated their fate. For years she had been casting spells upon herself designed to protect her should she ever find herself attacked by a phantom. Apparently she had done an effective job.

Effective, but not perfect. She could tell her heart had damaged itself. She suspected she would never live to be a crone. She would become frail prematurely. But then, she had already lived longer than her sisters, two of whom had succumbed to childbed fever, and the other to childbirth itself. If her decision to study the lore and become a sorceress had come with a price, it was one she had long since chosen to pay.

In the short term, though, she was in more pain than she had ever experienced.

She clawed at one of the pouches on her belt. Withdrawing a tiny vial, she removed the stopper and quaffed the entire draught. The medicine seared her throat as it went down, for it contained much alcohol along with the more potent ingredients. She waited for the relief to spread from gullet to her heart and to the bruises on her knees, elbows, and chin caused by her hard fall onto stone.

Darkness surrounded her, but it was not the lightlessness of un-consciousness. She recognized the stone couch beside her, the dusty paving stones beneath her. Starlight glinted in from the open portal.

No moonlight. Yet the moon was at first quarter and should have remained in the sky half the night. It was past midnight, then.

The revenant must have been roaming the land for many hours. She knew she had to track him down.

She leaned back against the couch. She tried to distract herself from the agony by regarding the urns, murals, and stellae across the passageway. It was her habit to glean whatever knowledge she could from the vestiges of the Ladians. No one in Quona was better at it than she. Even the minimal light could not hide the abundance of the trove.

An urn displayed a Ladian noble and his wife reclining on pillows near a fountain amid dinner guests, sharing wine and laughing. The difference between their era and that of Tecia was immediate—not only in the upper-body nudity, but in the fact that women could dine with men, and that the women could drink wine, an offense punishable by death in modern Quona and its neighboring provinces. Tecia had only once tasted it, in secrecy.

There were those who might not allow her to include alcohol in her potions, were she not the niece of a headman. There were those who would destroy "obscene" relics such as the urn, were it not housed in a tomb protected by a warrior ghost and other enchantments.

Yet however much she admired the bygone age, at the moment the living needed her. As the pain lessened, she staggered to her feet. The numbing effect of the concoction would dull her wits for hours. She was capable of activity.

She stumbled out into the landscape. A flicker caught her eye. Out in the valley a fire was consuming a hayloft. Men shouted. Pigs squealed.

All the way down there, she thought. She had no strength to cover such a distance.

A pair of silhouettes separated from the lee of a minor crypt a few dozen paces away.

"Mage Helper!" a man cried. "You still live! The river be praised."

Tecia recognized the two men as Kell and Rosvoi, two of her uncle's laborers.

"You were left to watch the tomb?" she queried.

"Yes. But we didn't dare enter it."

She waved off the apology. Even with the ghost gone, staying clear was a wise choice. Had anyone violated Vicedis's resting place in search of her body, they might have fallen victim to curses she knew how to avoid.

"The revenant started the fire?" she asked, gesturing at the valley.

"Yes." It could not literally be true, for the ghost had no physical presence, but he could startle a farmer into dropping a lamp.

"What else?"

"We don't know the whole of it, because none have brought news since the moon set," Kell replied. "Early in the evening the creature frightened the headman's best stallion to death, and ran off the field slaves."

Her uncle would be fuming about the loss of his favorite breeding horse for years to come, Tecia thought. The flight of the slaves would trouble him less. It was unlikely they could make it out of the province. When their terror was vanquished, most would return of their own accord, rather than risk flogging or castration.

"Does the ghost call for a man named Zaeghus?" she asked.

"He calls for someone constantly. That may be the name," Rosvoi answered.

Tecia concentrated. "Zaeghus…"

"Mage Helper?"

"If he was a contemporary of King Tobasi," she continued, thinking aloud, "he would have a crypt here in the mounds. If he was great enough to slay the man chosen to be the guardian of Tobasi's chief counsellor, he himself would have been chosen to guard an even more prestigious tomb."

Rosvoi shrugged, as if to say he was only a common man, unlearned in such things. And so he was. In all Quona, Tecia alone possessed the scholarship to puzzle this out.

What was the name of King Tobasi's own tomb guardian? The drugs in her belly dulled her memory, but she recalled that it was not Zaeghus. That left one likely burial site of that era: The tomb of Princess Ula, Tobasi's twin sister, and co-ruler until Tobasi's eldest son became old enough to take on his share of the ruling house's duties. The Ladians of that dynasty had never allowed a single monarch to claim total authority. The junior co-ruler was often a woman, particularly during transitional periods.

Tecia turned and gazed north at the shorter of two prominent knolls. "There," she said. "Help me walk. We will find help there."

Kell and Rosvoi went so pale she could see the change even in the starlight. "Are you certain?" Kell asked.

"Am I versed in magic or not?" she retorted.

They took up positions beside her and supported her by elbows and armpits as she travelled. She would have tripped over stones hidden in the grass if not for their help, but with it she soon arrived at the portal of a large house of the dead.

She knelt at the door and caressed the effigy carved into it. She murmured Ladian words of appeasement.

Digging into the largest of the pouches at her belt, she withdrew her double flute. The old yellow wood gleamed in the starlight. Wetting her lips, she began to play the sacred dirge of the Ladians — but backwards, for this was not the version meant to put the dead to rest, but that meant to wake them.

Kell and Rosvoi closed hands over their ears. The music was sweet, but few people cared to hear that tune, played on an instrument that had all but died out with the Ladians.

The song ended. Tecia lowered the instrument and listened — not with ears, but with a different sort of attentiveness.

A stirring came from within the tomb. It was a whisper, little louder than the susurrus of grass in the wind. Though it was what she hoped for, it chilled her. Kell hiccupped. Rosvoi backed away.

"Respectfully, we beg your assistance," she called in the old tongue.

Stepping away, she waved the two guards to approach. "Break the seal. Pull away the slab."

They hesitated.

"The ghost will not harm you," she said.

Her confidence won them over. As they worked, she waited

nearby with arms folded, feigning composure. In fact, ghosts were never so predictable. This one might be as murderous as the one wreaking havoc in her uncle's fields.

The tink-tink-tink of the chisels went on for some time. Finally, licking dry lips and murmuring prayers to the river, the men braced and pulled. The slab, well weighted like many of the best crypts, swung aside so easily one man would have been enough to do the job.

"Yah!" Kell called. He and Rosvoi leaped away.

A ghost stood in the vestibule. He wore leather torso armor, draped with sheaves of bronze, and held a bronze short sword.

"Guardian of Majestic Ula, hear our plea," Tecia called. "Be you the shade of Zaeghus?"

The warrior touched his collar, where a bronze disk fibula held together the corners of his cape. His fingers stroked the inscription, a traditional glyph of mourning.

"Am I dead?" he inquired.

"Yes," Tecia replied. Thank the river this ghost perceived so fully what the other denied. Otherwise she surely would have multiplied her troubles.

"Then…it appears I am the shade of Zaeghus, for such was my name. And now I guard that most ingenious of princesses? Why, better that than the bones of the king himself!"

"It is apparent that you served well," Tecia said. "Would you serve the living for an hour? An old enemy of yours needs killing again."

"What is his name?"

"That I do not know. But he calls for you in anger. I believe you killed him once."

The ghost grinned. "I killed many men."

"He was a noted warrior, middle-aged, with false teeth."

"Ah." Zaeghus laughed. "Ghinnis. I gutted him like a sow on feast day."

"So you will help us?"

"With delight. Promise to respect my lady's place of rest while I am absent, and I will do as you ask."

"I do so promise," Tecia replied.

The ghost of Ghinnis returned to the tomb of Vicedis in the crepuscular light of early dawn, as Tecia knew he would. The ghost of Zaeghus stepped from the lee of the edifice to meet him.

"You!" cried Ghinnis. He lowered his pike and rushed forward, as quick on his feet as Tecia had experienced.

Zaeghus side-stepped at the last moment, grabbed Ghinnis by the neck, expertly slid the sword through the laces of his armor, and disembowelled his opponent with a single wrenching motion.

The twice-slain man gawked at the intestines pouring from his belly. His eyes turned up and he collapsed. No worldly sword could have touched him, but the weapon of his known enemy was real to him.

As soon as his body stopped twitching, it melted away. A puff of vile mist trailed back to the tomb of Vicedis.

The people watching, which now included the headman and the men who had attempted to rein in the chaos created by the revenant, burst into a cheer.

The ache in Tecia's chest eased. She smiled. But she was also quick to reach into a pouch at her belt, and close her fist around the contents.

The surviving ghost strutted before his audience and spat on the dirt where Ghinnis's phantom blood had gushed, though no stain lingered there.

"Our thanks," Tecia said. "Now, if it please you, your sepulcher awaits. Dawn is coming, and I would spare you its bite."

Zaeghus waved his hand dismissively. "Nay, it would please me not."

Tecia groaned.

Zaeghus regarded the valley and river. The growing light splashed pleasingly over the rectangles of cultivated earth. "The land is not so crowded as in my day. Perhaps I will explore it."

"Perhaps not," Tecia stated firmly. "If you do, I will take back my promise to revere the tomb of Princess Ula. I will see to it her body is stripped of its finery, and her bones scattered on open ground."

The specter bared his teeth at her and raised his blade. "You will not," he growled.

"I will unless you abide by what is right. The 'most ingenious of princesses' would admire such a decision."

Zaeghus scowled. But gradually, his swordpoint dropped.

"You are most unfair," he muttered. "You remind me of my wife."

"Death is unfair," she responded. "But even so, it is inevitable."

Tecia flung out her hand, showering Zaeghus with dust she had gathered from the threshold of Princess Ula's crypt. "By the ancient rites, you are confined to your post," she yelled in ritual Ladian.

Zaeghus's scowl evolved into startlement. His "body" spasmed, became intangible and fluid. His feet rose from the earth. He was whisked back to the royal knoll like a sheet of rainwater in a gale.

Tecia finally let herself breathe. Thank the river for a ghost that could be swayed by his obligation, and therefore remained vulnerable to the old magic. She turned to Kell and Rosvoi. "Go back and seal the crypt. The sunrise will protect you."

They bowed and did not even wait for the headman to concur before they ran off to accomplish their task.

Tecia's uncle reaffirmed his authority by commanding a similar detail to close the tomb of Vicedis.

Tecia sat down on a broken column and rubbed her sternum. She let the headman come to her. He gazed down at her dusty, bedraggled self with the lordliness it had been his privilege to indulge in all his adult life. He pursed his lips and nodded. "So, niece. You have done well. I thank you."

She gazed back steadily, waiting for more. It did not come.

"The matter we spoke of yesterday afternoon?" she murmured.

"That was before I lost my horse," he said.

She straightened up, as much as the throbbing in her spine

would allow. "Did I or did I not risk my life to complete this task?"

The headman sighed. She understood his dilemma. It was one thing to sanction a female to take the duties of her late father, a clan sorcerer whose son and heir had also recently expired, leaving no other viable candidates but her. It was another to grant her the status of full mage, and enjoy the privileges that came with the rank — privileges that ordinarily came with the assumption of the duties, so long as the magician was a male. The most important of which was the ability to teach apprentices.

She had abided by her uncle's restrictions, kept the rank of Mage Helper these past five years, and undertook the twelve tasks to prove herself. Now he could only deny her her reward by breaking a sworn promise.

To her astonishment, the headman's expression softened. "Ah, girl. When I thought you dead in that tomb, the feeling was as bitter as one of your potions. So be it. As of this moment, you are Mage. You are free to choose your students."

She rocked back. She had expected at most a begrudging concession. The elder's tears took her by surprise. With a voice gone husky with emotion, she replied, "If it please you, I will begin with the traditional candidate."

He cleared his throat, as if expecting her answer. The traditional pupil was always a younger son of the headman, if one was available. And one was. She would not only teach, but teach a male.

"As you have chosen, so it will be," the headman said.

He strode off quickly, muttering about the need to set his farm in order. Several of the observers lingered, especially the women, to help Tecia back to her house in the walled city.

But first she stayed to watch the sun rise on a new day, the sort seldom seen since the age of the Ladians.

Trading Swords

THE RAIDERS CAUGHT UP with them on the open heath. The Islanders made their stand on an ancient Dyrie barrow — little more than a bump on the broad expanse of moor grass and wildflowers, but at least it was high ground. Above them clouds gathered into a dark, oppressive mass.

The bond-warriors and other fighting men formed a human wall around the barrow. Reila joined the bond-witches at the summit. There was no time to erect the ritual tent. The women would be un-shielded from the screams of their husbands; they would smell the blood as it spilled. Reila forced the prospect from her mind, seeking the concentration essential to her magic.

The Hrogi closed in with characteristic ferocity, as if to annihilate the party of Islanders as rapidly and thoroughly as they had obliterated a dozen Islander villages. The invaders outnumbered the natives four to one.

"Fight to the end," High Witch Maer called, both to the warriors and to her sisters. "If we make good account of ourselves, there will be too few of them left to endanger the heartland."

Reila spared one last glance at Kelf. Her spouse already had his back to her. Sword high, he braced to meet the coming charge.

Reila closed her eyes, folded her hands in her lap, and cleared her mind. To her great relief, the earth did not resist as she tapped its essence. The high witch had guessed well. The barrow must have been an ancient site of power.

Suddenly, without opening her eyes, Reila could see the entire battlefield. The tableau unfolded from a point high above the witches' circle. At the same time, she could feel the firmness of the barrow marker stone beneath her. All of her senses, except sight, remained lodged in her body.

The witches extended their protective auras around their husbands. The Islander party was as ready as it would ever be.

The Hrogi wave crashed against a breakwater of Islander steel and armor.

Kelf hacked off the point of an extended spear and kicked out the knee of his assailant. He had no time to deliver a mortal stroke. A flurry of six Hrogi raiders crowded around him. His flanking allies, occupied with their own opponents, could not reach him.

An axe struck Kelf's side. The blade sheared skin and muscle away from his ribs. Fragments of chain mail punctured blood vessels. He staggered.

Reila accepted the pain. She cried out, as she always did on the first blow. Kelf, freed from the agony, drove the point of his blade through the axe wielder's hauberk and into the man's heart.

Reila funneled her suffering into the earth as fast as she could. It never seemed fast enough. In exchange, the goddess sent the forces of renewal. The energy struck Reila with a potent kiss. She shaped it and thrust it toward Kelf.

The bond-warrior's slashed muscles knit together. His body spit out the fragments of metal. His skin closed over the wound. The healing was nearly complete by the time Kelf started to withdraw his sword.

Kelf's steel hung up in the axe wielder's armor. The bond-warrior yanked it free, but the delay cost him. A mace grazed his helmet. Broadswords slammed against his upper arms.

Reila stopped the ringing in her husband's head. She neutralized the effect of the sword blows—the blades had not penetrated his armor, but without her intervention his limbs would have gone nerveless from the sharp impacts.

One of the Hrogi, expecting to take advantage of a stunned

opponent, left himself open, and died.

Reila drained off more agony. Perspiration soaked her hair and dripped from her nose. The goddess once again gave generously of her essence. Reila sent the gift toward her husband.

Though she concentrated on Kelf, she took in the overall struggle. The Hrogi pressed in on every edge of the circle. Several Islander soldiers lay dying amid grass, crumpled shrubs, and barrow cobbles. All five of the bond-warriors fought on, thwarting their foes' momentum. The circle grew tighter around the barrow knoll, but at a dear cost to the raiders.

As the Hrogi witnessed the bond-guardians surviving damage that would have sent ordinary men into shock or death, they concentrated their attack on the five. Reila could hardly make out Kelf amid the horde. So many men tried to attack at the same time that they interfered with each other. High Warrior Fonis, given so many convenient targets, laid waste with his battle axe.

Dazed from the pain, disoriented by the constant, horrendous amounts of energy she was forced to channel, Reila's trance-induced gaze drifted past the battle. A barrel-chested Hrogi warrior stood at the periphery. He wore a horned helmet, inlaid with tiny rubies. One of his arms rested in a sling. He cradled a drawn but unsullied broadsword in the opposite gauntlet, waving it idly as if it were a willow switch, rather than a weapon designed for two strong hands.

Chieftain. Reila wished one of her party's fighting men would break free, and cleave that ornate helmet down the middle. That man had to be the spur behind the relentless Hrogi pursuit these past two days.

It was fortunate that Kelf could not hear her wish. Even without the weapons flailing in his face, he did not dare charge. Spilled blood — some his, but mostly that of his enemies — had turned the sod at his feet to muck. He could barely maintain his balance on the slick surface. He kept to his task, fighting Hrogi. He had found his rhythm. Each exchange left another enemy dead or gravely wounded.

The pain became a constant, hypnotic tide. Reila let the energies flow at their own pace along the path she had established. What little coherent thought remained she devoted to observing the enemy chieftain.

The man gazed straight at the bond-warriors. He slowly nodded his head. Then he stared even more intently at the bond-witches. He nodded more deeply, and his lips moved, as if counselling himself.

A scream from Sandel, the youngest of the bond-witches, brought Reila's attention back to the battle. The body of Sandel's bond-mate, Flin, lay nearly decapitated at the center of a knot of Hrogi warriors. A giant, thickly muscled raider brought a heavy battle axe down on Flin's abdomen, splitting through armor and internal organs to Flin's spine.

Sandel collapsed. She had taken no wounds of the flesh, but nevertheless she was dead before she struck the ground.

The death of the first pair of bond-guardians shifted the stream of energy flowing through the bond-witches. For the span of two heartbeats, the surge drove away every shred of Reila's pain.

In a moment of clarity, she saw the Hrogi chieftain, staring in fascination, not at the defeated bond-warrior, but at the lifeless bond-witch. Then the energies stabilized, and the suffering resumed.

Kelf had erred, letting himself be distracted by the defeat of his fellow guardian. He took deep wounds.

Reila grappled with the misery. She healed her partner.

Kelf regained his equilibrium, and in a deft display of skill, slew four opponents almost at once. His victories totalled nearly twenty. But Reila had been dealt too potent a blow. The brief interlude of comfort had erased her ability to cope with the severity of the anguish. She misdirected the shaping.

The owl of shadows took her consciousness away to its roost.

Reila woke to a tug at her neck, and to the caress of light rain, soft as fog, on her cheeks. The newly moistened heath shrubs cast up a fecund aroma, almost enough to quench the fetor of blood and intestines. If this were the afterworld, it felt and smelled too much like the one she had left.

She opened her eyes.

A filthy Hrogi warrior leaned over her, knife in one hand. He held her pewter-and-schorl pendant, the sigil of her cult, in the other palm. The severed ends of the leather loop tickled her exposed throat.

The warrior grunted in surprise as she stirred. He turned and spoke to someone behind her. She could not understand his harsh inflections, though the Hrogi and Islander languages had evolved from the same roots.

The chieftain came into view. Fresh blood stained the cloth that held his wounded arm. The battle had apparently reached him, after all, though his stride indicated no loss of vitality.

He waved his sword peremptorily. His warrior moved away from Reila.

"Alive? This is new."

The chieftain spoke with the clarity of a scholar, only the accent betraying that Island speech was not native to him. He gazed at her with fervent, almost sexual intensity, yet it was not physical lust she read in that glance.

"For years, over many raids, I have fought the *hrolf* warriors — the sons of your goddess. I have seen them kill so many of Hrog's best that we have run in terror back to our longships. Not until a month ago had I seen an entire cadre of *hrolf* defeated. Do you know what we found after that battle?"

He jabbed the High Witch's ribs with his boot. Reila winced, to see Maer's body tainted. "For every slain magical warrior, we found an equal number of women, lying in a tent. Dead, but unmarked, with no trace of poison on their lips." He knelt down, and said softly, "Why do you still live?"

She did live. And as the shock of the battle and the confusion of reawakening faded, she realized what that meant.

As if the chieftain could read the widening of her eyes, he turned and swept his sword across the site of the battle.

"Search the bodies. See if one of the *hrolf* is alive. Do *not* kill him."

Though the chieftain used Hrogi, the timbre and fine elocution of his voice allowed her to grasp his meaning. She moaned silently, deep in her throat. The chieftain verged on discovering the secret that had kept her people's small, low-lying homeland unconquered for two hundred years.

Struggling, Reila raised her upper body and perched unsteadily on her elbows. She watched as two Hrogi warriors abandoned their looting and began to systematically examine the dead. The one with her necklace joined them.

Three men. Four counting the chieftain. The only other surviving enemies lay on the bloodstained sod, making peace with their patron gods. Their wounds would kill them soon.

The raiders had barely carried the day.

"You cost us more men than I could believe," said the chieftain. "More than I would have risked, had I foreseen. Yet it may have been worth it after all."

He sheathed his blade. From the folds of his sling he removed the necklace of a bond-guardian. She recognized it as that of High Warrior Fonis, husband to Maer. The Hrogi chieftain bent down and placed the pendant beside the one that rested on Maer's breast.

"I always find a match," the chieftain said. "The pattern of the gemstones differs from one *hrolf* talisman to the next, but for each there is another of the same pattern around the neck of one of you witches."

The bond-guardians should never have worn their sigils into battle, Reila thought bitterly. Yet how could any of them have surrendered the symbol of their covenant?

"I am Thros," the chieftain said as he stood up. "And you?"

She turned her face away, denying him not only her name, but the sound of her voice as well. She would not sully it on Hrogi ears.

The chieftain sniffed. "Perhaps we will have other chances to be introduced."

She knew then that he meant her to survive. Not for rape, though that would probably be included. He wanted her for what she could tell him.

Thros. She knew that name. Nephew of the king of Hrog. Commander of the invasion. He had wanted to chase down their party very badly, then, to risk his own safety on a pursuit so deep inland.

Reila could understand now why this Hrogi invasion had been so overwhelming, far more so than that of a decade ago, and more threatening than any since the unification of the three kingdoms, and the creation of the bond-guardians.

The searchers called out suddenly. Thros turned. Reila opened her eyes.

The enemy soldiers had uncovered Kelf. Bloodied, chainmail and woolen garments yawning with gashes, he looked the part of a corpse, but Reila knew he must be alive. As did Thros.

"Bind him thoroughly, and bring him here," Thros ordered. His gaze had already shifted to Reila, and to the expression she could not banish from her face.

Tears cut through the mud on her cheeks. Her mate was so pale. The enemy warriors grunted under his limp weight as they brought him to the top of the barrow. They dropped him on top of Hara and Sandel's bodies.

He did not stir.

Thros ordered the man who had cut off her necklace to guard her closely, then the chieftain kneeled beside Kelf.

He pulled cloth and mail away from wounds, held the flat of a small knife under Kelf's nostrils until Kelf's otherwise imperceptible breath fogged the burnished metal.

Hindered by his wounded arm, Thros clipped free Kelf's pendant. Taking Reila's from the guard, he compared them.

He nodded.

"This man will die within the hour," Thros said. He dangled the matching talismans before her eyes. "But you can save him, can't you?"

She knew she should let him die. Then she would die as well, and Thros would learn nothing more than he had already deduced.

Kelf would have argued so, had he been conscious.

But as she looked at Kelf's lacerated gauntlets, she saw the strong, manly hands that had lifted the cup of bonding to her, the day they began the seven-day rites required to become guardians. As she looked at his grimace-locked eyelids, she saw his eyes, pale grey and intent, as he pledged his devotion to her on the final day of the rites. And as she shifted her gaze to his bruised lips, she remembered their touch on her body the night the rites concluded — and their touch over the years since, and the fine children that had sprung from their passion.

If it had been her life alone at stake, she would have made the sacrifice with no hesitation. She could kill herself, but she could not kill him, not even through inaction.

The trance claimed her almost before she was aware of her decision. The earth stirred, as full of power as ever, but the vessel of her body could barely channel that strength.

She reached out and found the flame still burning in Kelf's chest. She stoked the blaze as if with a bellows. The vents in his organs sealed shut. New blood filled drained channels. His bodily defenses rallied to attack the infections that had already taken hold in his abdomen and one of his legs.

Reila collapsed to the sod, head ringing, faintly aware of the gasps and murmurs of the Hrogi. Then even that sound vanished.

The clouds had broken, and the light from the setting sun was gleaming off of the droplets on the grass as Reila woke again. A tiny mason was inside her skull, chiseling at the bone from the inside. It hurt merely to hold her eyelids up.

Kelf, stripped of armor and bound more securely than ever, lay a few paces away, on top of a skirt obviously torn from Sandel's body. She was bound as well, though only with leather laces around her wrists and ankles.

Their glances met. Though scabbed, scarred, and still vividly bruised, Kelf had regained the alert demeanor so characteristic of him.

Color filled his formerly pallid countenance. She had not been able to restore him completely, but the injuries were now far from mortal. In some ways, he was in better condition than she.

A fen hawk caught a mouse and disappeared into the distance with it. Still the bond-mates stared at each other, saying nothing.

"Ah, awake at last," called a merry voice.

Reila turned as Thros approached. He had donned a fresh sling. Behind the Hrogi chieftain the other three raiders clustered around a bed of coals. A brace of flatland hare sizzled on skewers, blessing the site with their aroma. Reila felt no hunger, but she thanked Mother Earth for another means to stifle the lingering stench of carnage.

"That was fascinating," Thros said, waving at Kelf's nearly-healed form. "Our magicians have speculated that it is possible to channel the power of the earth, or the sun, or the sea. Many have tried, and been killed or robbed of their minds by the forces they tried to focus. To think that what was needed was to use one adept as the con-duit, and another as the recipient."

"The Hrogi have always been slow thinkers," Kelf said.

Thros scarcely glanced in the bond-warrior's direction. "Even if that were so," the chieftain said calmly, "we are good learners, once we are taught a thing."

"I will teach you nothing," Reila said.

"Ah, you have a voice," Thros said. "But it speaks nonsense."

Thros sauntered over to Kelf. Kneeling down, he seized a bit of earlobe between the thumb and middle finger of his mail gauntlet. And squeezed. Blood sprayed. Kelf flinched.

"You can imagine other ways I might have given him pain," Thros said. He stood. "I am not drawn to torture, but sooner or later you *will* cooperate, for your man's sake. You have already shown me that it is not in your nature to let him die. Surely you will not allow him to suffer, either."

She could not hide her emotions. Her expression told her enemy what he wanted to see.

"I thought not. I have only to keep you both bound, and see that your partner does not harm himself."

"It is a long way to Hrog," Kelf said.

"The swiftness of the journey will amaze you," Thros promised. He grunted in deep satisfaction. "When my people begin their next campaign in this land, we will be able to match your *hrolf* warriors with *hrolf* of our own. My lord had thought to abandon these costly raids. Now he will judge otherwise."

He caught Reila by the chin and tried to make her look him in the eyes, to see the triumph shining there, but she lowered her lids. He chuckled, flipped her head dismissively to one side, and moved off to enjoy his share of the victory meal.

Bile, bitter as heathwort soup, rose in Reila's throat. Of all the possible outcomes of the battle, few could have been worse.

Inevitably, she turned to Kelf. The newborn dusk had filled out his pupils. She saw into them as if they were windows, straight into his thoughts. He now agreed that she had been right not to let themselves die. The purpose of their survival was laid out for them.

They could only let themselves die now if they took Thros with them.

The Hrogi took no chances with Kelf. They checked the knots on his bonds and tied him securely to the bulky corpse of High Warrior Fonis. Kelf couldn't roll over, much less break free.

The captors paid less attention to Reila. Slight of build, thin, and obviously exhausted from channeling magic, she gave them no cause to feel threatened. They checked the bindings on her wrists and ankles, and tossed her on the opposite side of the sleeping area from Kelf. They knew the intricacy of their knots and the awkwardness of her position, hands behind back, would keep her from freeing herself. The distance would prevent her from aiding Kelf to untie his bonds.

The three soldiers did little to hide their lust for her.

"Save your strength," Thros ordered. "We've a fast, hard march tomorrow."

The men shrugged. Obviously weary from the battle and two

days of constant pursuit, they didn't argue.

But they continued to peer in her direction.

Thros himself carried bits of the cooked hare to the few of his wounded comrades who had not expired by sunset. He fed them, let them drink as many draughts of pungent Hrogi liquor as they could tolerate, and spoke soothingly to them.

By the close of twilight, the poison in the liquor had done its work. The chieftain uttered a prayer, and turned away from the bodies.

The Hrogi retired early. Thros promised Reila they would all be underway toward his army's beachhead before dawn.

Soon the only sounds coming from the raiders were rhythmic, sleep-deepened breaths and the scuffing of the lone guard's feet as he paced, and even these drowned within frog croaks and cricket songs.

Early in his watch, the guard banked the fire. With the loss of the light from the coals, the gloom closed in, heavy with the reek of corpses and wet heath. A new mass of clouds slowly drew a curtain over the stars. The moon, waning through its final quarter, would not rise until after midnight.

Now, thought Reila, while their sleep is deepest, while the night is darkest.

Reila's exhaustion vanished. The power of the earth goddess came arcing into her from the far side of the camp.

From Kelf.

The energies did not heal her bruises, nor the lacerations on her wrists. Kelf shaped the magic his way, according to his skills. She received it her way, as she had practiced in the hall of her sect.

She checked the position of the watchman. His silhouette told her he was looking the other way. As silently as possible she shifted over the ground to the body of an Island warrior. The Hrogi had taken away nearby weapons and thrown them in a pile, but before daylight had faded, she had memorized the location of a cutting edge they had missed.

Her bindings made her effort extremely awkward, but she managed to maneuver her wrists toward a sword shard that protruded a finger-length from the body of the warrior. She began sawing at the leather around her wrists.

The watchman turned. She stopped. Perhaps he had heard her. Even if he had not, he might decide to walk toward her. If he did, he would immediately realize she was not where she was supposed to be.

The Hrogi stretched, sighed, and turned to watch a pair of bats flitter past and disappear toward the fens.

The leather parted. Wrists bloodied from the task, Reila brought her hands to the front of her body. She cut through the cords around her ankles and waited for sensation to return fully to all her limbs.

She rose in a fluid, confident motion. Catlike, she padded rapidly to the source of the nearest weapons — those lying beside the Hrogi who had cut off her necklace. She could not see them in the murk, but she found them with the instinct of a warrior — a light sword and small mace, well-matched to her limited upper-body strength. She grasped the handles of both.

The sleeping man woke to the rasp of his blade leaving its sheath. Abandoning silence, Reila brought the mace down, crushing the man's skull before he could rise.

The watchman turned, reaching for the pommel of his blade. Sprinting forward, Reila drove the point of her steel into his throat just as his weapon cleared the sheath. He gurgled, raised the sword as if to strike, and abruptly lost his balance.

Even in daylight, only the most expert of swordsmen could have placed a thrust as precisely as Reila had, in the narrow gap between the man's jaw and the collar of his hauberk. But for the moment, she was such an adept.

The watchman was still staggering when she reached the third Hrogi warrior. He had spun from his bedroll to his feet, and peered in her direction as if confused, in the dark, as to which of the combatants was his enemy. When she leaped forward, he raised his battle axe.

He fended off her sword thrust. Steel sparked against steel. He charged. Light-footed, unencumbered by armor, she stepped to the side and tripped him. As he went down, she slammed her mace against the back of his neck.

He sprawled onto the sod, arms wide, and stayed there. She couldn't tell if he were unconscious or dead, but with luck, she could make sure later.

She sensed, rather than heard, the hiss of a swinging broadsword. She ducked a stroke that would have decapitated her. She sprang forward and whirled.

Thros cursed her, and levelled his blade at her. They stood apart, he in his armor, one-handed but clearly strong, she in her simple woolen tunic and skirt, invigorated by the energies of the goddess, but lacking in physical brawn.

He waded in, slashing. She darted backward. Her blade licked out, hit chain mail. She danced away from his backhand slice.

She had mobility, but he had protection. Thros jabbed again. She side-stepped, parried, thrust quickly while he recovered. Her sword point met only steel.

"I should have killed you this afternoon," Thros said.

"Yes, you should have," Reila taunted. She wanted him angry enough to lose his calm. Perhaps that would earn her an opening.

But the opposite happened. Fully awake now, given time by the stalemate to think, Thros found his strategy. "I should have killed one *or the other* of you."

She said nothing, but inside she shuddered. He had found her weak point.

He wasted no time taking advantage of it. Immediately he pressed in the direction where Kelf lay bound, stripped of armor, incapable of avoiding a deathstroke. Even a lesser blow would break her husband out of his trance. Once she lost her ability, the skirmish would end just as poorly.

Reila tried to hold her ground. She forced Thros to parry. His vicious slash drove her back. She dared a thrust at his face, but he blocked it. The sword penetrated the chain mail just enough to blood his forearm.

Not enough. The best she could do was slow him down for a few exchanges.

She couldn't give up. One way or another, the Hrogi must not win. She struggled against mounting desperation.

She knew that in the heat of battle, she could not find her own solutions. But she had Kelf, who sat apart from the fight, able to observe, able to counsel. No words could pass through the conduit of sorcery, but he guided her hands and feet.

She let his influence take root deep in her muscles, and refused to overlay her own concerns, her own judgments.

Thros pressed again. She retreated. Her riposte was thwarted.

She waited for her body to tense, to adopt some special tactic, but it merely continued to retreat. Thros advanced straight into her. She ducked, parried, and danced, but nothing more. The night wind blew over her sweat-drenched hair, and the chill raced down her spine.

Her heels bumped against a human leg. She read victory in the shadows below Thros's eyebrows.

She had to stand her ground. She couldn't leave Kelf unguarded. She would rather be cut down herself.

But her feet said jump. She trusted the message.

As she leaped clear, Thros seized the opportunity. He stabbed downward.

And skewered the lifeless body of an Islander warrior.

Kelf had altered her retreat slightly to one side. In the dark, neither Reila nor Thros had realized they were fighting over the wrong dark lump on the ground.

The dead warrior still wore armor. Thros had thrust with such force that he had penetrated it, but now his sword was lodged. Though expecting Reila's thrust, he could not avoid it. She drove her sword into his throat.

He let go of his weapon and sank until he was supine on the bloodied grass, not two paces from Kelf.

A small gap appeared in the clouds. A handful of bright stars peeked through. Their light, though scant, revealed the expression on Thros's face. Shock. Surprise. Disbelief.

With the threat gone, Reila allowed herself to pity her foe. Over-confidence had done him in. He had solved so many mysteries, he had been convinced there were none left.

The chieftain of the Hrogi sighed deeply. The sigh became a rattle. Reila turned from the body and cut her bond-mate loose.

The Sassy and the Naegg

CLAERI COULD GET A BOY to do anything she wanted. Her mother said it was her curse.

With some boys, she didn't even have to try. Of those, Gannen was the worst. He would follow her around like a new-hatched duckling if she'd let him.

One morning Claeri wanted to walk along the west trail. She hoped it would help her mood. Salt Dell was not as confined as some safeholds. It stretched three leagues north to south, and even wider west to east. It was home to over five hundred plainfolk. It had brine fields and mills, farms and berry brambles, and two separate villages. The river was a joy, from the five-tiered waterfall to the huge mill pond where she'd learned to skate when no taller than her father's knees. But by now Claeri was the better part of twenty years old and it seemed as though she had seen behind every stack of hay and climbed every tree and knew every single person in the enclave. She was corsetted by familiarity, and on that morning the laces were drawn too tight.

At least when she walked the west trail, through the woods and the mushroom mounds, she was at the verge of the Wild. She could gaze over the low stone fence and contemplate the unbounded world.

She could not walk the trail alone. Custom did not allow it. And so she asked Gannen to walk with her. She knew he would.

Gannen did not try to get her to talk. Wise of him. He simply walked beside her, half a step behind so as not block her vantage of the Wild.

The woods were quiet, the dew still so heavy the moisture dulled the echo of their footfalls. She inhaled until her chest could expand no further, savoring the crispness of the air. Only the shadiest spots cradled any unmelted snow but the breeze was still northerly. She loved winter. Summer was an ordeal of workshifts in the fields, gnats flying up her nostrils, sweat touching her too intimately. Winter was perfect for leisurely strolls. It was all going so well until they spotted the elk.

"Look," Gannen said.

She frowned, annoyed because she had already noticed them for herself, and because at the sound of his voice, the animals realized they were not alone.

A stag was standing just inside the safehold boundary. A calf stood next to it. The sentry charms that kept out inimical beings had not prevented their entry. Elk were welcome to pass through — particularly when they lingered long enough for hunters to fetch their bows. The cooking sheds never smelled finer than when fresh hunks of venison were turning on the spits.

The stag made a huffing sound that declared its reluctance to be observed. It turned around. A quick hop and it was across the barrier. The youngling leaped over with even greater ease. Two cows and two more calves greeted them on that side. Together the little herd turned and began heading back the way they had come.

Their way led through a natural passageway in the trees. The stag lowered its head, but its left antler grazed a branch.

Claeri blinked. Had she seen what she had seen? Yes. The antler that had struck the branch was now dangling beside the stag's neck, clinging to the skull by a shred, on the brink of detaching.

"Gannen," she murmured.

"I see it," he whispered back.

Lifebone. The bone that needs neither death nor bloodshed to free it. Found when fresh, and coaxed with the right incantations, it could cure the pox or turn a barren womb fertile.

"Can you believe our luck?" she asked.

"Our *bad* luck, you mean? 'Tis the wrong side they're on."

"It's on *this* side they'd be if you hadn't spoken."

"I'm sorry."

How many times had she heard him utter those words?

"Never mind," she said. "Follow them. The ancestors will smile on us, make no mistake. The antler will fall off and you can come right back."

"But..."

"You'll be the talk of the safehold." She smiled at him. "Proud of you I'll be."

She reached out and took his mittened hand, closing it inside both of her own. He was so startled he almost pulled it back.

She already knew he would do it. He had to straighten up, wipe the branch-drip from his forehead, and gaze at the elk tails disappearing between the boles of the trees before his faith rose to the level of hers. He slid his hand free, eased over the stone fence, and was soon gone from her sight.

She waited where she was, expecting him back at any moment given how tenuously the antler had hung.

He did not return. Not while she stood there on the west trail. Not for the rest of that morning. At noon, she mustered the courage to tell the elders what had happened. The searchers went out, protected by fetishes, fortified by elixirs, and armed as well as the plainfolk knew to arm themselves. They did not find him, not even with his brother's dog to sniff along his track. Spring came and went before any denizen of Salt Dell learned what had happened to Gannen son of Ayn.

One humid morning, not long after Claeri had started her shift at the loomhouse, her father sought her out. "You're to go to the elders' keep," he said. "It's about the boy."

"There's news?" she asked.

Her father shrugged. "I expect it's you who'll be telling me, come supper time."

She hurried off at once, so distracted by the possibilities she tripped on her way across the rope bridge and nearly tumbled into the river. Her hair was matted with sweat by the time she marched up the slope to her destination.

The elders' keep stretched as long as four barns — the largest structure in all Salt Dell with the exception of the festival lodge. Even so, the audience was overflowing the gallery of the main council chamber.

So many faces, and all regarding her. And the only one with any sympathy was Maerea, her mother's aunt.

A burly young man stood off to one side, his red hair standing out sharply above the horizon of grey-haired and white-haired heads. She knew him well. Ollsos. The woodchopper. One of Gannen's friends.

The way was cleared and Claeri proceeded forward to stand right in front of the dais, facing a half-circle of elders seated behind their heavy table of oak and sigil tile. In the center chair sat Dame Haddah. Spindly as a skeleton she might be, as well as blind in one eye, but no person in Salt Dell had shown surprise when she had been reelected as speaker of the council for the fourth year in a row.

"An emissary of the Eyeless appeared at the west gate at dawn," Haddah said. "They have Gannen. They have offered to return him to us alive and unharmed. All they demand is an item coveted by one of their warlords."

Claeri's breath caught in her throat, trapped. She wanted to cry out in joy that Gannen was not dead, and at the same time, the anguish she had struggled to dampen for five months was now rekindled. A captive of the Eyeless?

"Wha-What do they ask for?" she stammered.

"They want *this*."

The speaker's voice was deep and male. Out of the crowd emerged a figure in work leathers and heavy boots that said he had come straight from his forgeworks to the gathering. He carried a sword.

Embruss was his name. He was Gannen's uncle.

The blacksmith was a hale man, still active in his craft, but the creases in his face had deepened to canyons, and he held his burden with a profound unsteadiness.

Embruss had made many swords in his time. Most had gone to customers outside the safehold. Blades were among Salt Dell's most important trade goods. Once and only once, Embruss had made a sword for himself. No other piece contained so much of his essence. He had been offered great sums for it in times past. He had always said no.

Embruss placed the sword on the council table, unsheathed. Five heartbeats later, he let go of the hilt.

"This is to be taken to Gibbet Rock and bonded to the warlord," Haddah said. "When all that is done, Gannen will be released. We have decided the duty falls to you, Claeri."

Claeri lowered her glance to the floor. "I understand."

"And you accept?"

"I do," she answered.

"Good."

"When is it to be done?"

"Tonight. Before the sun sets, out the gate you'll be."

"Oh."

"Revered elders. If it please you, I will go with her."

Claeri's head darted to the side. Ollsos had taken a step forward and, wrists crossed in official supplication, was awaiting the reply.

Her heart began to race. To not have to face the ordeal alone — that was honey on bread, cool water on a hot day. She nearly rushed over to hug the woodchopper, no matter that the last time she and Ollsos had spoken, he had called her names and spat at her for encouraging his friend to cross into the Wild.

Haddah shook her head. "The Eyeless are oathbound not to harm our envoy, but treachery is as common to them as dung in a pasture. Better to risk one of our number than two."

Ollsos picked up his ax from where he had left it in a corner and he exited the keep. Despite the frown on his face, Claeri knew that was that. The elders had spoken, and Ollsos was not the sort to defy their judgment.

Haddah set a knobby hand upon the table beside the sword. "We will spend the afternoon teaching you the ritual and supplying what advice we can," she told Claeri. "Take an hour or two now and go say your farewells to those who matter most to you. If all goes well, you will see them all again tomorrow. But best get it done, for their sake."

The expressions on her parents' faces tore at her heart, and it was nearly as bad with the others she chose to seek out. Agonizing as the process was, she was almost relieved when the agreed-upon hour arrived and she had to journey back to the elders' keep.

Her great aunt was waiting for her at the threshold.

"We'll prepare you the best we know how," Maerea promised.

"Helpless I'll be," Claeri warbled. "And hopeless, too. I've never even learned to set a snare or bait a hook. I can't even run all that well."

"Who's to say, that may give you an edge. The Eyeless won't be on their guard with you — certainly not the way they'd be with Ollsos. And you make friends easily."

"I've no wish to be *friends* with the Eyeless," Claeri objected.

Maerea clucked her tongue. "Hear me with your good ear, not the one you've stuffed with straw. I am saying, child, look to your strengths, and don't forget what those strengths are."

The old woman gave Claeri one last hug, then urged her through the doorway.

Claeri departed through the south gate late that day and set out along the wagon ruts of Traders Way, soon entering a rolling terrain of scrub, woodland, and breeze-bared hilltops. The sun set not long after she veered off onto the footpath she'd been told to take, her route winding a little toward the west now, not strictly toward the south.

The brightness of the horizon faded, the sky giving way to twilight, and then to dusk. It felt to her as though she was being covered over by Death's cloak, but a gibbous moon hung behind her to her left and she had no difficulty seeing where to place her feet. She had a small glowstone with her. Should clouds appear and hide the moon, she would use it. For the moment, she did not need it. In fact, she could see so well that when a small creature crossed the trail a hundred paces ahead and disappeared down the bank of a small creek, she could tell from the white striping it was a skunk even before its stench wafted her way.

No, it was her mood that was dark, and so it should be. All manner of Other Folk roamed the Wild, and now that she was away from the safehold, if any decided she would serve as a meal or as entertainment or as property to be seized, there might be little she could do to thwart their designs. Brutal her luck would be if she had to deal with something worse than the Eyeless tonight, but when she considered the odds, dark her spirits remained.

She trudged on. She knew she was climbing, but the increase of elevation was so gradual her legs felt no more taxed than before. Mostly the change manifested in the disappearance of boggy spots, and in the speed with which the rivulets trickled along the creases of the landscape.

Gradually she became certain she was being followed. She had heard nothing. When she turned, she saw nothing. It was more a matter of her hair stiffening at the nape of her neck, and goose pimples rising from her wrists toward her armpits.

At the end of another hour, she understood the cause, and was embarrassed it had taken her so long to puzzle it out.

She pulled the glowstone from her pack, cupped it so that its light was steered toward her right, where clumps of summerdrop heather formed a natural hedge.

"If you want to sneak around after me like that, you should try doing in some other form," she called out. "As it is, I smell you every time you catch up."

The skunk appeared in the gap between two leaning shrubs and ambled to the center of the path. It stood up on its hind legs and started to shiver. Or at least, shivering was what it resembled at first, but the disturbance evolved in an odd manner. Eventually Claeri began to wonder if her eyes had forgotten how to remain steady in her head. All she could be certain of was that the newcomer was getting larger, and then larger still.

Finally the shape was man-sized, and indeed, what stood in front of her seemed to be a man in fact—a gnarled, hairy, and very naked man. Quickly she put the glowstone away. Moonlight gave her as much of a view as she cared to be granted.

At least the smell was fading.

"That's close enough," she told him.

He made no move toward her. But then, his sort would not, so she had been schooled. With his sort, it was what you said that would ruin you. Or save you.

He smiled. For all the scruff and dirt that adorned him, his teeth gleamed white and straight and were perfectly intact. His breath was blossom-sweet.

"Now what would a maiden such as yourself be doing so far from her warded glen all alone on a night of woe and portent?"

She put her hands on her hips. "It's a maiden I've become? My! They say the Wild will change a person. Quick it is about its business, I must say."

Her companion laughed. "A sassy you are, then. Good. That's some protection, at least. I will not describe what happened to the last virgin who wandered this—"

"Was it my safety on your mind?" Claeri interjected. "And why should that be your concern?"

"Considerate I am," he said. "The kindest of fellows, to those I like."

"So you say. A moment ago you were a skunk."

"And a *kind* skunk I was. Naeggs may take a thousand shapes, but our natures are as fixed as stone."

"I've heard much talk of the nature of naeggs," Claeri said. "So…is it my escort you've made of yourself? Will I have your kindness beside me the rest of my journey?"

"A little way, perhaps. Who do you think is keeping that shadow man over there at bay?"

Claeri almost turned to look at the spot the naegg indicated, but she caught herself in time.

"There's no shadow man there," she stated.

"A poor and desperate thing my eyesight is tonight," complained the naegg. "I suppose next you'll be telling me *you're* not really here!"

Claeri sighed. "Unfortunately, I *am* here. Much as I'd prefer to be back in my warded glen, as you put it."

"Well, you're here, then, and I'm here. Let's get to the important matters. Have you any five-fold leaf in that belt pouch of yours?"

"Maybe. Maybe a pipe as well."

"*Salt Dell* five-fold leaf?" the naegg added with eagerness.

"What other kind would I have?"

"Oh, and it's a cruel wench you are, to put me on the brink of begging."

"I liked 'sassy' better than 'wench' if you must know. And anyway, now hardly seems like the time to be lighting up a pipeful."

"Any evening's a time for five-fold leaf! And what better occasion than on your way to likely doom and torment?"

"Are you a seer as well?" she asked.

"It's to Gibbet Rock this trail leads. You're not on the way to a midsummer dance, are you now?"

"I am not."

She rummaged through her pouch and brought out her pipe. She tossed it to the naegg, who cradled it reverently. She uncorked her bottle of leaf, poured a measure into the bowl, and poised the striker.

A spark. The naegg inhaled. The longer he held his breath, the more peaceful his smile became. When at last he opened his mouth, only a whiff of vapor was left to escape his lungs.

"Ahhh," said the naegg. "If ever I'd a mind to work, I'd labor in the fields, and this would be my crop."

"No food?" Claeri asked.

"No. I would share this, and my friends would set their baskets in my larder and their kettles of soup in my fireplace, and I'd get by very well."

"You've a house and a larder and a fireplace?" Claeri asked.

"And so I would have, were I a farmer. To go with the fields and the barn."

Claeri took a long draw. It was ordinary leaf by her measure, but she was willing to concede her perspective was different than a being who owned no pocket and carried no pouch. She handed the pipe back.

"Your first time beyond the boundary?" the naegg asked, voice squeaking as he held his breath.

"When I was sixteen I went in a caravan to Wheathaven. For spring carnival."

"And how was that?"

"Different boys. That was nice. Alas, not different enough."

"Isn't that the way?"

"I wish I'd gone again this year," she said. "Might have been my last chance."

"And why is that?"

She couldn't ken why his questions didn't strike her as nosy, but they did not. It wasn't just the leaf — though goodness knows a bit of leaf was known to bring out the garrulous side of her nature. It was something about *him*. In any case, as they walked on, continuing to smoke, she told him the whole account of Gannen's capture and the task she'd been assigned.

"Well," he said when she was done, "'Tis quite the nettle patch you're in."

"Isn't it, though?"

"Do you know what I heard through all that?" the naegg commented when she was done.

"What did you hear?"

"You didn't blame the boy. You didn't blame the elders. You didn't even blame the Eyeless."

She scoured the dregs out of the pipe and let the bits fall to the ground. "If I think that way, where does it stop? Should I blame my mother for giving birth to me, or my father for the glint in his eye, nine months before?"

"Some might," the naegg said.

"Could be. I suppose I'm not made that way."

The path was beginning to curve. Claeri recalled that as one of the signs to indicate she was nearing Gibbet Rock.

"I'll take my leave now," the naegg said. "You've listened well and given back better. Most plainfolk tire of my blather, and rude they are in telling me so."

"Whereas I am sorry we are at the end," Claeri responded. "The conversation was a kindness. A distraction from what lies ahead."

"And what lies ahead? Doom and torment did I say? Well, meet me early of a night, and it's a pessimist you'll find. Meet me later, and it's an optimist I am. Go forward, young lass. Perhaps all will be well."

"Not everything changes as readily as do you," she said. "I set out on a path to peril and it's to peril I'm goin' still. You've been good company. That was a bounty I'd not expected, and I thank you for it."

"A joy it is to know you," the naegg declared, and he stopped in place, and held entirely still. "I grant you the favor of a wish."

She turned. He remained where he was, more steady of form and motion than he had been since he'd emerged from the hedge as a skunk.

"I've heard about shifters' wishes," she said.

"They are as dependable as we are," cackled the naegg. "But may come a time when you've naught to lose. If so, wish away. Keen my ears will be."

The naegg resumed his characteristic jiggle and wag. Soon it developed into the peculiar shiver she had witnessed before. When her vision settled, she found her companion had become a treefrog. He bounded away with astonishingly robust leaps.

Her dread stretched the remaining journey in her heart and mind, but when she rounded a shoulder of a hillside and saw Gibbet Rock looming in front of her, the moon was straight overhead. That meant it was still well before midnight.

The formation looked nothing like a gibbet. It was prominent in the landscape and possessed a flat top. When the Eyeless or the shadow men wanted to leave a morsel dangling for the crows, that was where they would do it. Nothing stood up there at the moment, the plain folk having torn down the most recent butcher's tree, but she could sense the lingering miasma of death. When the Eyeless themselves emerged from the shadow of the rock and ambled out to meet her, they seemed to bring the mephitis with them.

They had arms and legs, faces and hands, but the Eyeless would never be confused with the plain folk. Horns grew from their head, curling down like ram's regalia. Their chins came to points. Their skin was grey. Their knees bent backward.

They weren't actually eyeless, but Claeri saw at once how they had acquired the label. Their eyes were uniformly black — pupils, irises, and sclera — and so the sockets appeared empty except when they stood close.

Unfortunately they soon were all too easy to see clearly. They did not come to a halt until they were only a few paces away. There were five of them. The one in the center stood slightly taller, though all of them were too tall to suit her. He wore the most accessories, including a necklace of what appeared to be severed fingers. He took another two steps forward, leaned in, and studied her.

They *were* severed fingers. She was glad that at least they were grey, clawed fingers, clearly taken from his own kind. She did not let herself tremble. She stared straight back at him, no matter that it felt like she was staring at holes in his skull.

He did not touch her. The bargain did not allow that. But he was so very close. Her nose filled with the ripeness of his body, the ripeness of his breath.

And still she did not let herself tremble.

He smiled.

"I am Hadren."

"Is it to you the blade will be consecrated?" Claeri asked.

"Of course," he replied.

She reached behind her back and drew Embruss's masterpiece from its scabbard. She held it level at the height of her chin, letting them get a good look at the folded steel and at the intricate roping of the hilt.

All five stared at it with an intensity she could only call ravenous, and yet they all, even Hadren, kept their distance. Iron was poison to the Eyeless, as it was to so many of the fey. That in part was why they craved iron weapons — the better to kill enemies among their own kind, for any cut might be fatal, even a small slice on an arm, or a jab into a thigh. That was why she could be certain she would live at least a few more minutes. She still had to complete the ownership enchantment.

"I've shown you the sword," she said. "Now show me my compatriot."

Hadren shrugged. "In due time."

"Now."

He mocked her with a laugh.

She slid the sword back into its scabbard, folded her arms, and glanced off to the side and upward, barely keeping Hadren in her field of vision.

Hadren ignored her. A bat fluttered across the face of the moon. It had already fluttered back the other way before he spoke.

"As you wish."

He raised a hand and gestured. Two more Eyeless emerged from the shadow of the rock formation, bringing with them a human figure in tattered winter garments. His hair was matted, his face dirty, his shoulders were bowed rather than broad and even, but she recognized him as soon as the moonlight struck him. It was Gannen.

Tears brimmed on her lower lashes. She almost spoke, but then she saw the vacancy behind his eyes. He walked between the escorts like a cow plodding from one stack of hay to another, too pasture-dazed even to raise its tail and give its flies a slap.

"What have you done to him?"

"He was being uncooperative. We took the fight out of him.

There's nothing awry with him that your wisefolk can't mend. See for yourself. Have we bled him? Have we broken his bones?"

She went to him. He gazed straight ahead as if he did not see her, but his eyes were open. His chest filled with each breath. She pressed and prodded and found no indication of wounds or bruises. He was unbathed and had lost weight, but not to a degree any worse than could be explained by the deprival for five months of a roof, a hearth, and his mother's kettle.

"You have him. Now fulfill the bargain. The moon is high. It's time."

Claeri swallowed the temptation to keep him waiting. After all, she wanted to be on her way back as soon as possible.

She unlaced the scabbard and lifted it and the sword from her back.

"Where is it to be done?" she asked.

Hadren led the way around to the far side of Gibbet Rock and slightly farther up the ravine. From the tenth step onward the sound of falling water grew more distinct. They came to a waterfall the height of Claeri's waist. A rock shelf permitted a person to walk right up to one side of the feature. Near the spot stood a bucket adorned with the glyphs of the Cloudwalkers.

The place had the necessary conditions.

"Begin," demanded Hadren.

Claeri fully recalled the steps the elders had drilled into her that afternoon, but how she would have loved to introduce a "mistake" in the ritual. She dared not. Hadren was observing her carefully, and she had no doubt he knew the required elements even better than she.

With the bucket, she filled a granite hollow some twelve to fifteen paces from the waterfall. It took several trips until the water was deep enough that it would cover the sword, assuming the sword was laid down flat.

She gestured to Hadren. He placed a forearm over the puddle and cut a slice in his own flesh with his obsidian blade. His blood dripped into the puddle. She took a wand of rainwood from her pack and stirred the blood until it was thoroughly mixed with the water, then threw the wand away.

She drew the sword, set the scabbard aside, and went to the waterfall. She turned and tilted the weapon until every part had been rinsed in the torrent, then she did it again. All the while she murmured gentle incantations of release beneath her breath. She felt the bonds that had dedicated the artifact to Embruss weaken and one by one, slip away. Finally none remained.

She walked back to the puddle, where Hadren waited, his sneer now gone. His eagerness was obvious from the way he leaned forward, gaze following every move she made.

She saw the puddle was not quite ready. Four transformative attributes were required: Water. Blood. Moonlight. And finally, stillness.

Hadren bared his teeth, as though about to growl at her, but apparently he understood the need for the delay. Gradually the water finished settling. When it was mirror smooth, she opened her mouth and said, "Hadren." Immediately thereafter she bent down and set the sword down in the water, submerging it completely.

She let go of the hilt and straightened up. Her part was now done.

Again the wait. She feared she would chew the inside of her cheeks raw before the water grew still again. Finally, for the second time, the water became motionless.

Hadren grabbed the hilt and lifted the sword out. He did not writhe in pain. His hand clutched its prize steadily. No tremors. No odor of burning flesh.

He cut the air. Smiled at the swishing noise it made. His companions, though they eased back to a safer distance, regarded him as though he had become one of their gods.

Claeri went to Gannen, took him by a wrist, and tugged. He moved in the same desultory manner as before, but he did enough that she would not have to drag him all the way back to Salt Dell. She set off along the trail with him.

"No, no, no." Hadren chuckled. "It's not really my sword until I've spilled blood with it, is it my girl? Your blood will do nicely."

"You are sworn not to harm me," Claeri exclaimed.

"Nor will I. It's the sword that will harm you."

Hadren sauntered three steps forward. Claeri retreated, pulling Gannen along.

"So quiet you are," Hadren jeered. "This is usually the point where your ilk tries to throw a curse or two at me. By all means, give it a go."

Claeri had been supplied with a chant verse and had rehearsed the words and the activating rhythm, but she could see by Hadren's cocksure pose that she was unlikely to inflict harm. He might well be enough of an adept to reflect the assault back on her.

The bat fluttered past again. Strange how it lingered. Bats tended to like places where insects hovered. Stagnant puddles. Sedge ponds. Slivers of meadow. All of which she had noticed on her way up the ravine, but none of which existed here near the waterfall.

Bats, she considered, have keen ears.

"Nothing to say?" Hadren cut the air again. "How disappointing."

"If it's words you need, you shall have them: *I wish I had a horse.*"

Hadren tried to charge, but the bat swooped in, expanding so rapidly it was a stallion by the time it reached the ground. Hooves flashed in Hadren's face, and he back-pedalled so suddenly he fell back on his rump. The sword bounced from his grip and clattered away in the direction of the puddle.

The horse lowered itself down. Gannen stood there dully, as if nothing was going on, but Claeri shoved him forward and he ended up draped over the horse's midsection. She vaulted into place behind him, grabbed his belt with one hand, and a fistful of mane with the other.

The stallion surged away. Claeri thought she heard Hadren cackle in triumph, but perhaps terror alone put the noise in her ears. In any case, her back was not split open, nor did the horse scream. She didn't look back to see how close their escape had been. She put all of her concentration into hanging on to Gannen and keeping the both of them atop their saddleless mount.

An arrow whisked by, then another, but then they were around Gibbet Rock, and not long after, around the curve of the hillside.

The whole way along the ravine and through the scrubland, retracing her outward route in reverse, she worried that formerly unseen members of Hadren's band might rush out of hiding places, but they covered the distance without further attack. The most frightening aspect of the journey came from another source entirely. The naegg apparently was not accustomed to being a horse. Twice he skidded on muddy ground and at other times, his hooves landed poorly and kicked up small rocks. Claeri was sure they would all tumble over in a gigantic somersault. Much as she wanted to go quickly, she was relieved when he ceased the gallop and fell into a brisk but stable trot.

At last the brush and brambles and trees vanished to either side, leaving only grass and clumps of wildflowers. Claeri realized they were on the Traders Way and were at the verge of the buffer zone just outside the south gate.

There they stopped.

"Oh my achin' back. Heavy as boulders, you two are." The body beneath Claeri and Gannen was still that of a horse, but mouth had transformed, and the naegg's voice came from it as distinctly as a bard from a stage.

Claeri dismounted. She wasn't certain how she was going to get Gannen off without making a mess of it, but all at once, he slid off of his own accord. Her breath caught. Was he freed of his affliction? Unfortunately, once his feet were on the ground he just stood there, staring at nothing and showing no further indication he was in command of himself.

Meanwhile the presence beside her was no longer a large animal drenched with horse sweat. It had become a hairy naked man drenched with horse sweat.

"Thank you," Claeri told the naegg.

"The pleasure was mine," he replied. "Been wanting to give that fellow grief for ages now."

"You certainly did that."

The naegg's amusement put a bounce in his limbs and a lilt in his voice. "Hee. That I did. That I did." He waved her onward. "Now off with you. Tend to your friend. He is only half-rescued."

"I will."

"And come back, of an evening, and tell me how he fares."

The naegg shivered and shrank. She blinked, and by the time her vision cleared, a bat was fluttering off toward the midge meadow.

Claeri could not get Gannen to do more than stumble a few steps forward at a time, but as her wits returned, she realized she did not need to deal with the matter at all. She pulled out her glowstone and waved it back and forth over her head. It wasn't long until four strong sentries arrived from the direction of the gate. Two picked up Gannen and hauled him off. The other pair bracketted Claeri as she followed.

Claeri was sure some calamity would befall her at the last moment, but everyone moved efficiently and carefully and soon they had crossed the threshold to safety. Just inside the gate, she dropped to the greensward and kissed the grass.

They were taken at once to the elders' keep. Despite the hour, many of its denizens were still up, including Haddah. When Gannen was laid out on a bench, the woman limped over and studied him carefully with her one good eye.

"Many a trick I've known the Eyeless to play," she muttered. "And here is another to add to the list."

"What's been done?" Claeri asked.

"His spirit has been untethered. In his present state, any restless ghost could force its way into his body and nevermore would Gannen be free of it."

Haddah was trying to be kind, but Claeri knew perfectly well that restless ghosts were the least awful thing likely to seize the opportunity.

"Can it be un-done?"

"Yes. But quick we must be about the task, or Gannen will know suffering worse than any the Eyeless might have caused him on their own."

Haddah beckoned to others who had just entered the council chamber. They carried sticks of spirit incense and bottles of trance brew.

A hand settled upon Claeri's shoulder. It was her great aunt.

"This will take many hours. Meanwhile you will come with me."

"I want to be here," Claeri objected.

"No. Your presence will be a distraction, and in any case, you need cleansing. You were among the Eyeless. No one returns from that untainted."

"They did not touch me."

"Glad am I to hear it, but you're to come with me nonetheless. Don't make me pull you by the ear."

The cleansing was a matter not only of magical ritual, but of soap and hot water in the crones' tub room. Maerea kept Claeri company, but it was a trio of white-haired sorceresses that tended to her. Between that ordeal, and the soporific effect of the bath, and the exhaustion stemming from her encounter with Hadren and his cronies, Claeri lacked the energy to argue she should be allowed to return to Gannen's side. Barely minutes after she had been shown to a bed, sleep reached out and snatched her.

She woke to Maerea's hand on her upper arm.

"What's the time?" Claeri asked at once. "Is it done?"

"Nearly noon," her aunt replied. "And yes, it's done."

"Did they save Gannen?"

"That they did."

To Claeri, it was as though a breath she had been holding for five months could finally be released.

"He'll need to be left in peace at home for a time," Maerea continued. "No busy-bodies asking him lots of questions about things he'd rather forget. His father has come to fetch him. Get dressed and come to the council chamber. You've just enough time to say the words you need to say."

Maerea went on ahead. Claeri followed in short order.

Her footsteps echoed from the far corners of the chamber, a

startling emptiness compared to the day before. Those in attendance now consisted of not much more than the elders who had performed the ritual upon Gannen, along with some of the attendants who had assisted them.

Claeri smiled to see Gannen on his feet, standing next to Ayn. He turned as she entered, and she could tell by the alertness of his glance that he was "there."

She opened her mouth and was on the verge of blurting her apology — about to make a tangle of the careful words she had rehearsed — when his hand shot up, palm toward her.

"Say nothing to me."

She froze in place, mouth open. Then, reading his expression, she did just as he requested.

He looked away from her and began walking toward the door. His father stopped him halfway there.

"Son. Whatever else, 'twas she who rescued you."

Gannen turned his head only halfway, not enough to face her. His mouth contorted one way and then the other, and finally two sullen words came out: "Thank you."

Ayn let loose his hold, and together father and son left the building. Gannen did not look back.

So many times in the past few years, Claeri had wanted less devotion from Gannen. Now there was not a trace left, and already she missed it.

She turned back to the council. Two of those who had participated in the re-anchoring of Gannen's spirit were heading away, their stumbling gaits and lowered chins showing they could not remain awake any longer, but a small cluster of others including Haddah and Maerea sat down in the common area, away from the dais. Haddah gestured Claeri to approach.

"Tell us the tale, child. What did you see, and how did you make it back to us?"

The elders never passed up the chance to learn more about their neighbors in the Wild. It was not as though they could obtain that knowledge routinely.

Claeri gave a summary of the whole excursion from the first glimpse of the skunk to the moment when the four sentries came out of the gate to ferry her and Gannen back inside. To her surprise, she described more of the seemingly idle conversation with the naegg than she expected she would.

"I'm grateful it went so well," she concluded. "And humble I am to know I had such luck. I'm unhurt, and Gannen is no longer lost."

Not one of the elders smiled at that assessment. Haddah wore a particularly somber expression. Gradually Claeri caught up to their thinking.

"I haven't seen the last of this matter. Have I?"

"Certainly not the last of that naegg," Haddah said.

"I understand. He granted me a wish, and now I owe him."

"For the wish? From what you've told us, that was freely given, was it not?"

"Well. Yes. I suppose it was."

"Then you owe him nothing for the wish. 'Tis the other thing."

"What other thing?"

"You owe him for saving your life."

"Um. Wasn't that part of the wish?"

"You wished for a horse. Did you wish for a *brave* horse?"

"I didn't specify."

"Then it was his choice to be the sort of horse you needed."

"I see," Claeri said. "But—if I'm to ever save his life, I'll need to…"

"You will have to frequent the places where he is to be found."

"Oh, dear."

"Yes. Oh, dear, indeed."

Shapeshifters were fey folk, and no manner of fey folk were to be found at any time within Salt Dell. The sentry charms were not refined enough to allow an exception, not even when the individual in question was trustworthy. The ban was absolute. Claeri was facing at least one more excursion into the Wild, and probably many.

"You've much to think about, child, but plenty of time to weigh and ponder and plan." Suddenly Haddah was overtaken by a huge yawn. "As for me, I'm off to bed before I'm reduced to curling up right here next to Bluebell." With her toes, she nudged the dog sleeping beneath her chair.

The other elders rose with Haddah and began limping and wobbling toward their rooms. They waved away Claeri's fumbling attempts to thank them all over again. Soon she was making her own way from the council room, and from the keep itself. Maerea walked beside her as they took the path that led to Claeri's home.

She contemplated what she was facing. A few months ago she had been aching for the chance to venture beyond the boundary, but this was far from what she had been after. Her situation was not unlike a sentence of exile, and exile was the worst punishment a condemned member of the safehold could suffer.

"How do I begin?" Claeri asked her aunt.

"Do you like him?"

"Who? The naegg? Not well enough to be his mare, if that's what you're getting at."

"What I meant was, did you enjoy the time you spent with him? Was he good company?"

"I've had worse," she admitted.

"In that case, you know that plot of five-fold leaf your father is tending?"

"Yes."

"Tell him that when harvest comes, he should hold onto a reserve. You won't want to run short."

"I see. I'm to keep the naegg in a good mood."

"It's always a good idea to keep a shapeshifter in a good mood," Maerea replied, "but it's not just him I'm thinking of. It's you. Takes steady nerves to be out in the Wild. As you learned last night. And frankly, you're better company when you're relaxed."

Claeri blushed. Her aunt made it all sound straightforward—something within her means to accomplish. But she knew perfectly well it would not be anything like that. On the contrary, she was quite certain she had managed to mire herself in a destiny.

"I may die," she said plaintively.

"Child," Maerea said. "We all die, sooner or later. On the way to that moment, while you still bide among the living, I think you will find there are worse things than getting to wander the Wild, with a naegg as a friend."

Acknowledgments

The twelve stories contained in this volume were published over a span of thirty years. The number of people who helped me make these works better adds up to quite a tally. I appreciate all they did and I appreciate them, too. Not to mention that I miss those who passed away during those three decades.

First of all, to my wife Connie and children Lerina and Elliott.

To my feedback horde, most of whom did their critiquing as part of the meetings of the writing groups The Spellbinders, the Melville Nine, and Will Write For Food: Bob Fleming, Cherie Kushner, Risa Aratyr, Shirley Johnston, Brent Anderson, Pras Stillman, Armando Gomez, Margaret Raymond, Marian Gibbons, Marge Windus, Janet Berliner, Joel Fruchtman, Jim Killus, and Eliot Fintushel.

And special gratitude goes to the editors who acquired these pieces for their anthologies or magazines: Marion Zimmer Bradley, Elisabeth Waters, Kit Kerr, Jo Clayton, Jennifer Roberson, Deborah J. Ross, Shawna McCarthy, and Shannon Page.

About the Author

A Nebula Award finalist, Dave is the author of novels, short fiction, comic book scripts, and screenplays. His writing spans several sub-genres of science fiction and fantasy including sword-and-sorcery, hard sf, contemporary fantasy, superhero, martial arts, and horror.

His books include The War of the Dragons trilogy (*The Sorcery Within, The Schemes of Dragons,* and *The Wizard's Nemesis*), other novels *X-Men: Law of the Jungle* and *Piper in the Night,* and the collections *Embracing the Starlight, Futures Near and Far,* and *Raiding the Hoard of Enchantment.* Those last three volumes, along with the one you have in front of you right now, contain some of the more than one hundred stories of his that have appeared in magazines such as *Asimov's Science Fiction, Realms of Fantasy, The Magazine of Fantasy & Science Fiction, Pulphouse,* and *Dark Regions,* and anthologies such as *Full Spectrum 4, David Copperfield's Tales of the Impossible, Peter S. Beagle's Immortal Unicorn, Dragons of Light, Far Frontiers, Vol. VI, Future Earths: Under African Skies,* and *In the Field of Fire,* along with nineteen installments of the Sword and Sorceress series.

In addition to being an author, Dave is a book-cover artist and designer, and from time to time, a karate instructor, having trained in goju-ryu karate-do for fifty years. He lives in Santa Rosa, CA with his wife and son.

For addition information: davesmeds.com.

About Book View Café

Book View Café is a professional authors' publishing cooperative offering DRM-free ebooks to readers around the world. With authors in a variety of genres including mystery, romance, fantasy, and science fiction, Book View Café has something for everyone.

Book View Café is good for readers because you can enjoy high-quality DRM-free ebooks from your favorite authors at a reasonable price.

Book View Café is good for writers because 90% of the profit goes directly to the book's author.

Book View Café's authors include New York Times and USA Today bestsellers, Nebula, Hugo, Lambda, Chanticleer, and Phillip K. Dick Award winners, World Fantasy, Kirkus, and Rita Award nominees, and winners and nominees of many other publishing awards.

BOOK VIEW CAFE

bookviewcafe.com